Sophie couldn't stop thinking about that afternoon, when a set of elevator doors opened, leaving her face-to-face with Meyer Cartell.

He'd been staying with John Skinner. A last hurrah, evidently, before they'd donned their Air Force uniforms. And her sister, Corinne, had been collateral damage.

Nobody in the Lane household had talked about it around Sophie. But she'd already been twelve years old. She'd still known.

Maybe her father could stand being involved with the Cartell family now all these years later, but not Sophie.

She could be glad for the help Meyer provided to Meredith and the kids since John's death, but that didn't mean she would ever forgive him for what he'd done to Corinne.

She just wished she didn't see his face every time she closed her eyes.

Dear Reader,

Welcome to Cape Cardinale, a small coastal town in the Pacific Northwest that has as many secrets as the shore has shells. Pilot Meyer Cartell has to figure out how to coexist with his half siblings following the death of their father. In order to inherit the aging beach house their eccentric and neglectful father has left them, they first all have to live together in that house. The stipulation is destined to put a wrinkle in their lives, and Meyer is no exception, even though he's made his home in Cape Cardinale for several years now.

But that wrinkle has a silver lining in the form of nurse Sophie Lane, who lives nearby.

Meyer's had an eye on Sophie for a while now, but it's been a pointless exercise since she's never had any use for him. But all of that is about to change...

I hope you'll enjoy this trip to the coast as much as I have!

Allison

The Pilot's Secret

ALLISON LEIGH

HARLEQUIN

SPECIAL
EDITION

HARLEQUIN®

SPECIAL
EDITION™

PLEASE RECYCLE · THIS PRODUCT IS RECYCLABLE

Recycling programs
for this product may
not exist in your area.

ISBN-13: 978-1-335-59455-6

The Pilot's Secret

For questions and comments about the quality of this book,
please contact us at CustomerService@Harlequin.com.

Harlequin Enterprises ULC
22 Adelaide St. West, 41st Floor
Toronto, Ontario M5H 4E3, Canada
www.Harlequin.com

Printed in U.S.A.

Though her name is frequently on bestseller lists, **Allison Leigh**'s high point as a writer is hearing from readers that they laughed, cried or lost sleep while reading her books. She credits her family with great patience for the time she's parked at her computer, and for blessing her with the kind of love she wants her readers to share with the characters living in the pages of her books. Contact her at allisonleigh.com.

Books by Allison Leigh

Harlequin Special Edition

Cape Cardinale
The Pilot's Secret

The Fortunes of Texas: Hitting the Jackpot
Fortune's Runaway Bride

Return to the Double C

A Weaver Christmas Gift
One Night in Weaver...
The BFF Bride
A Child Under His Tree
Yuletide Baby Bargain
Show Me a Hero
The Rancher's Christmas Promise
A Promise to Keep
Lawfully Unwed
Something About the Season
The Horse Trainer's Secret
A Rancher's Touch
Her Wyoming Valentine Wish

Visit the Author Profile page
at Harlequin.com for more titles.

Prologue

"Is that the widow?"

The spectator's voice was hushed, barely audible to her companions who'd also ventured to the big church on the forbidding cape that overlooked a wind-churned ocean. They stood as close to the church as they could get considering the unsmiling faces of the security guards positioned between them and the mourners who'd been arriving all morning.

"I don't see any more limos coming up the road." Her friend was squinting through the rain. "So, I assume so. Otherwise it's too hard to tell with her umbrella and all. But judging by the wailing?" She snickered slightly behind her hand that she raised to her mouth only because it *was* a funeral and laughing outright—even from their distance across the road from the church—was unseemly. "Who else would it be?"

"The man had kids," someone behind them reminded, also in a quiet tone. "Maybe she's one of his daughters."

"Don't be sexist. Could be one of his sons."

"Wailing away like that?" Someone else snorted softly. "That's a woman, sure as shootin'."

"Oh, hush up, Burt."

In general, the dozen people huddling beneath their bubbled canopy of crowded umbrellas had been quiet and mannerly. As befitted any funeral, but particularly when those security guards had already given the boot to a bunch of reporters who'd gotten too rowdy—shouting questions to the mourners alighting from the steady stream of vehicles.

The guards couldn't do anything about the news helicopters hovering in the sky, though. They added a constant buzz beneath the crash of waves and the beat of falling rain and were a constant reminder that this wasn't just any funeral.

It was an *event*.

Pietro Cardinale had perished in a storm during his latest maritime adventure, which had only increased the public's interest where the famous photographer was concerned. Especially when he'd transmitted his last photograph only minutes before his ship had capsized in the Mediterranean.

His three crew members had been rescued.

But Pietro had been lost.

He'd been larger than life. Death obviously hadn't changed that. For days, the town had been awash with mourners coming in from around the world for the so-called "private" funeral.

Their small group of spectators weren't devastated mourners. It wasn't as if the photographer had done anything special for their part of the world. The galleries that sold his works for millions of dollars were in New York and Paris and the like. Certainly not down on *their* Main Street.

"I heard there was a prenup," someone mused while across the way, the wailing reached a fever pitch and the woman's umbrella fell to the ground, slowly rolling down the wide, shallow steps of the church. Supporters all dressed in black clustered even more closely around the desperately weeping individual, practically carrying her the rest of the way up to the church doors. "Everyone knows Cardinale was loaded. I'd be crying, too, having all that money out of my grasp."

A snicker *was* heard then. "You always were a mercenary soul, Donna."

"What about his other wives?" The first spectator turned her back on the church. "He had five, right? Prenups all around, I bet."

"Except maybe the first one." Finding herself at the center of attention, Donna preened in her yellow slicker and matching hat.

"What was her name?"

"Sharon something or other. No, Susan. I think that was it. She was a local, too. Same as Cardinale." Rainwater streamed off her glossy hat as Donna nodded. "Married him before he got famous."

"Divorced him before he got famous, too, from what I've heard," another woman said.

"She found out he was cheating on her and took their kid and left town for good," Donna said with authority. "Moved to Seattle and never came back."

Another woman crossed her arms beneath her rain poncho, looking challenging. "You've only lived here for five years. What makes you an authority on Pietro Cardinale? He might have been born on the cape, but he left a *long* time ago!"

Donna rolled her eyes. "Bartender, remember? I listen to people all the time. Pietro's roots are still here even if he isn't. Peter Cartell, you know. That was his real name. Four kids before the fifth wife?" She jabbed her chin in the direction of the church as she clucked her tongue. "Bet the widow's just plumb out of luck if everything goes to his children." She let out a long, envious whistle. "Talk about being set for life."

"Shoot," the first woman said. "I'd be happy if I had enough money for dinner at the Cliff for my anniversary."

Their little crowd gave a collective nod and huddled even closer as the wind continued to drive the rain, more punishing than sorrowful, while across the road, the steps finally cleared, the church doors finally closed and the forgotten umbrella slowly rolled down the steep road.

The weeping no longer audible, the helicopters seemed more noticeable. Or maybe they were just coming closer. Not that even their long-range lenses would be able to see anything through the stained-glass windows or the solid door any more than the spectators could from right across the road.

They remained there a while longer, until Donna finally sighed loudly. "Whad'ya say? Back to the pub? I could stand some hot chowder about now."

"Good whiskey will warm me a lot better than soup," Burt said while they all began tramping away from the church. They'd seen what they'd come to see.

The helicopters, though, stayed in place.

As did the rain.

Chapter One

"And that's it." Fitzgerald Lane closed the leather folder sitting on the desk in front of him with finality. "The only thing left in your father's estate after all the debts were paid is the coast property, currently valued around two million dollars."

Silence ensued.

Meyer Cartell pushed himself out of the wing chair he'd occupied for the duration of the lawyer's explanation and moved over to the window on the far wall. Fitzgerald's office was located in the tallest building in Cape Cardinale, and the view was as spectacular as all views of the cape were, even when the sky was a dull heavy gray, matching the whitecaps crashing on the rocks five floors below. Since the funeral two weeks ago, the weather had been the same. But at least the rain had stopped.

"We should've known," he murmured more to himself than the others.

His half sister, Dana, still heard. She was sitting in the

chair closest to him. Four of them in total. All positioned in a semicircle in front of Fitzgerald's desk so that he could deliver Pietro Cardinale's last wishes.

"Why should we have known?" she asked.

Meyer didn't answer. He doubted Dana expected one. No more than Cutter or Alexa. They'd known their father as well as Meyer had.

Which was to say not at all.

Silence still reigned, and Meyer sighed, pushing his fingertips against the pain centered at the nape of his neck. Smoke and mirrors, he thought. Everything about their father had always been smoke and mirrors. Including his supposedly massive wealth. Admittedly, a property worth two million dollars—even in its currently dilapidated state—was more than most people would ever see.

But it was also less than the selling price of a single one of their father's photographs.

He turned his back on the familiar view and looked at his siblings. The only thing they had in common was their father.

Peter Cartell.

Pietro Cardinale.

Didn't matter what name the man had used. His presence in their lives had been less than minimal, his lack of attention for each one of them enduringly constant.

"We *are* talking about the beach house." Meyer addressed the lawyer. "The house he inherited from his parents. The house he's neglected for more than thirty-five years. That's all that's left from the man who was supposed to be worth billions." Just to be sure, even though there was no reason to think they'd misunderstood the situation.

Fitzgerald refrained from pointing that out and nodded. "I'm afraid so. But once the last stipulation is met, you're free to do with it whatever you like."

Stipulation.

A simple word bearing a boatload of inconvenience.

"Why the hell would the old man want us to live in that house for a month, much less a year? Aside from the fact that we have lives, the place is a wreck." Days before that carnival of a funeral that Lotus had arranged, Meyer had driven down to the house on the beach where their father had been born. The house where Meyer had been born.

He remembered playing in the surf a lot more than he remembered the small house. Probably because he'd been barely five years old when his mother had hightailed out of there. She still lived in Seattle. Dana's mother in Portland. Alexa's in San Francisco, and Cutter's in Los Angeles.

Despite the years, the divorces, the bitter feelings, they'd all come to the funeral. Sat alongside Lotus, the latest Pietro Cardinale wife, who was younger than Meyer.

"Does it really matter why?" Alexa's question broke into Meyer's reverie again. He'd been ten when she was born. By then he'd been less confused about why his newest sister lived in another house than he'd been at five when Dana had been born—ergo his mother's abrupt departure from the beach house.

"The bottom line is that if we want to sell the place, we all have to agree to live there first," Alexa finished simply, as if she were talking to the second-grade children that she taught in San Francisco. "And the only thing we've ever been able to agree on is that our father was a complete failure in the parental department."

"Staying there for twelve months is one thing. But there's no *if* when it comes to selling," Meyer said flatly.

Unfortunately, Fitzgerald had already made it plain that if the four of them didn't comply with the stipulation, the property would be donated to a local charity. Save the dogs or some such.

The dogs would benefit. Cartell flesh and blood would, as usual, be forgotten.

He looked at Dana, who was sitting quietly, her attention on her hands folded on her lap. Both of his sisters were blonde. They both had the same blue eyes. But that was where they differed. Dana was tall, even-keeled and favored neutral-colored classics. Alexa was short, emotional and hadn't met a color she didn't like. "What about you, Dana? How's your husband going to like you being down here for an entire year?"

She spread her fingers, and the cluster of diamonds on her ring finger sparkled despite the dreary sky outside the windows. "Tyler's in real estate," she said calmly. "The property includes a half-mile cove of Oregon coastline. The beach is pristine because just getting to it involves a difficult hike. Ty would still say the time's worth it no matter what we decide to do with the property—renovate the house, tear it down to build more or investigate commercial development. All we need to do is stick it out. The possible return could be five times the current value if we're smart." She swept her long, waving hair off one shoulder. "I can deal with a few months of—"

"Roughing it?" Alexa didn't hide her faint smirk.

Dana's lips compressed slightly, but she didn't respond.

Alexa was right, though. No matter what she said, Dana was used to fine homes and fine things. Neither described the beach house.

Meyer looked toward Cutter—the youngest of them at twenty-eight. He was a head taller than Meyer and a hell of a lot smarter. He already ran his own business managing IT for other companies and worked wherever the hell he felt like. He lived his life exactly the way he wanted, but that same quality he'd inherited from their father was mostly devoid of their old man's arrogance. Unlike Pietro, there was nothing ostentatious about Cutter. And unlike Meyer, Cutter was usually as easygoing as a person could be.

His response was exactly what Meyer had expected. "I can work anywhere," Cutter said. Even though he looked around the room, his fingers never stopped working over the screen of his cell phone. "Twelve months is plenty of time to decide what to do with the place," he added, which was not quite what Meyer had expected at all.

"There's no decision to be made," Meyer said. He pushed his fists into the pockets of his weathered jacket. "If we're going to do this, then we sell the house the day it's legal to do so, pocket our share and go our separate ways again. We don't put a dime in it that we don't have to."

"Nobody put you in charge, Meyer." Dana's voice was still calm. "We're equally responsible when it comes to deciding." She released the deep blue shell hanging around her neck from a long chain and raised her palm, forestalling. "And yes, I realize spare dimes are at a premium for everyone."

Except for her, since her "in real estate" husband, Tyler Mercer, was one of the most successful developers in the Pacific Northwest. She and Ty owned several different homes—the closest of which was in Corvallis, some sixty miles away from Cape Cardinale. Meyer wasn't privy to the financial state of his siblings, but it was pretty safe to say that Dana was the only one of them who didn't need anything from their father's estate.

"I say we vote now on whether we want to proceed at all," Dana added, "or leave it to the dogs." It wasn't a metaphor. She lifted her hand again. "I'm a yes."

Meyer's jaw felt tight. With his share of the proceeds, he could put another chunk in the kids' college funds and still have enough left to finish cementing JCS Aviation's position at the airfield. "Yes," he said.

Cutter didn't look up from his phone. "Count me in."

"That leaves you, Alexa," Dana said.

Looking disgruntled, Alexa uncrossed her pretzeled legs and stood. The green-and-purple dress she wore stopped above her knees and looked wrinkled despite her tugging on it. Combined with the glittery gold sneakers on her feet, her outfit might have been chosen by one of her students. "Fine," she said abruptly. "But it's not just a few months." She gave Dana a telling look. "It's a full year and that's a real problem. I have a job in California, for Pete's sake. I'm expected to just give it up and hang out here?"

Fitzgerald cleared his throat softly. "I know it doesn't help, but the local schools are always looking for good teachers. Maybe you'll *like* Cape Cardinale and decide to stay."

Alexa tossed up her hands. "Well, then, goodie," she muttered facetiously.

Fitzgerald sighed. "I know this isn't easy for anyone. There's no time limit for deciding when you want to start your time—"

"Sentence," Cutter corrected. "If this were a horror movie, we'd all be doomed."

Fitzgerald didn't dispute it. "The stipulation was only that your stays in the house be concurrent and last for twelve months. Uninterrupted." Fitzgerald gave Meyer a warning look. "I know you, Major. Appearing now and then for a weekend isn't going to suffice. You'll all have to stick out the whole term. Live together. In the house. If one of you drops out, all of you will lose." He'd already explained that his involvement with the estate was only because he was local and could monitor the situation more easily and more affordably than the legal firm from New York could.

Meyer had spent fifteen years in the Air Force, the last several in Italy. It wasn't the prospect of spending a year in a run-down shack on the Oregon coast that bothered him. It was knowing that their father was reaching out from the grave to screw with things that he'd never given a rat's ass about while he'd been alive.

"Drop the 'Major'" was all he said to Fitzgerald, who knew perfectly well that Meyer had left all of that behind when he'd moved back to Cape Cardinale and taken over JCS six years ago. Fitzgerald Lane had been the attorney then, too.

Cutter slid his phone into his pocket as he rose. "I have a plane to catch," he said. "When y'all decide the D-Day, just text me the details. I'll be there."

The second the door closed behind him Alexa made a production of looking at her watch. "I had no idea it was so late. I still need to check out of the hotel, too." She took in both Dana and Meyer. "How *do* we decide when D-Day is? Meyer, you've got JCS to worry about, and Dana…" She smiled weakly. "Well, you've got, um—"

Dana lifted her hand. "Don't hurt yourself, Alexa. We all know I'm the unproductive member of our quartet." She stood. She'd been sitting just as long as Alexa while the lawyer had pedantically gone through the grim details of their father's estate, but her narrow white dress possessed none of the wrinkles that Alexa's bore.

"That's not what—"

Dana looked skeptical. "Forget it." She leaned down and brushed her cheek against her sister's. "You and Meyer decide the date." She gave Meyer the same glancing kiss. "I really don't care. And Ty won't, either." Without waiting for a response, she thanked the lawyer for his time and left, too.

Alexa looked up at Meyer expectantly. "Well? How are we going to work out this whole thing?"

Meyer's head throbbed harder. "Damned if I know," he muttered. "There are four of us. The beach house has three bedrooms and one freaking bathroom." After so many years of neglect, he expected that the plumbing wouldn't even work, but he kept that to himself.

Alexa made a face. "One bathroom will bother Princess Dana a lot more than it will me. You boys can bunk together because she and I are *not* sharing a room as well as a bathroom. Bad enough I'm going to have to give up a perfectly good job in the process."

The last thing he cared about was the longstanding tension between his sisters. Aside from an occasional holiday when their father had exhibited an inexplicable desire to gather them all together, the four of them had rarely spent time together under the same roof.

The only reason they stayed in occasional communication at all was because of Dana, who'd been insisting on it since she'd been a teenager.

"Maybe you can get a leave of absence," he suggested.

She just grimaced and tossed up her hands when thunder suddenly rumbled through the room. "Honestly! The rain here never stops. And stupidly, I used one of the hotel bicycles to get here."

"I'll give you a ride back," he said absently. Rain wouldn't affect their charter schedule, but a thunderstorm was another matter. He'd need to check in with Hannah. Plan for contingencies.

The lawyer accompanied them down the carpeted hall to the elevator, but before he could press the button, it slid open to reveal a young woman wearing a red-and-white polka-dot raincoat over narrow jeans and boots. "Sophie," he said, clearly surprised. "What are you doing here?"

"Hi, Daddy." She practically bounced out of the elevator and came to an abrupt halt when her bright brown gaze landed on Meyer. Something in her eyes glinted frostily before she recovered and stretched up to kiss her father's cheek. "Thought I'd treat you to lunch if you're free."

"I am, and I accept," Fitzgerald said with a smile. "Go on to the office while I finish up."

She gave Alexa a polite nod and ignored Meyer completely as she turned on her heel and strode away.

Didn't stop him from watching the way her honey-colored ponytail bounced between her shoulders and her polka dots swayed.

"I've arranged an inspection for the house."

Meyer realized the lawyer was holding the elevator doors open with his palm.

"I'll notify you when I have the report," Fitzgerald continued. "You all can decide how you want to proceed from there and let me know. Reasonable costs for necessary repairs can be charged to the estate until the final settlement."

"At least there's that," Alexa muttered under her breath as she shook the lawyer's hand before stepping into the elevator.

Meyer followed suit, and the doors slid closed. The image of Sophie Lane, though, stayed fresh in his mind.

"Twelve months," Alexa muttered under her breath as the elevator descended. "Not that I can't use half a mil after all is said and done, but seriously?"

"Preaching to the choir," he told her. At least she seemed in favor of unloading the property at the earliest opportunity. "Fitzgerald Lane wasn't exaggerating, though. They do need schoolteachers here. I'm sure you'll be able to find work if you want."

"Whoop-de-doo," she said glumly.

"Plus, you wouldn't need to pay San Francisco rent while you're here," he added.

Her expression brightened slightly. "Is that what you'll do? Give up your apartment?"

He hadn't even thought about it. Rent in Cape Cardinale was a lot different than rent in San Francisco.

"Except, even with the inheritance, I won't be able to buy anything bigger than a coat closet when I go back home." She rubbed her forehead, sighing.

He almost reached out to squeeze her shoulder but refrained. Sister or not, it seemed too familiar.

"What's the real estate market *really* like around here anyway?" She looked up at him. "The property is only worth what someone's willing to spend. What happens if the place doesn't sell and all we've ended up doing was wasting an entire year of our lives?"

"It'll sell. Even in the state it's in, it'll sell. Beach properties always do."

They reached the ground floor, and she stepped off the elevator. "Are you in the parking garage?"

He nodded. "I'll drive around to the front and pick you up."

As soon as he reached the front of the building, she darted forward with her bicycle. He got out long enough to toss it into the truck bed and get soaked in the process. He glanced up at the top floor of the building as he moved back to the cab of the truck.

Sophie Lane stood in the window. The light from behind her made her glow a little. Golden. Warm.

He exhaled, ignoring the usual surge of heat she always inspired, climbed behind the wheel and drove away.

Chapter Two

"I saw your business partner this afternoon."

Meredith Skinner looked over her shoulder at Sophie and raised her eyebrows. "You were out at the airfield?"

Sophie shook her head. She focused on stirring cream into her coffee, but in her mind, all she could see was Meyer Cartell when she'd come off the elevator. Six feet of perfectly sculpted brawn topped by short rusty hair, a cruelly exceptional jaw and faithless blue eyes. "At my father's office."

"Oh, right." Meredith turned back to the mountain of pots and pans she was washing in the sink. Two teenage children made for a lot of dishes despite the dishwasher. "They did the reading of his father's will this morning. Can you imagine what that must be like?" She turned on the faucet to rinse a pan. "Not the will, I mean. But having a father as famous as Pietro Cardinale?" She set the pan on the drainboard to dry. "I didn't even know mine."

Sophie reached over to the box of cookies she'd brought

from the school bake sale and selected a sugar cookie. She dipped the edge into her coffee and nibbled at it. "What do you think he's going to do? Now that he'll be rich, I mean."

"Meyer doesn't care about money."

"The only people who say that are people who have it."

Meredith laughed outright. "I just said it, and we *know* I don't have any to spare." She gestured with one sudsy hand, taking in the cozy kitchen made even cozier because of the round table and chairs where Sophie sat. "Proof of which is all around us." She lifted her eyes toward the ceiling at a sudden burst of yelling coming from upstairs.

A few seconds later, feet pounded on the stairs and Meredith's fourteen-year-old daughter appeared. Leda's unruly brown hair was twisted on top of her head with two pencils stuck in it. "You have to make Grange stop," she said through her teeth. "I have a test tomorrow, and I *need* the computer!"

"Leda, you've been studying for that history test for weeks," Meredith said. But she leaned back her head and addressed the ceiling again. "Grange," she yelled, "leave the computer to your sister."

There was no response except the stomp of feet and a resounding door slam.

Leda rolled her eyes. "He's such a child," she muttered and started back up the stairs.

Meredith exhaled and waited until the steps were silent again. "Just another day in the Skinner household," she said wryly. She grabbed a towel to dry her hands and pulled out the chair opposite Sophie. She emptied the rest of the coffee pot into a fresh mug and took the cow-shaped pitcher that Sophie nudged her way. "It's a good thing I'm not a drinker, or I'd be adding something a lot stronger to this coffee than cream." She tilted the pitcher over her mug.

"They're good kids," Sophie said.

Meredith's lips curved, and she nodded. "Just teenagers, heaven help me." She raised her eyes again, even though there was no yelling. "How did he seem? I should have thought to call him. It had to be stressful. Everything concerning his father is stressful."

Sophie managed not to grimace. She knew her best friend felt grateful to Meyer Cartell for the way he'd left the military and stepped in to take over his best friend's aviation business when John Skinner had died six years ago. On the surface it sounded selfless—one friend keeping another friend's dream alive. But she herself remembered Meyer Cartell from much further back when he'd dated her sister, Corinne, for a summer.

He'd left her brokenhearted, and as far as Sophie was concerned, Corinne had never been the same.

She toyed with her mug. She had her own feelings of guilt for not calling her sister more often. "He seemed like he always seems." Too damned good looking for such a waste of space. No matter how much he'd done for Meredith and her kids. "What if he takes his money and runs?"

"I'd miss him," Meredith said promptly. "But he won't. JCS is finally profitable thanks to him. If John had lived—" She moved the box of cookies to the table and studied the contents. "I wonder sometimes if he'd have been able to accomplish as much with JCS as Meyer has." She raised her eyes toward the ceiling when they heard a loud thump, but after a couple seconds with no fallout, she looked back at Sophie. "Did I ever tell you that he refused to take a salary that whole first year after the plane accident?"

Sophie shook her head. She and Meredith had been friends for ten years. Ever since Sophie had left her job working in a Portland emergency room to come back to Cape Cardinale and join Doc Hayes's practice, where Meredith had been an office assistant.

John Skinner had been alive then, making a modest success of his fledgling flight-charter service. Leda and Grange had been in preschool.

A lot had changed since then, but not Sophie and Meredith's friendship. Even if Sophie didn't believe that Meyer Cartell was as pure of heart as Meredith seemed to think.

"He even paid our mortgage payments for a while," Meredith finished. "Him. Not JCS."

If only Saint Meyer had been as caring with my sister.

Sophie forced the thought aside, making an appropriately impressed sound. She shoved the rest of the dry cookie into her mouth, swallowing it down with a long drink of coffee that left her throat feeling a little singed.

"Meyer's going to do what Meyer's going to do." Meredith set down her mug and slowly rotated it between her fingers. "That's what John always used to say. If this were even two years ago, I'd be panicked at the idea of him leaving. John poured everything into JCS, and all I had was—" She broke off for a moment, shaking her head. "All I had was a high school diploma, a part-time job with Doc Hayes and John's old Camaro. I barely earned enough to cover the cost of childcare, much less our mortgage or the money-suck of JCS."

None of which was news to Sophie. "And now?"

Meredith inhaled deeply and let it out slowly. "Now JCS is bigger and better than ever. It's solid. Profitable. And employs more people than John ever imagined. I *hope* that continues under Meyer's management, but even if it didn't, thanks to the way he's managed the profits, my debts are paid. I'm still just a high school graduate, but I run Doc's office now. I own a company that I could actually sell for a profit. The kids—teenagers or not—are healthy and usually happy and…" Her voice trailed off.

"And you have Walker now," Sophie finished.

"I didn't say anything about Walker!"

Sophie pushed her tongue into her cheek and focused hard on her coffee until she'd conquered the urge to grin.

Walker Armstrong was fairly new to town. An associate at her father's law firm. He and Meredith had been dating for a few months now, and the blush on Meredith's cheeks was answer enough.

She switched subjects entirely. "What do you hear from Doc?" Their employer was four months into his six-month sabbatical. "Where's he this month? Egypt?"

Meredith nodded. "He says he spends every day wishing he were back in his rooms even if he's treating Burt Griffin's gout."

Sophie chuckled. "I'll be glad when he's back, too."

"Subbing for the school nurse getting old?"

"Oh, it's fine." She waved her mug. "But I can only wipe so many noses without feeling a little—"

"Bored?"

"Let's just say less than challenged."

"What about your cases with Cardinale Cares? They less than challenging, too? I know they're keeping Olivia busy. Every time I've tried calling her lately, she's been busy."

Olivia was a physical therapist from Doc Hayes's office who'd also gone to work for the new home–health care company during his sabbatical. But in her case, she was doing it full-time whereas Sophie was only taking assignments on the weekends. "We have a patient in common right now, so I get to see her occasionally. She's got a full schedule, for sure."

"Just so long as you both remember Doc's coming back in two months." Meredith pointed her cookie at Sophie. "We've got a perfect team there."

Sophie smiled. "You don't have to remind me of that. I can't wait for things to get back to normal." She loved working in private practice where she had a chance to develop real client relationships that lasted. "So, when you talk to Doc, you'd better make sure he doesn't get some wild hair about extending his sabbatical." The doctor hadn't left his staff hanging for the duration of his sabbatical, but even a generous man like him couldn't afford to pay his entire staff their full salaries for six entire months. With the exception of Meredith, who had JCS, they'd all had to take on temporary positions. "Doc's partial salary is great, but I much prefer not having to work a bunch of different jobs to pay my mortgage."

"Wouldn't have that mortgage if you hadn't moved out of your dad's *very* spacious house," Meredith drawled. "I still can't believe you bought that old bungalow down on Bluff Road when you could be living in the lap of comfort, complete with a housekeeper *and* a cook."

"I'm thirty-three years old. Lap of comfort or not, it was high time I had a place of my own, and I *love* it," Sophie said. "I can sit on the deck feeling the ocean spray on my face and watch the sunset every evening." It was just unfortunate that after she'd purchased the place a year ago, Doc Hayes had announced the plans for his sabbatical a few months later.

"You *have* to sit outside because it has a kitchen even smaller than this one!"

She laughed. That was true. "The only person it needs to fit is me. I am not feeding two other mouths."

"Oh my god, talk about feeding." Meredith shook her head. "Grange ate an entire box of cereal one day after school last week and *still* consumed half the roast that I'd thought would have at least *some* leftovers. He has hollow legs—I am convinced of it. He's going to be thirteen in June! What's he going to be like in a few years?"

Sophie smiled. "Nearly as tall as John was?"

Meredith nodded. "Probably." She chewed the inside of her lip for a moment. "Walker wants us to go away for a long weekend," she suddenly blurted. "Just, um, just the two of us."

Sophie raised her eyebrows. "And?"

"I can't leave the kids alone."

"I'll stay with them," Sophie offered immediately. "Unless—" she peered closely at Meredith "—you want a reason *not* to go?"

Meredith closed her eyes and tilted back her head. "I don't know what I want, Soph. Walker is so…good and steady, but he's not…" She sighed again.

Sophie set aside her cup and covered Meredith's hand with her own. "He's not John?"

Meredith looked pained. "I wouldn't want him to be like John," she said quietly. "John *wanted* to be a good family man, but wanting and being are two different things." She smiled, bittersweet. "Hindsight is so clear."

"Then what's the hesitation about Walker?"

"We haven't, um…" Meredith made a face. "You know."

Sophie managed to keep her jaw from hitting the table. "You guys have been dating for months!"

"He hasn't wanted to rush me. And there hasn't been anyone else since John died. You know that. And if I *had* slept with him, I would have told you."

"I just thought you were being private." Sophie sat back in her chair, still feeling stunned. "Haven't you wanted—"

Meredith's cheeks flushed again. "Well, yeah. Obviously I've wanted." She suddenly scrubbed her face with her hands. "This is so ridiculous. I'm nearly forty years old, but I feel like I'm a schoolgirl all over again." She dropped her hands, suddenly irksome. "I didn't like school the *first* time around!"

Sophie couldn't stop her smile this time. "Where does Walker want to take you?"

"He says anywhere I'd like to go, but his family does own a cabin in Colorado that we could use."

"Very nice. A romantic weekend in the mountains."

Meredith leaned closer. "I can't agree and not expect to sleep with him, can I?"

Sophie made a face. "What makes you think I'm an expert? Every guy *I* go out with ends up getting an itch to marry someone else." She hadn't had a date, much less sex, since Ricky Scarpa had dumped her more than a year ago. She picked up her mug again. "And I definitely haven't had any weekend invitations from handsome lawyers. Of *course* he expects the two of you to do the deed. But don't talk to me about it. Talk to Walker. And if you decide—whenever you decide—to go, I am happy to watch Leda and Grange."

"That's what Meyer said, too."

Sophie felt suddenly irksome herself. "You talked to Meyer about this?" She stopped the *before me* from emerging, but it bounced around inside her head all the same. Talk about schoolgirl.

Meredith snorted softly. She'd returned to the sink and the dwindling suds. "Not about Walker. We were going over all the things he's planned at the airfield celebrating Memorial Day, and we got to talking about how long it had been since either one of us had even a semblance of a getaway. Everything I do is centered around the kids. Soccer tournaments. Spelling bees and science fairs." She turned on the tap.

Sophie swirled the dregs of coffee in her mug. "And what was his excuse?" As if she didn't know. JCS Aviation and Meredith were Meyer's excuses. She just had never been able to tell which superseded the other.

And the fact that she continued to wonder annoyed the daylights out of her. Ordinarily she could go for months at a time without Meyer even being a topic of conversation between her and Meredith.

She blamed it on him being at her father's office.

Of all days to surprise him for lunch.

"I learned the Memorial Day parade route ends at the airfield," she said. "That's a switch." It usually ran the other direction, ending at Friars Beach.

"Yeah, I'm not sure if Meyer bribed the mayor or what he did to accomplish that." Meredith smiled. "The route's been the same for as long as I can remember. You going to volunteer at the first aid station again for the parade?"

"Probably. Imagine the planning committee will send out the notices—" She broke off when Leda squawked from the top of the stairs.

"Mother," the girl yelled. "Grange is being an annoying little creep!"

"*Muh...ther,*" Grange mocked, knocking into Leda deliberately as he raced down the stairs, the tablet computer he'd snatched right out of her grasp in the process in his hand. His hair was as curly as Leda's and nearly as long, and Leda caught a hunk in her fingers and yanked. Grange yelped and stopped short on the stairs, scrabbling furiously at his sister's grasp even as he held the tablet out of her reach.

"Let go of your brother," Meredith said, walking over to the staircase. She slid the tablet from her son's hand but didn't give it back to Leda. "And both of you go and do something that does not involve computers. I said *go!*" she added over their immediate protests.

Leda let go of Grange, who muttered something goading under his breath as he pushed past his sister again to beat her back up the stairs.

"If I fail my test tomorrow it is *your* fault," Leda accused Meredith over her shoulder. She stomped loudly on each step, the better to communicate her ire.

Meredith sighed and looked at Sophie. "Oh, for the days of hungry babies and sleepless nights. So much easier."

"I'll have to take your word for it," Sophie said dryly. She took her mug to the sink and washed it before giving Meredith a quick hug. "I'll talk to you later."

"Sure that you're willing to watch them for a long weekend?" Meredith asked as the kids upstairs started yelling again. "I know you're a nurse and all, but that—" she jabbed her thumb toward the ceiling "—takes nerves of steel."

Sophie chuckled. "I'm sure," she said before letting herself out the door as Meredith headed up the stairs again to deal with her feuding offspring.

The sun had set by the time Sophie made it across town. When she passed Oceanview Church, located at the highest point of the cape, she turned on the narrow road that zigzagged its way down the southern side of the cliff toward Cardinale Beach.

It had stopped raining, but the wind grew stronger the closer she got to her home, making her mini SUV rock. With every zig, her headlights swept over the choppy water beyond the cliff topped with Sitka spruce that were blacker than obsidian in the dark. With the next zag, she saw spiky beach grass swaying in the wind, a waltz of gentler waves than the water that crashed against the cliffs. When the road leveled out at the bottom, she passed the turnoff for the little house on the beach that had been abandoned as long as she could remember, turned once more and finally pulled into the neat carport the previous owners had built onto the backside of her bungalow.

She pulled her oversized purse out of the car and let herself in through the side door.

The wind carried the door shut with a bang, and she shivered slightly at the chilliness inside the house. Turning lights on along the way, she tossed her purse onto a narrow table and grabbed a chunky cardigan from the hooks next to it. Humming under her breath, she pulled on the cardigan and exchanged her flat-heeled boots for fleecy slippers. She poured a glass of wine from the bottle she'd opened a few days ago and returned it to her dorm-sized refrigerator. Then she hit the switch for the gas fireplace, watched the flames leap to life around the lifelike logs and walked over to the bare windows that overlooked her covered porch and the fifteen feet of cantilevered decking beyond that.

The waves were not any calmer in front of her house. Despite expending considerable energy over the stretch of boulders below her deck, a swirling froth of misty spray still blew up and over the five-foot plexiglass wall surrounding the deck.

Sophie clasped the lapels of her sweater under her chin with one hand and rested her shoulder against the thick windowpane, feeling the soft roar of the surf as much as she heard it.

She loved this spot, had known it was exactly what she wanted the moment that she'd stepped foot inside the house. Yes, just the down payment alone had cost every cent that she'd been squirreling away since she'd been a fifteen-year-old babysitter, and yes, it was cozy.

But the only one it needed to fit was her, just as she'd told Meredith. That didn't mean she wasn't aware of just how alone it felt, though. Particularly on evenings like tonight—going from the weeknight chaos of a home with kids to a home where the only squawking came from seagulls fighting over food.

"You need a date, Soph," she said to her faint reflection.

Her reflection sipped the buttery chardonnay and stared back.

She sighed and reached out to turn on the porch light, sending her reflection into oblivion. The round patio table and chairs appeared instead. Beyond them, the wet boards of her deck glistened. The circle of light reached far enough to illuminate the sea spray when another wave hit.

As mesmerizing as the sight was, Sophie couldn't stop thinking about that afternoon when a set of elevator doors had opened, leaving her face-to-face with Meyer Cartell.

Corinne had gotten an abortion after that summer spent dating Meyer. He'd been staying with John Skinner. A last hurrah, evidently, before they'd donned their Air Force uniforms. And Corinne had been collateral damage.

Nobody in the Lane household had talked about it around Sophie. But she'd already been twelve years old. She'd still known.

Maybe her father could stand being involved with Meyer Cartell all these years later, but not Sophie.

Objectively, she could acknowledge the help Meyer provided to Meredith and the kids since John's death, but that didn't mean she would ever forgive him for what he'd done to Corinne.

She just wished she didn't see his face every time she closed her eyes.

She flipped off the porch light again. Hiding the sea mist. Hiding the wet deck. Her faint reflection returned again and stared back at her until finally, Sophie turned away. She turned off the gas fire, dumped out the wine that she hadn't finished and went to bed.

Chapter Three

"Don't forget we have the tour this afternoon with the kids from Howell Elementary."

Meyer looked up from the report he was studying and focused on the woman standing in the doorway of his office. Hannah Blackstone had been with him from the beginning. She'd been the first pilot Meyer had hired when he'd realized how precarious JCS was. Now Hannah was retired from flying, but she did damn near everything else—from cleaning the bathrooms if necessary to her actual job of marketing their services up and down the coastline.

His brain was still on the home-inspection report that Fitzgerald Lane had emailed him that morning. "Tour?"

Hannah raised an eyebrow and propped her hand on her hip. "The school tour that I reminded you about just yesterday?"

He pulled off his reading glasses and rubbed his eyes. "Yeah. Right." Two classes of fourth and fifth graders from the local school. Hannah had set it up as part of their Career Week or something. "When?"

"Two o'clock."

He glanced at the plain round clock on the wall above the ancient filing cabinets. It was already half past one. He closed his laptop—the one truly modern piece of equipment in an office that had been furnished with serviceable items circa 1970—and stood. "What am I supposed to do?"

Hannah rolled her eyes. "Sometimes I feel an urge to pin a note on your shirt that says *If lost, return to*—"

"Yeah, yeah." He automatically looked through the windows in front of his desk out to the enormous hangar below. Three sleek jets were parked inside. Two belonged to JCS. The third was being serviced by them for the owner—a tech billionaire out of Seattle. The other two aircraft owned by JCS were out on private charters.

He passed by Hannah and headed down the catwalk to the metal stairs. She was nearly as tall as he was and kept pace with ease. "Tater's polishing up the Stearman, and Tanya's setting up the conference room."

He nodded. The Boeing Stearman biplane, with its brilliant yellow-and-blue paint and open cockpit, was always popular for people to see whether they were eight or eighty. The fact that JCS had one that was still airworthy was one small detail that set them apart from other charter services in the area. "What kind of food is she putting out?"

"Why? Did you forget to have lunch again?"

He didn't bother answering.

Hannah snorted softly and clattered down the metal stairs after him. "Hot dogs and chips," she told him.

His stomach was growling. A hot dog wasn't high on his list of favorites, but it would fill the hole.

They reached the bottom of the stairs, and he crossed between the two JCS jets. Unlike the colorful Stearman, the jets were white with two stripes of deep blue running from the nose to a curl up the tail. Meyer had made a lot of changes in how JCS operated since he'd taken over, but he hadn't changed the paint scheme that John had designed himself back when they'd been in officer training school.

We'll own our own aircraft, John had said, doodling on his pad and dreaming about the future outside of the Air Force even when they'd been barely inside. *That way we control everything.*

Meyer and Hannah walked beyond the yawning hangar into the sunshine and turned in the direction of the executive terminal.

It was a glorified term for the building, but that hadn't stopped Meyer from having the sign placed on it. Cape Cardinale Airfield was owned by the town of Cape Cardinale. But the operations on it was owned by JCS, including the terminal with its two lounges—one for passengers and one for flight crew—restrooms, office and conference room, all designed to bring comfort and ease to the pilots who chose to stop there for refueling before heading elsewhere.

Until a few years ago, Cape Cardinale had rarely been the ending destination of choice. Now Meyer envisioned a future where the town held its own among the finest coastal towns in the Pacific Northwest.

"Glad the weather is finally acting like winter is over," Hannah commented when they reached the gleaming glass door of the building.

"Only took us halfway through spring." Meyer could see a school bus out on Perimeter Road. He lifted his hand in response to the rag Tater Jones was waving at him before following her inside, where she immediately made off for her own office.

Whereas the one he used in the hangar was ancient and serviceable, the interior of the terminal was modern and sleek. He'd negotiated with local businesses to kick in the funds to make it so, since they were the ones who also benefited from the upgraded impression. He was having more of a challenge with the mayor and the city council agreeing to fund the next expansion he wanted—a longer runway.

The seed money from his inheritance would be a good lure, though.

He found Tanya in the conference room. She was Tater's daughter and, besides owning a popular eponymous restaurant in town, was the go-to when it came to events utilizing the room. They'd had six weddings in the last year, countless business meetings and whenever it was raining, the Church of Sunshine and Harmony held its Sunday service there.

"Couldn't get the school to spring for barbecue brisket, I guess," he said, stopping next to the banquet table where she was arranging air-swollen bags of potato chips in a basket.

"Good thing." Tanya's nimble fingers didn't stop arranging. "Have barely had time to breathe since the circus left—" She broke off, giving him a chagrined glance. "Sorry."

He shrugged. "The funeral *was* a circus," he agreed. The town had been besieged by the people that Lotus had invited from far and farther as well as the media clowns that had followed them everywhere they'd gone. Lotus had chosen Cape Cardinale for the funeral only because of the tie-in to the name that Meyer's father had adopted. She'd counted on the attention it would draw.

And it had. Even the local hotels and restaurants had made a killing. So had JCS, for that matter. For the first time in its history, they'd had to turn down charter requests.

"Saw the school bus out on Perimeter." He lifted the lid off the pan of hot dogs long enough to grab one with the tongs and set it back in place. Tanya beat him to the buns, deftly placing one into a paper basket and handing it to him. "Be here in five minutes."

She immediately pulled off the thin plastic gloves she'd been wearing, tossed them into the trash and donned a fresh pair. "Shoot. Are they early?"

"Not really." He pushed the dog between the bun halves and returned the tongs to the handle of the steam pan. While she moved even more quickly, arranging fat, frosted cupcakes on a tray, he pumped ketchup and mustard onto the dog and lifted it to his mouth. Holding the plate close to his chin to catch crumbs, he moved out of Tanya's way when she shooed him, and he glanced at the colorful brochures placed at precise intervals on the narrow tables facing the front of the room where a big rolling whiteboard had been placed.

You, too, can fly! And fifty other career ideas in the aviation industry.

He smiled slightly.

When he'd been a kid, he hadn't needed any school field trip to inspire him. He'd known he wanted to be a pilot since he'd wound the rubber band on his first balsa-wood airplane.

He'd wolfed down the hot dog and was just throwing away the plate when the yellow bus rumbled past the windows overlooking the airfield's two runways. It continued out of sight, and he left the conference room, heading for the lobby entrance.

He pushed the doors wide until they were locked open, and Hannah returned with a basket of souvenir wing pins just as the bus doors opened and spewed young adolescents out onto the sidewalk. They immediately ran helter-skelter until a thin-lipped woman lifted the whistle hanging around her neck and blew into it sharply.

"Order!" Her voice was almost as shrill as the whistle,

and Hannah slid a look Meyer's way as every single child immediately shuffled into an orderly line. "Remember, we are here to learn! Where are my chaperones?"

"School's hiring drill sergeants now," Hannah murmured while two women wearing floppy hats against the sun and a man in dark sunglasses fanned out, spacing themselves along the line of children. Hannah was trying to hide her smile and doing a bad job of it.

He didn't bother trying at all and stepped forward, extending his hand toward the Whistle in Charge. "Mrs. Maitland." He knew pulling the teacher's name out of the hat would impress Hannah, who routinely accused him of not paying attention. "Welcome to JCS Aviation. I'm Meyer Cartell. I run the operation here."

"Mr. Cartell." The teacher shook his hand briskly and turned to survey the students. "May I present the members of our fourth and fifth grades at Howell Elementary School? We're very grateful for your participation in our Career Week. Children." She raised her voice slightly. "What do we say to Mr. Cartell?"

"Thank you, Mr. Cartell" was the immediate singsong response.

His smile widened. He remembered Leda and Grange at this age. Back then, Meredith would have been one of the chaperones on the fieldtrips they'd had—always to her children's dismay because they'd have preferred anyone else's mother over their own. "We have snacks inside waiting for you—" that garnered some shifting and murmurs of interest "—but before we get to that, how many of you have been out here to the airfield before?" He lifted his hand, and a few went up in response.

"My dad is a private pilot," a ginger-haired boy near the front of the line boasted. "He's here all the time."

Meyer lowered his hand. "What's his name?"

"Nick Dowling."

"We know Nick, don't we, Ms. Blackstone?"

"Sure do." Hannah's smile didn't so much as flicker even though Nick Dowling was a pain in the rear, complaining about everything from the price of fuel to the quality of coffee provided free of charge in the crew lounge.

Meyer gestured with his hand, taking in the buildings around them. "For those of you who haven't been out here, in addition to offering private charters, JCS Aviation is what's called a Fixed Base Operator, or FBO for short."

"You're a gas station for airplanes," the Dowling boy said. "And my dad says the prices you charge—"

"Are based on what we have to pay for it from our distributors," Meyer spoke over him. Like father like son.

His conscience pricked hard. He didn't want to be compared to *his* father. Wasn't fair to compare ginger-boy to his old man, either. He grabbed a couple plastic pins from Hannah's basket and tossed the first one to the Dowling boy. He caught it easily and grinned, offering his thanks even before his teacher prompted.

Meyer tossed out the others he held, and Hannah took up the rest. "Yes, we sell fuel to the aircraft that require it. We have a line crew that does all the servicing. They'll take care of refueling and cleaning and anything else the aircraft might need. We also have mechanics who can do engine repairs and other specialists who can fix cabin-interior problems like torn upholstery. We also have a marketing expert—" he didn't look at Hannah in case they both laughed "—who handles advertising and social media. So, you can see there are lots of different kinds of jobs involved."

Hannah was almost halfway down the line of kids. "If the pilot is leaving his or her aircraft for any length of time, we store it for them until they're ready to get back in the air. We *are* like a gas station, but we're more like a big truck stop than a corner convenience store with a pump."

A shy-looking girl lifted her hand cautiously. "We stop at a truck stop whenever we drive up to Seattle. They have a restaurant, and the bathroom has *showers*." She lifted a diffident shoulder. "Anyway, I... I like the brownies they sell."

Meyer grinned. "Well, we don't have brownies, but we do have cupcakes from the best baker in town for all of you a little later on. So why don't we go visit the hangar first, where you can see our latest jets, and then Ms. Blackstone will show you around the executive terminal. And after that, we'll head into the conference room where one of our pilots, Jason, is going to talk to you about learning how to fly."

He stepped out of the way as Hannah took the lead and the kids trooped after her toward the hangar.

Only when it got down to the chaperone positioned at the rear of the line did Meyer realize that her broad-brimmed hat was hiding a distinctive honey-colored ponytail.

"Sophie." Her name came out unintentionally. "I didn't know it was you under the hat." He knew she was a nurse. "School chaperoning seems a long way from Doc Hayes's office."

"I'm filling in for the school nurse." Besides the hat, she wore sunglasses. She didn't bother taking off either, even when the shade of the hangar cast over them. "As for *this* gig, I was drafted."

She didn't sound pleased, and for a minute, he wondered if he was supposed to apologize for it. Then he wondered why he wondered.

A perpetual problem where Sophie Lane was concerned.

She was Meredith's best friend. As a result, some encounters over the last six years had been unavoidable.

Sophie was never entirely rude to him but never exactly friendly, either.

Maybe she blamed him for John Skinner's death.

If so, they had that in common since Meyer blamed himself, too.

"Maybe you'll enjoy the cupcakes at least," he told her. "They're from Tanya's."

He left her and joined Hannah as the kids clustered around the gleaming jets. He was impressed with the questions—everything from how fast they flew to how many people they could carry to how much they cost to rent.

"What's up there?" A girl with tangled brown pigtails down to her rear pointed up at the catwalk.

"That's where my office is."

"Why not in the terminal?" Sophie asked.

Meyer looked at her, more surprised that she'd asked a question at all than by the question itself. "It suits me better."

"He likes being closer to the planes," Hannah added and widened her eyes when Meyer shot her a quick look. "He used to be a pilot with the Air Force," she told the students, which set off another tangent of whose mom or dad was in what military service while they jockeyed for position in line as they headed back to the terminal.

At least the kids seemed to be having fun so far.

Sophie, on the other hand, looked like she'd rather be anywhere else.

When he figured he was focusing too much on her rear view, he strode ahead until he caught up to Hannah.

She gave him a sidelong look. "You're like a long-tailed cat in a rocking chair store. What's wrong?"

"Have a lot to do besides elementary school tours."

She made a sound. She obviously didn't believe him, but they'd reached the terminal again and the kids filed inside.

There was a lot more to explore in the terminal than in the hangar, but Mrs. Maitland still relaxed enough that she only threatened to bring out her whistle one time. After the students had prowled through the lounges, peered and poked at the various items they carried for visitors to purchase, and run up and down the steps a few times to the weather center, they headed finally into the conference room where they eviscerated the supply of chips and hot dogs.

Mrs. Maitland and her whistle stepped in at that moment before they could descend on the cupcakes.

"I advise waiting until the end before giving them the cupcakes," she told Meyer. "It will be a helpful—" she broke off long enough to witness Sophie catching the Dowling kid before the chair he'd climbed on tipped over "—enticement to encourage good behavior," she finished in a rush as she hurried over to them.

"*Mister* Dowling," she said severely. "What were you thinking?" She took his shoulder in her hand and steered him toward the door. "Nurse Lane, you're in charge while I speak with our budding acrobat."

Somewhere along the way, the chaperones had discarded their hats and sunglasses, and Meyer saw the vague alarm ripple across her face.

He clapped his hands together. Loudly and just once, a trick he'd learned in the service. It served him well now as he walked through the kids who'd all turned their attention his way. "Before we head outside where you'll meet Ollie, I want to introduce you to our newest pilot, Jason."

The little girl with the liking for truck-stop brownies raised her hand again. "Who's Ollie?"

"Ollie—short for Olive Oil—is our oldest member here at JCS," Meyer told her, "and I think she works harder than all of us. She'll blow your socks off, I promise." He dropped his arm over Jason's shoulder. "And this is Jason, who is the *youngest* member here at JCS. How old are all of you?"

He got a chorus of "nines" and "tens," which was what he'd expected. "Jason was only sixteen when he earned his first certification as a sport pilot. Anyone ever been up in a hot-air balloon?"

The children were looking around at each other, and almost reluctantly, Sophie, standing in the back of the room, raised her hand.

"I always wanted to go in a hot-air balloon." The brownie-lover was rapt. "I bet it was awesome."

Focused on the girl, Sophie's expression turned soft. "It was awesome," she said with a smile. "I'd do it again in a heartbeat if I had a chance."

"Ballooning is great," Jason agreed. "But I didn't want to pilot only balloons. I wanted to pilot all sorts of aircraft like Major Cartell does. He has a lot more stories about flying than I do."

Meyer felt fifty pairs of eyes latch onto his face. It was worse than having fifty hard-as-nails airmen staring him down. His neck felt hot, but he waved his hand casually and shook his head. "Nothing that's as interesting as becoming JCS's youngest flight instructor." He nodded toward Jason. "He earned his private certificate when he was seventeen, his commercial when he was eighteen and his flight-instructor cert a few months later. Which means that he can teach anyone in here right now how to become a pilot."

Jason tugged his ear. "But you would have to wait a few years before you could test for your own license," he warned.

"I wanna be like the Jetsons," one of the kids said, "and drive flying cars."

The comment earned both agreement and jeers.

"I think a flying car would be cool," Jason agreed, "but for now we have more traditional aircraft. And I'm pretty lucky to be already earning my living at it before I'm even twenty."

"How come you wanna be a pilot, anyway?"

Meyer was glad to move aside now that Jason had gained the focus, and he walked to the back of the room near Sophie and the other two chaperones. He leaned back against the wall and crossed his arms while Jason—less than ten years older than some of his listeners—told his tale.

Through the window beside him, he could see Mrs. Maitland. She was obviously still giving the Dowling kid a stern talking to.

He angled his head toward Sophie. "How long is she going to lay into him? Standing on a chair is hardly a federal offense, is it?"

Beneath her dark purple Howell Elementary T-shirt her shoulder twitched. She kept her voice as low as his. "Why ask me?"

Good question.

He focused on her face and waited out the usual tug in his gut. "What's the beef that you've got with me, anyway?"

She raised an eyebrow. "I can't imagine what you mean."

His snort was louder than intended, and he covered it with a cough. In front of them, several of the kids' hands had shot up to wave excitedly, and he realized he didn't even know what it was that Jason had said to earn the response.

Jason had pointed out two students, a boy and a girl, and they were all suddenly pushing out of their seats and hurrying for the door. Meyer's mind caught up. Jason was taking them out to see Ollie.

He pushed away from the wall just as Sophie did the same; and he gestured for her to go first.

"By the way." She offered a glacial smile. "You have mustard on your chin." Then she pushed her sunglasses onto her nose and followed the children out of the conference room.

Swallowing an oath, he wiped his chin.

Sophie Lane: one. Meyer Cartell: zip.

As usual.

He hung back in the conference room and watched through the windows until the kids appeared on the other side. He was slightly relieved when he saw that Mrs. Maitland no longer had young Dowling pigeonholed. The boy was standing with his friends again, and the second that Hannah taxied Ollie into sight, he looked just as attentive.

Once again, the bright yellow-and-blue Stearman was wielding her magic.

There wasn't a single face that didn't look rapt as Hannah cut the engine and the prop slowly stopped spinning. When she pushed herself up and out of the rear cockpit and jumped lightly to the grass, she pushed the flight goggles that she'd worn only for effect to the top of her head and glanced around.

He didn't need to be able to hear her "Who's first?" when the two kids that Jason had selected immediately trotted over to the plane.

Jason and Hannah helped them up into the tandem cockpits, with Jason standing on the wing walk so he could point out some of the features of the plane that dated back to WWII.

Meyer would have gone out to join them except for one thing.

Sophie Lane was finally smiling.

It was a sight worth seeing.

Good old Ollie. She never failed.

Chapter Four

Meyer stood on the pale gold sand, looking at the house.

The weather was clear. The morning sun warm and welcoming against the wind pushing in from the ocean behind him. The sand under his feet was wet but packed. The tide had already receded and along with it, the two wet-suited surfers who'd spent more time falling in the waves than riding them. When the tide was in, it reached halfway up the boulders leading to the seawall. And if there was a king tide, it would easily swallow that as well.

The breeze rippled the inspection report in his hand, drawing his attention. He'd already read it through more than once.

On paper, things seemed much better than reality.

He looked at the house again. The siding paint was peeling. Some indeterminate shade of blah. Maybe it had been gray at one point. Who knew? Who cared? The roof, though—which by rights ought to have been falling apart— was sound. No leaks.

The house had been exposed to the extremes of coastal weather since it had been built. Either the roofer who'd done the work more than forty years ago was the best roofer in history or someone had been making sure it stayed in good repair.

Even though the house was vacant.

"What was your deal, Dad?" He spoke the question aloud even though he knew there would be no answer.

He sighed and folded the report in half again, tucking it once more into the back pocket of his jeans. Then he walked over to the stone seawall that was as tall as he was and found enough footholds to scale it.

It was simpler and a lot quicker than walking the long way down to the north end of the seawall to the stairs that—according to the inspection report—were crumbling anyway.

He hefted himself up and over the last few inches of the wall and wiped his hands on his jeans as he stood. Sand, pebbles and mounds of dried seaweed were strewn across the ground. Routinely wiped away by waves as routinely as they were deposited.

The house had a cedar deck running the length of it, but it was too shallow to have ever been much good for anything. It also hadn't received the care that the roof had and was nearly rotted through on one side. Pulling it off, though, would mean a good three-foot drop from the front door down to the ground.

He pulled out the two keys hanging from a small round key ring. Fitzgerald had told him that one of them opened the door onto the deck; the other opened the door around the rear of the house, where a metal carport was meant to protect the parking area and the oversized closet designed to contain everything from a washer and dryer to surfboards.

Meyer chose the rear.

The carport didn't protect his truck. He'd left it parked up on the road because the driveway down was half-buried in a sand dune. The roof of the carport was metal, and the siding at the back side of the house was in slightly better condition than the front.

At least the paint was less chipped. Not as exposed to the elements.

He didn't bother looking in the closet, though it was obvious the inspector must have because the sand mounding against the house had been swept away from the closet doors.

The door had a dead bolt only, and the second key worked.

He turned the knob and pushed. The hinges squeaked, but it still swung easily enough.

He didn't move, though. Just stood there, looking through the doorway. He wasn't sure exactly what he expected to greet him.

Nothing was what he found.

He jingled the two keys from the small ring.

From his position, he could see straight down the narrow hall through to the door on the opposite side of the house that opened on the deck.

What was he waiting for? He didn't know why he felt a strange reluctance to go inside. He just knew that he did.

It wasn't because of bad memories, since he hardly *had* any memories of the house.

He grimaced and stepped through the doorway. It smelled like years of bottled-up air. Musty. Stale. Disused.

He followed the ugly brown linoleum floor to the first opening on the right. Bedroom. There was no furniture to help cover the wrinkles in the thin green carpet. Faded marks on one wall outlined the position of a long-gone mirror. Or maybe a framed picture. Regardless, the only thing left behind was a dirty octagonal shape against the yellowing wall. A small grimy window was on the wall opposite the door. There was no closet. The second room was much the same, only the dirty outline on the wall was in the shape of a narrow rectangle.

He looked in the bathroom. Wood cabinet. Chipped pink sink. Matching pink bathtub. Too shallow and too short to do anyone any good. At least there was a showerhead, though it looked clogged with minerals. He lifted the lid on the toilet and frowned slightly.

He'd expected a decade of disuse.

The ring of minerals around the edge of the water in the bowl was thick and yellowing. But the water itself looked clean. He pushed down on the flaking gold handle, and the toilet flushed. Smoothly. Easily.

The sink faucet had the same worn gold finish. He turned one of the cross-shaped handles, and water rushed out of the spout. He waited a minute and felt it.

Hot.

He turned the handle, and the water stopped flowing.

Maintained roof. Maintained plumbing.

The inspection report that Fitzgerald Lane had given him had said as much, but seeing the proof of it was strange. Surreal.

But then again, nothing was stranger than Pietro's decree that in order to inherit the place, they would have to live in it for a freaking year first.

He left the bathroom and glanced into the third bedroom across the narrow hall. Slightly larger than the other two and possessing two windows. He opened a hall closet that was only large enough to hold a mop and bucket and then moved around to the kitchen area. The cabinets were yellow and made of metal, the electric stove white. The counters were avocado green—who knew what they were made of. No refrigerator. Just a narrow space for one between two lower cabinets. He tried opening one of the drawers. It was rusty and only moved a few inches.

He turned and looked at the living area, which spanned the width of the house. The linoleum continued here, too. A narrow fireplace had been built on the south wall. The red brick was stained with soot above the firebox. No mantle. No hearth. Maybe at one point in its life it had been useful for staying warm on a cold evening, but not anymore. The inspection report said the fireplace wasn't safe to use.

Evidently maintaining the chimney hadn't been important enough to make the cut on Pietro's maintenance list. It needed a total replacement.

He walked over to the swinging door leading out to the deck. It was old, solid, made of wood panels with an inset window on the upper half. The window was caked with decades of baked-on crud, just as the two windows flanking the door were. He unlocked it and pulled the door open. The hinges didn't squeal. But they also didn't do a lot of good when the swollen wood caught on the floor, preventing the door from being opened more than a few degrees.

He pushed it closed with an effort. Relocking it was laughable—who would want to break in?—but he did it anyway.

He pulled out his cell phone and called Cutter first, then conferenced in the girls.

He'd already sent them copies of the inspection report, and he added his personal observations. "I'd hoped maybe the house could be condemned, which might have allowed us to circumvent the twelve-month stipulation, but no go. It's small and ugly as hell, but it's not falling down or uninhabitable."

"High praise," Cutter said dryly. "Suppose pitching a tent on the sand outside the house is allowed?"

"What *are* we going to do about furnishings?" Alexa

asked. "Cutter can do what he wants, but I'm not interested in sleeping on a camp cot for an entire year."

"I'll take care of furniture," Dana offered. "Assuming no objections."

There weren't. But the same couldn't be said of the date, which set off an argument between Alexa, who wanted to at least finish out her school year before she had to give up her job for the duration, and Dana, who wanted to get things resolved sooner.

Though Meyer was personally more of a mind to agree with Dana—get it over and done with—he also had other practical matters to consider. "My schedule's going to get tight in May leading up to Memorial Day. JCS is pretty involved in the town's activities that last weekend of the month."

"Then I vote for the end of June," Alexa said, and Meyer had no problem imagining the smirk she was directing toward Dana.

"*Beginning* of June," he said, hoping to stave off more debate. "We'll be done by next summer, and everyone can go back to enjoying their own damn lives."

"Sounds good to me," Cutter added as if he, too, just wanted an end to the matter.

"Fine," Alexa said crankily. "June first. Gives me a whopping month and a half to entirely rearrange my life." She hung up.

"I'm sure we'll be in touch more," Dana said much more calmly before she left the call as well.

"We gonna survive them?" Cutter asked when it was just him and Meyer left on the line.

Meyer looked around once more at the legacy left to them. "Think the question is more like will they survive each other."

Cutter laughed shortly, and he, too, hung up.

Meyer pocketed his phone and locked the back door again to work his way back up to his truck. He'd parked as much off the side of the road as he could, but without being able to use the driveway, it was too narrow at this stretch to turn around.

The simplest solution was driving further on in the direction he was already facing. He knew from his last time down there that the road widened again in front of the only other bungalow that far down Bluff Road before it started climbing up the cliff that protected the southern end of the small cove. The road inexplicably dead-ended a couple hundred feet after the bungalow, as if whoever had been building the road had simply run out of the strength to make its way up an even sharper cliff.

He also knew that Sophie Lane was the owner of said bungalow.

It didn't take a mental leap to predict her reaction when she realized he'd be her neighbor for the next year.

He made the tight U-turn. Sophie's bungalow had probably been built around the same time. Except hers had enjoyed more than just a maintained roof.

The siding was a cheerful blue, the trim a pristine, creamy white. The windows—and there were a lot of them—sparkled in the morning sun. She even had a patch of grass growing along one the side of the house before it gave way to the staircase that led in one direction up to her deck and the other in a terraced trajectory that jogged around a stand of spruce and crossed over jagged rocks before it eventually reached the sandy beach.

Either nurses earned a lot more than he thought or she'd had help from Daddy the lawyer to buy the place.

He drove past the beach house—looking even more run-down compared to its bright and shining neighbor—and had reached the first hairpin turn on his way back up the northern bluff when another vehicle appeared, coming his way. He pulled to the right as far as he could and slowed nearly to a stop as the other vehicle—a small white SUV—did the same.

When their windows came abreast, Sophie stopped her vehicle altogether. "What're you doing down here?" she demanded.

Her hair was wound in an untidy knot on the top of her head, and loose strands were escaping around her somewhat flushed face. The color only made the gold flecks in her brown eyes seem more pronounced.

"Public road, Sophie."

"And nobody's house is down here except mine," she countered swiftly. "So, what do you want?"

He waved the folded inspection report. "I beg to differ." He tossed it aside and rested his arm on the door, mimicking her position.

Barely four inches separated his elbow from the sleeve of her pink sweatshirt. One nudge and he'd brush against her.

She pulled her arm inside her vehicle. "What's that supposed to mean?"

He smiled, knowing it would irritate her. "Your house isn't the only one down there."

"Yes, it—" Her gaze shifted as if she were looking beyond him toward the sandy beach. When she looked back, her eyes were narrowed. "What do *you* want with that abandoned house?"

The real issue was what he wanted *out* of that house. But that was months down the road, and right now the only thing on his mind was the woman an arm's reach away. "About eighty years ago, a couple named Edna and Albert Cartell lived there with their toddler son."

A tiny wrinkle bisected her forehead right between her eyebrows.

"My grandparents," he added, even though he could see she didn't need the added information.

"You're trying to say that it's *your* house?" The wrinkle disappeared, and she gave a sniff that had a *who cares* tone to it that wasn't the least bit convincing.

"Mine and my half siblings'." Technically it wouldn't be entirely accurate until they'd met the terms of the will, but close enough.

"Good," she said abruptly. "About time someone gave that poor shack some attention."

"Who cares about the house? The property will be a great place for a couple dozen McMansions," he said as she put her engine into gear. "When we sell it."

Her lips parted slightly, then firmed again. "You're not going to sell it."

"Why wouldn't we?"

"Because—" She floundered for a millisecond. "Because even you wouldn't want to chop up that beautiful stretch of land for a bunch of places that get occupied two weeks out of every fifty! Don't we have *enough* places like that in Cape Cardinale?" She jabbed her finger in the air between them. "And don't pretend you'll need the money. Not with inheriting your father's estate."

Not that Meyer had ever wondered about it, but the statement proved that Fitzgerald Lane didn't share client information with his daughter. "Rumors about my father's estate are just rumors."

Her lips twisted. "What did he do? Cut you out? My heart bleeds."

Before he thought better of it, he reached through her window and caught her arm. Beneath the thin fleece, it felt lithe. Strong. Distracting. "What *is* your problem, Sophie?"

She yanked her arm away. "Maybe you should ask that of Corinne." She didn't wait for him to respond but hit the gas instead. Her tires spun momentarily before gripping, and she shot off down the road.

The only thing he could do was watch her in his rear-view mirror.

"Corinne." He said the name musingly. He hadn't thought about Sophie's sister in years. He'd dated her briefly what felt like a hundred years ago when he'd stayed with John before their final year of college. It hadn't been remotely serious. Corinne had only gone out with him because she'd had eyes for John. Pointlessly because even then he'd had eyes only for Meredith.

Meyer was tempted to turn around again and follow Sophie. Have it out once and for all and damn the consequences.

But his responsibility where Meredith was concerned kept him from doing so. It was the same thing that had held him back for years. Ever since returning to Cape Cardinale.

He'd let John down in life. He wasn't going to let him down in death.

Finding out that little Sophie Lane was all grown up and Meredith's best friend had been a surprise. But nothing would be served by shining a light on the antagonism Sophie felt for him. Being attracted to her, despite the chip on her shoulder that she had where he was concerned, was nobody's problem but his own.

And he intended to keep it that way.

She was driving too fast. Sophie knew it even before she hit the next turn and felt her tires bump over gravel toward the suddenly inadequate-looking metal barrier between rough road and open air. She managed to get back on the pavement and slowed to a complete stop.

Her hands shaking, she turned off the engine, set the

parking brake and dropped her forehead to the steering wheel.

Why had she let Meyer get under her skin?

"He's not worth it," she muttered.

Even at twelve years of age, she'd known it. Had said the very same words to Corinne when she'd found her sister in her bedroom sobbing like her life was over. Sophie had wrapped her arms around her sister, chanting it like a mantra until finally, Corinne had stopped weeping.

You don't understand, Sophie. I hope you never know what it feels like to be so betrayed. So...used. All 'cause I don't fit into his...his plan.

Twenty-one years later and Sophie could still hear Corinne's words like it was yesterday.

She finally lifted her head and stared out at the glittering ocean. She was only halfway down the bluff. She'd just come from the yoga class she took on Saturday mornings. She ought to be calm and restored.

Five minutes with Meyer Cartell and she was agitated enough to nearly drive herself off the road.

When her cell phone jangled noisily, she nearly jumped out of her skin.

She reached into the pocket of her yoga bag and pulled out the phone. Meredith's image was displayed on the screen, and she pressed the speaker button. "Hey there."

"Is your offer still open?"

Offer. Sophie's mind felt scrambled. "Uh. Yeah." Brain cells engaged. "You told Walker you'd go!" She grinned even though she had to rub her eyes to get rid of the image of Meyer stuck behind them. "Meredith, that's great. When?"

"Weekend after next. We'll, um, we'll leave Friday morning after I get the kids off to school."

Sophie's schedule at the elementary school ended a half

hour before the junior high let out. "I'll be able to pick them up after school—no problem."

"Meyer's already said he'll take care of that. Leda has chess club, and Grange has a baseball game. Meyer always goes to see Grange play, so there's no reason for you to worry about that part."

Sophie's nerves had frayed a little more the second Meredith uttered his name. "Okay. I can just stay at your place with them. When are you coming back?"

"They actually said they wanted to stay at your place, if that's all right." Meredith barely waited for Sophie's response before adding in a rush, "And we're not coming back until Tuesday evening. Is that too long?"

"You could go for the whole week, and I wouldn't say it was too long." No matter her personal feelings, she was seriously delighted for Meredith. "Tuesday'll be fine."

"Yes, well, we both have things we need to get back for. Really, the timing *isn't* the best, but—"

"But some things can't wait," Sophie said knowingly.

"Heaven help me," Meredith said on a nervous laugh. "Soph. I don't even own any pretty undies."

Sophie felt her own tension fade away. "Well, I guess we'll have to do something about that. We can go shopping this weekend. Today if you want. I just need to clean up." She'd already seen her weekend client, Otto Nash, that morning before her yoga class.

"And I need to drop off Grange at a birthday party. Leda's already off with friends for the day. How about we meet at Tanya's in an hour for lunch first?"

Tanya's made Sophie think about the school trip to the airfield. Which just led to Meyer Cartell's infernal face hogging her mind's eye all over again. "See you there."

They ended the call, and Sophie put her SUV in gear again. She was determined not to give Meyer Cartell another thought. He wasn't going to ruin what had otherwise been a perfectly lovely Saturday.

She drove as circumspectly as she ordinarily did down the remainder of the hairpin turns. She definitely didn't need any more episodes of sliding off the road around a curve.

Despite her intentions, she still found herself slowing as she approached the turnoff for the abandoned little house. She'd lived in Cape Cardinale nearly her entire life. Why hadn't she known the property belonged to the Cartell family?

Not that it mattered now. Meyer had said the place was to be sold.

She looked beyond the house to the shallow crescent-shaped beach. She had a view of that beach, had been freely accessing it for the last year because her own property ended at the boulders beneath her deck. Now some enterprising developer could buy the land, slap Private Property signs all over it and have every right to do so. They could neatly slice off any way for her to easily access the strip of sand through their property. Which meant having to drive all the way to the top of the cape and hike down the difficult trail on the other end that constituted the only public-access point to the beach.

It'd be easier to just drive to Friars Beach instead, which was about a mile down from her house in the opposite direction. Friars was much larger and more accessible than Cardinale Beach. It also easily had three times the surfers.

Sophie had been surfing since she'd been a kid. She made no claims to being an expert, but she far preferred the less congested waves at Cardinale Beach.

Two hours later, yoga and unwanted Meyer encounters showered away, Sophie asked the plaguing question over their iced tea and crab-salad croissants. "How did I not know the place was owned by the Cartells?"

She and Meredith were sitting at an outdoor table at Tanya's. On such a beautiful day, the place was packed and they'd had to wait nearly thirty minutes for a table.

Meredith looked surprised, then shrugged. "I never thought about it, either, until Meyer mentioned it." She stirred sugar into her tea. "Why?"

"I ran into him this morning," she managed offhandedly. "He says they're going to sell it."

"Not surprising. Meyer's never been the beachside type. Have you seen his apartment— Oh, duh. Naturally you haven't. He could have had an ocean view if he'd wanted, but he chose the valley and the airfield." She shrugged. "Are you worried about who might buy it?"

"Not who. But what ends up there? That's another matter." Sophie plucked a meaty piece of crab from her salad and popped it into her mouth.

"You've been spoiled," Meredith said with a nod. "You've basically had that cove to yourself since you moved there. Nobody would want to share it if they didn't have to."

"I do sound spoiled."

Meredith laughed. "I didn't mean it in a bad way. You're one of the *least* spoiled people that I know." She glanced at her cell phone. "The afternoon's halfway gone. We'd better eat quickly."

"Planning on buying up a lot of lacy lingerie?"

"I haven't cared what my underwear looks like in a long time." Meredith's voice was low, her cheeks flushing slightly. "I'm used to buying it at Shop-World, for heaven's sake."

Sophie grinned. "Fortunately, despite the desert of my own love life, I do know a few places that are a bit of a step up from Shop-World."

"I was counting on that." Meredith leaned closer, confidentially. "You know the best thing I remember about wearing pretty bras and panties?"

"Feminine confidence?"

"Sure. There's that. But even better?" Still flushing, Meredith's eyes turned dreamy. She propped her chin on her hand and lowered her voice even more. "The way it felt to have a man slowly...pull...them...off."

Sophie choked a little on her sip of tea. She was wearing mascara—rubbing Meyer's face from behind her eyelids *again* would have to wait.

Chapter Five

Sophie checked the clock for about the twentieth time in an hour.

On Meredith's way out of town with Walker that morning, she'd called Sophie to go over the kids' schedule one more time, even though she'd already done it earlier in the week.

Sophie knew it was nerves over the weekend with Walker more than nerves over Sophie watching her off-spring that had prompted Meredith's repeated instructions. Even though Sophie had her own nerves to contend with, she'd mmm-hmm'd in all the right spots and repeated re-assurances that they would all be fine until Meredith and Walker returned.

Sophie's nerves, however, had nothing to do with Meredith's kids. She was looking forward to having them stay with her.

It was the fact that Meyer was involved in even the slightest of ways.

She turned off the oven, leaving the foil-covered lasagna inside, and looked at the clock again.

Where were they?

It was after seven. Meredith had told Sophie that Grange's games were always done by six o'clock. Even allowing for time after the game to celebrate—or, as was more often the case with Grange's baseball team, to commiserate—and driving across town to the beach, Meyer should have been there by now to drop off the kids.

Unlike so many parents, Meredith hadn't allowed her kids to have their own cell phones yet. So, it wasn't as though Sophie could just contact Leda or Grange directly to ask them.

Even though it set her teeth on edge, Sophie copied the phone number that Meredith had provided her and pasted it into a new text message.

This is Sophie. Why haven't you dropped off the kids yet?

Being curt to Meyer was second nature to her.
She deleted the draft.

This is Sophie. I thought the kids would be here by now.

Admittedly, she was biased, but she thought that seemed less accusatory.

Can you give an ETA? I have supper in the oven.

She decided it would do and had just sent it when she heard a noise at her door. A second later, it pushed inward and Leda and Grange practically tumbled inside, bearing suitcases and school backpacks.

"We won!" Grange crowed the second he saw Sophie. He dumped his backpack right in the path of his sister to stride into the house, pumped full of adolescent male pride. "And *who* hit the winning run? Yeah, that's right. The Grange-Man!" He gave Sophie a palm-stinging high five before running through the living area, where she'd left the sliding door open and out onto the deck. "We can boogie board tomorrow morning, yeah?"

His energy was palpable. "If it isn't pouring rain," she said. Her eyes were on him on the deck as she leaned over to pick up his backpack.

Her hand encountered another—larger, warmer—and she jerked back, leaving Meyer to it.

If he noticed the way she scrubbed her hand down the side of her jeans, he didn't show it.

Leda shimmied around Sophie, clutching her own backpack to her midriff.

"How'd chess club go?"

"Fine," Leda mumbled. She turned in the opposite direction of her brother, going down the hall and disappearing into the bedroom that she always used when she came to visit.

Sophie looked at Meyer and raised her eyebrows.

He shrugged. "Got me. She's been like that since I picked her up." He hefted Grange's backpack. "Where does this go?"

"Bedroom across from Leda."

He turned and went down the hall. He was wearing his typical blue jeans, but today he wore a button-down white shirt with the sleeves rolled up. It was tucked in.

Realizing she was looking too hard at the backside view, she went into the kitchen and pulled the lasagna out of the oven. She set the heavy pan onto the stovetop and went out to join Grange on the deck. She was barefoot, and so far, the ocean spray hadn't gotten high enough to make it damp. "What's up with Leda?"

Grange had already picked up a handful of the smooth

pebbles that the waves constantly pushed onto the deck and was pitching them out over the water. "I dunno. What're we gonna do if it's pouring rain?"

She had a hard time not ruffling his disheveled hair. He'd tolerated it when he'd been five. Not so much now that he was nearly thirteen. "We'll figure out something," she assured. "Are you hungry? I made lasagna."

"Starving." He launched the last pebble out into the churning water and followed her inside again.

Meyer was just walking back up the hallway again and wasn't bothering to hide his curiosity as he looked around her home. "Nice place."

She hunted for some hidden meaning but found none. "Thanks." She turned quickly into her small kitchen and picked up the plates and flatware she'd already pulled from the cupboard. She passed the stack across the granite peninsula to Grange. "We'll eat outside." She knew that setting the table was an ordinary task for Meredith's kids, and Grange took everything without complaint and went back outside.

"Was it refurbished before or after you bought it?"

"Mostly before." She pulled open the refrigerator and extracted the Caesar salad she'd made earlier. "I had a few—" She broke off when Grange returned.

"We need another set," he said.

Surprised at her error, she set the salad on the counter and automatically pulled another plate from the cupboard. "Sorry. I thought I set out enough for the—"

"Four," Grange said over her *three* and gave Meyer a pointed look.

"Oh. Ah—"

"Smells good, doesn't it, Uncle Meyer?" Grange pulled the plate from the grip that Sophie had unconsciously tightened.

"Yeah," Meyer admitted. A knowing smile seemed to flirt with the corners of his lips.

She yanked open a drawer and pulled out another set of flatware. "There's plenty if you want to stay." Her tone was calm, even if she *had* said the words through her teeth. She couldn't seem to do anything else given Grange's automatic assumption that Meyer would be included.

She peeled the plastic wrap off the salad bowl and brushed past him to take it out to the patio table. When she turned back, Meyer was in her wake carrying the lasagna pan, holding it with the sunflower-patterned dishtowel that had been hanging on her oven door.

Something inside her stomach fluttered annoyingly.

She ignored it—and the cause—and returned to the kitchen for glasses. "Grange, you want milk or lemonade?"

"Milk."

She pulled out the gallon of milk that she'd bought specifically for the weekend. It had taken some rearranging in her little fridge to make room. She'd also stocked up on a box of Grange's favorite cereal—some horrid purple-berry thing—and strawberry yogurt for Leda.

She went down the hall to look in her.

The girl was sitting on the twin-sized bed, hunched over a thick textbook.

"Hey, sweetie, we're about ready to eat. Milk or lemonade?"

Leda shrugged and didn't look up. "Don't care," she mumbled. "Whatever."

Sophie swallowed a sigh and entered the room. She pushed back Leda's hair and saw the distinct track of tears on her cheeks. "Want to talk about it?"

Leda shook her head.

"Okay. But you're still going to have to come out and eat."

"I'm not hungry."

Sophie plucked a tissue from the box on the nightstand and handed it to Leda. "You know your mom is going to call me tonight and ask how the two of you are doing."

Leda made an impatient sound. She took the tissue and swiped her cheeks. "You can't tell her I was crying. She'll make Walker bring her home!"

Sophie nodded. "Yeah, well. Probably. You know your mom. I want to have your back, honey, but I'm not going to lie to your mom, either."

Leda sighed noisily. "It's nothing, okay? Just…just—"

She looked on the verge of crying again, and Sophie squeezed her shoulder. "You don't have to tell me. Right? But you have to come out and eat." She steeled herself. "Even…even Meyer's staying." As if they'd be the magic words to get a teenaged girl to sit up for supper.

"Why don't you like him?"

Sophie started. "What?"

"You always act weird when Uncle Meyer's around."

"Uncle Meyer's hardly around when I am. I'm not acting weird. I just barely know him." She plucked the tissue that Leda had balled in her hand and turned to toss it into the little trash can on the other side of the nightstand. "Now, come on. Supper. Do you want lemonade or milk?"

"Can I have strawberry in it?"

She nearly sagged in relief. It was such a Leda thing and had been since she was a little girl. She nodded, glad that she'd bought strawberry syrup along with the cereal and yogurt. "You bet."

Leda followed her back to the kitchen. In the small space while Leda doctored a glass of milk with the dark pink syrup, their shoulders touched.

"You're taller than me," Sophie observed. "When did that happen?"

"You're not wearing any shoes," Leda pointed out.

"Close enough," Sophie argued. Leda's flip-flops were barely a quarter-inch thick. "You're going to catch up to your mom soon."

"Yeah, then I'll be the *tallest* girl in my class with no boobs," Leda said on a soft snort. "At least you have those." She licked her strawberry-milky spoon and tossed it into the sink.

Sophie couldn't help her own snort. "Not like your mom." Meredith had an hourglass figure that would draw attention even if she wore a sackcloth. She bumped Leda's shoulder again and wondered if curves—or lack thereof— was at the root of Leda's upset. "Give it time, honey."

"That's what Mom says. But neither of you knows what it's like to—" She broke off, shaking her head sharply. She picked up her glass of pink milk.

"Hold up." Sophie handed her Grange's glass of plain white. "Take that out for your brother."

Leda did so without complaint.

Sophie watched her walk out to the deck. Leda's shoulders were rolled a little, basically announcing her blue mood. Sophie was a nurse—she knew teens had moods. Particularly teenaged girls.

Maybe the weekend at the beach would help Leda shake it off. She'd enjoyed staying there before just as much as Grange had.

She filled two glasses with ice and lemonade, grabbed a handful of paper napkins and a spatula for the lasagna and carried it all outside.

She didn't even have to turn her head to see the sweep of beach that belonged to Meyer and his family. Once he had his way, his honorary niece and nephew wouldn't have unfettered access to that beach, either. Not without trespassing on his land to get there.

She set his glass of lemonade in front of him. "It's fresh."

Then she felt her cheeks flush a little, as if she'd been bragging or something. "I have wine if you prefer."

"I'm a beer guy." He lifted the glass of lemonade. "And this is great. Thank you." He looked toward the kids. "What do you say, guys? Here's to your weekend with Sophie."

They all clinked their glasses, and Sophie began dishing out the lasagna. She'd made the Caesar salad with only a small amount of hope that anyone besides her would eat it.

She'd been wrong.

Meyer piled salad onto his plate alongside the lasagna and dug in as if he hadn't eaten in a week. "Only lasagna I have these days comes frozen from Shop-World," he said. "Meredith's never mentioned you could cook on top of everything else."

Was he being facetious? Sophie couldn't tell.

"Told you she cooks good," Grange said around a mouthful of food.

"Cooks *well*. And you're gross," Leda told him. "Wipe your chin."

Grange stuck his tongue out at Leda and wiped his chin.

Meyer looked like he was biting back a smile.

Sophie was doing the same thing.

It was distinctly odd to realize it.

She stabbed her fork into her salad. The sun was hovering above the horizon, cloaked only minimally by striations of gray-and-pink clouds. The evening tide was coming in, and though there was still an hour of good light left, Meyer pulled out a lighter and held it over the fat candle in the middle of the table that she kept inside a glass lantern.

"I didn't realize you smoked," she said.

"Because of this?" He held up the lighter.

She recognized it as a Zippo, only because her grandfather had been a cigar aficionado and had always used a Zippo-brand lighter.

"The pocketknife I always carry has a corkscrew on it. Doesn't mean I'm opening wine bottles all the time." He flipped the flat, rectangular lighter between his fingers and showed her the USAF insignia on the other side. "Had it a long time," he said and shifted in his chair enough to push it into his pocket once again.

"He has a whole collection of 'em," Grange said, leaning across the table to look at the lasagna pan.

She scooped another piece onto his plate. His third.

Thank goodness she'd bought the extra-large box of cereal.

"Sophie collects shells," Leda said and suddenly hopped up from her seat and went inside. She returned a few seconds later with the shallow lined case containing dozens of little shells that Sophie usually kept in the room that Leda was using. "She makes jewelry out of some of them. See?" She propped the corner of the case onto the table to show Meyer.

"It's just a hobby," Sophie demurred.

Meyer picked up a blue iridescent whorl that was as long as his little finger. "Dana has a necklace with a shell like this."

"Dana?"

"My sister. Half sister." He looked like he regretted even bringing it up as he replaced the shell on the green felt lining the case. He smiled at Leda, though, before she carried the case back inside the house.

"Meredith mentioned you have two sisters." Sophie told herself she was maintaining polite conversation.

He nodded. The angle of the setting sun reflected brightly on the water, and he was squinting slightly against it. For some reason, it made the slice of blue even more intense. "Dana and Alexa. My brother's the baby."

Sophie nodded, although it was information that Meredith had already provided somewhere along the way. She stopped pretending an interest in her salad and worked a sliver of lasagna free where the noodles and the cheese had a crusty edge. Using a fork was hopeless, and she picked up the edge with her fingers and ate it like a french fry.

Considering the size of the lasagna pan, she'd expected to at least have a serving or two left over, but aside from the nearly burnt edge still clinging to the pan, there wasn't any left at all, thanks to Meyer's two helpings and Grange's three.

Leda returned to slip into her seat again. Her plate was only half-empty, but she didn't look interested in finishing. Another unusual occurrence. Not that she ate at the rate of her brother, but Sophie's lasagna was one of her favorites.

"Can we go walk on the beach after supper?"

Sophie started to nod automatically, then looked quickly at Meyer. "It's *your* beach," she said instead. "Do you mind?"

A shimmer of impatience flitted across his face. With the unrelenting reflection of sun and water, she could see the web of lines arrowing out from the corners of his eyes and the fiery auburn in his hair that ordinarily looked more like muddy rust.

It wasn't fair for a man to be so darned handsome.

Particularly a man who'd broken her sister's spirit.

"It's not *my* beach, which you know good and well." He stood and picked up his dishes, obviously prepared to clear them away.

"Just leave all that," Sophie told him, but he ignored her and carried them inside anyway. It was polite. But it still annoyed her that he hadn't listened to her.

The kids' presence was the only thing stopping her from making some comment. Leda's eyes kept bouncing from Sophie's face to Meyer and back again.

Instead, Sophie suggested they *all* carry their plates inside. "Then we'll take our walk. I have cheesecake for after."

Grange whooped. He snatched up his dishes and raced inside. "Uncle Meyer, there's cheesecake!"

Sophie hoped the light wasn't illuminating enough to reveal her consternation. She could hear the murmur of Meyer's deep voice as she gestured for Leda to go inside first but could guess what Meyer had said by Grange's response.

"Oh, come on! You *have* to stay," Grange said.

"Yeah," Leda added, surprising Sophie. "You have to stay." She didn't try to enter the kitchen already occupied by Meyer and Grange but leaned over the narrow peninsula to place her dishes directly in the sink. "We have a chess match to finish."

Meyer's eyes met Sophie's over Leda.

Her imagination was really working overtime because it seemed as though he looked apologetic.

And Meyer never looked apologetic for anything.

But Leda seemed, at last, to have shaken off her doldrums.

"Maybe Meyer has plans," Sophie attempted. It was a Friday night, after all, and Meyer was an eligible, single male. If a person's taste ran to men like him.

A mocking laugh sounded somewhere inside her head.

"Plans like what?" Grange scoffed.

"I don't know. A date or something." Sophie wished to heaven that she'd just kept her mouth shut. She leaned over the peninsula herself to add the lasagna dish and her own plate to the sink.

Meyer smiled slightly. "You think I'd have dinner here with all of you if I had a date later?"

Her skin felt flushed. She waved at the dishes in the sink. "Let the lasagna pan soak," she said and started down the hall for her bedroom. "I need shoes."

And, apparently, a muzzle.

Chapter Six

When Sophie reappeared, she had tennis shoes on her feet. They were black. White laces.

If she was wearing socks, they didn't show.

Meyer figured he was safe enough if he kept his attention on her feet.

An impossible task, of course.

He had found a scrubbing sponge in the cabinet beneath her sink, and he continued scrubbing out the lasagna pan, watching her through his lashes while she moved around the living room. Turning on a lamp in the corner of the room even though it was still plenty light outside. Picking up a soft-looking gray blanket that she refolded needlessly before draping it once again over the back of an upholstered side chair. Pulling out a chess set and arranging it on her coffee table that looked like an old sea chest.

She hadn't changed from her white jeans. They were snug from hip to ankle, clinging to her lithe legs every inch of the way and making them appear longer than he knew they were. She was about a head shorter than Meredith. Meyer didn't know how tall that would make her, exactly.

But it was a lot shorter than him.

Nor had she changed the baggy gray sweatshirt that kept slipping off one shoulder to reveal a narrow white strap.

Maybe a bra strap.

Maybe one of those camisole things.

He didn't know.

But he'd spent most of dinner speculating while he'd been trying not to keep looking at the smooth skin beneath that strap.

The angle of the sunlight while they'd been eating had been relentless.

Clearly illuminating a tiny, faint scar on her shoulder. The velvety texture of her lightly tanned skin.

He looked down at the dish again, scrubbing harder at a particularly stubborn bit of baked-on lasagna.

It really had been delicious—including the overly crusty edge that probably wouldn't have been so crusty if he'd gotten the kids to her place sooner than he had.

She was still setting out the chess pieces, and he looked out to the deck, where Leda and Grange were bouncing a ball back and forth between them.

For a moment, he recalled them as young children, doing the very same thing. Only John had been there to run after the ball when it had escaped them.

He blinked, and the vision faded.

It was just Leda and Grange. Teenagers now, and at each other's throats as quickly and as easily as a ball could bounce over a plexiglass deck wall.

"Now look what you've done." Leda shoved Grange's shoulder.

Grange shoved back. "You're the one who catches like a girl."

Meyer shut off the faucet, but Sophie was already hurrying out onto the deck, pushing up the sleeves of her sweatshirt while ignoring the slipping shoulder.

Again.

"Hey, guys. It's just a ball. No need to push each other over into the boulders, too. Now, come on. Grange, grab a flashlight. You know where it's at."

Grange thumped back inside. He opened the drawer of the narrow table next to the door and pulled out a sturdy-looking flashlight. "Come on," he said to Meyer as he headed back outside again.

He'd stayed because of the kids, he reminded himself. Nothing more. Nothing less.

He spread the sunflower towel on the narrow counter and turned the pan face down on it to dry.

Wiping his hands on his jeans, he joined Grange, and they all followed Sophie down the wooden staircase that was even narrower than he'd realized as it jogged around the trees and spanned a jagged rocky crevasse before leveling out into a walkway surrounded on both sides by beach grass that finally ended with a foot-high drop down to the sand.

There was no need for the flashlight yet, but he believed Sophie had told Grange to bring it so they'd be able to see more clearly on their way back.

They were still a good hundred yards away from the seawall protecting his father's beach house, and looking back, the only thing that Meyer could see of Sophie's place was one corner of her cantilevered deck. Otherwise, thanks to the trees and the angle of the shoreline, the blue bungalow was completely hidden from view.

They still had a couple hours before the tide would come in, and Sophie set off across the damp sand. Somewhere along the way, she'd picked up a random branch, and she was dragging the pointed end in the sand beside her. The ball that had bounced over her deck had somehow managed to land near the end of the wooden walk.

It was either that or another ball had been left.

Either way, Grange grabbed it, and he was tossing it into the air while Leda did cartwheels along the line that Sophie left inscribed in the sand.

Meyer absently rubbed his chest and followed them. Aside from one glance over at his father's house to help orient their position, he didn't give the place another thought.

They walked all the way to the northern end of the beach, where it petered out again against another rocky morass of boulders. The public trail allowing access to the beach was clearly marked, working its way up the face of the cape until it eventually reached a small parking lot at the top that Meyer knew was rarely used.

If not for the difficulty of the trail and the absence of the uniquely distinct sea stacks for which the Oregon coast was known, the protected crescent-shaped stretch of sand would be a lot more popular. As it was, it was usually only the bravest of surfers who found their way around to the strong waves.

Grange was punting his ball into those waves now and chasing after it when the rolling, foaming water returned it.

Leda was laughing while Sophie showed off her own cartwheeling skills, and Meyer learned that the strap belonged to a sports bra of some sort. Not a clinging camisole. Nothing remotely sexy.

She had to be nearly ten years younger than him. Cartwheeling away like she was Leda's age.

He still felt in danger of swallowing his own damn tongue.

He pulled off his boots, stuffed his socks down inside them and walked barefoot farther down on the wet sand.

The water was cold and soaked the bottom few inches of his jeans.

Not a cold shower, but at least something other than Sophie Lane to hold his attention.

The sky overhead was a rainbow of color, streaks radiating outward from the glowing orb backlighting the clouds as it dipped even closer to the horizon. Even when it did, Meyer knew that twilight would linger for another hour. Only after that would the stars be fully visible.

Ahead of him, Sophie had fallen onto her back, arms and legs splayed.

He wasn't worried.

He could hear her breathless laughter as Leda hauled on her arm like she wanted to lift Sophie back onto her feet. "Leda, I'm too old for this."

Leda hauled a few more times before plopping down onto the damp sand herself. They were a few feet above the creeping edge of the tide, but neither one seemed concerned with getting wet. Meyer reached them after a few more strides, and Sophie squinted at him when he stopped and held out his hand.

"Come on," he said. "I've built up an appetite again." It wasn't for food, but there was no point telling her that.

"Me, too." Grange bounded over. He'd tucked the large wet red ball under his arm, evidently tired of his game of catch with the ocean. "I'm ready for cheesecake. Did you make strawberry sauce, too?"

"Of course." Sophie finally placed her hand in Meyer's and let herself be pulled upright.

Not that it took much pulling. He moved freight at JCS that weighed more than she did.

As soon as she was on her feet, he let her go and she set off in a jog, brushing sand off her rear as she went. "Last one to the stairs gets hosing-off duty in the morning."

Since he had to pull on his socks and boots again, Meyer was the last one. Grange was the first, with the strong flashlight beam leading the way.

"What's hosing-off duty?" he asked Leda, who was in front of him.

"Just rinsing off everything on the deck and wiping down the plexi wall. It all gets loaded up with sand and salt overnight."

He felt confident that he would never be around in the morning to be assigned the task.

The sun was down by the time they made it to the end of the meandering staircase, and the temperature had dropped. While the tide had been engulfing the sand down on the beach, here at Sophie's house, the waves hit the boulders with ferocity. The spray was already blowing up above the plexiglass barrier.

They wiped their feet on the abrasive door mat and trooped inside. Sophie closed the sliding door behind them. It muted the sound of the pounding surf but didn't shut it out completely.

And it suddenly made the cozy living area feel way too small.

Given the way Sophie's gaze had skittered away from him as she'd closed the door, he wondered if she felt it, too.

"I'll get the cheesecake," she said and gestured toward the chess set. "If you and Leda want to get back to your chess game."

Leda grabbed Meyer's hand and dragged him toward the couch before he could form a coherent excuse to escape. He sat down on the couch, and Leda knelt on the opposite side of the chest, quickly arranging the pieces to pick up where they'd left off last.

"You had both my bishops," he told her when she was finished. "Remember?"

She took the piece off the board, but her cheeks had gone pink, making him wonder why she'd pretended that she hadn't remembered.

She had a clear advantage. They'd been playing chess for nearly six years, since he'd first taught her. And these days, it wasn't a foregone conclusion that he could beat her.

"And it is your move," he reminded when she continued to just sit there.

"Right." She lifted her hand, hovering above the pieces as if she were debating what move to make. But Sophie returned with two plates of cheesecake, and Leda quickly took one of them and sat back on the floor, crossing her legs as she drove the fork greedily into the dessert.

Meyer waved off the plate that Sophie offered him. "It looks great," he said honestly, "but I already overdid on the lasagna. I can't fit in another bite."

"More for me," Grange said around his mouthful. He sat next to Meyer on the couch and continued eating at his usual ravenous speed. "Chess is boring."

"You're boring," Leda countered immediately. She was savoring her forkful as slowly as her brother was wolfing.

"Nobody is boring," Sophie chided lightly. She set aside the slice of unwanted cheesecake on the fireplace mantel and sank into a wicker chair, swiveling it around from facing the fireplace to facing the couch. She snatched a knitted throw out of a basket next to the fireplace and swung it around her shoulders.

She could have sat in the upholstered chair that was adjacent to the couch.

He figured she'd have done so if not for his proximity.

Leda was still slowly dawdling over her cheesecake. Meyer looked at his watch.

The action was lost on Leda and Grange.

It wasn't on Sophie, though. She stretched out her foot—

barefoot, he realized, and wondered when she'd taken off her tennis shoes—and nudged Leda on her back with her toes. "Quit stalling, kiddo." She pulled back her feet and hugged her knees to her chest beneath the blanket. "Meyer doesn't want to hang out here all night."

That depended on what he was doing.

He clamped down on the thought.

He shouldn't have turned down the cheesecake. It left him with nothing to keep his attention on.

"I'm not stalling," Leda denied, even though it was patently obvious that she was. She scooted closer to the sea chest again and made her move without hesitating.

He countered the move and saw her faint surprise.

"Still have a few surprises left in me," he told her.

She set her plate onto the rug beside her and positioned herself on her knees, more attentive to the chessboard.

Meyer clasped his fists together in front of his mouth, hiding his amusement. He made the mistake of glancing over Leda's head at Sophie.

She was hiding a smile herself, and their eyes met.

Heat streaked down his spine and spread, and he was glad when Grange jumped off the couch, his knee glancing against the chest.

"Watch it," Leda said, quickly protecting the chessboard.

"Yeah, right." Grange ignored her as he continued around her to exchange his empty plate for the one that Sophie had set on the mantle. "Like you don't remember where every piece goes and every move you've already made."

He returned to the couch and plopped down onto it.

Aside from a haughty look, Leda ignored him and made another move. The only move that she could make without proving to Meyer that she was delaying the game. "Checkmate."

"Good job." He winked and pushed to his feet. He reached

out to rumple Grange's hair but caught himself and turned it into a fist bump instead. "Have fun this weekend." He sidled between the chest and Grange's gangly legs. "Thanks again for dinner, Sophie."

She was tossing off her blanket and uncurling her legs. "You're welcome." She padded over to the door, opening it as she hit a switch on the wall, illuminating the entryway. "Mind the sidewalk. It gets damp at night."

He nodded. "If you need anything, let me know."

"We won't. I mean, I'm sure we'll be fine."

He smiled wryly. "Don't doubt it for a second." He stepped outside and wasn't surprised that she closed the door as soon as he cleared the threshold.

It would take more than lasagna and a walk on the beach to thaw Sophie Lane.

It was damp and chilly, and he had sand inside his socks. He still found himself smiling a little as he walked to the rear of her house where he'd parked next to her small SUV. He pulled his cell phone out of his pocket before climbing into his truck. He had several text messages that he read through after he started the engine.

Mostly from Hannah reminding him of one thing or another. The last one from Meredith—a thumbs-up response to the photograph he'd sent her of Grange's winning home run.

He tucked the phone in the console and was backing out of the parking spot when Sophie appeared in the bright wash of his headlights. He braked, and she hurried around his truck to his side.

"Here," she said, thrusting something at him when he rolled down his window.

Surprised, he took the plate. She'd covered the small, flowered plate containing a thick piece of cheesecake with clear plastic wrap.

"If you don't take it, Grange is going to make himself sick eating the whole thing," she added.

"Thanks." She'd even added a little bowl full of the strawberry topping nestled next to the slice. He set the plate on the passenger seat. "Always willing to do my part where Grange is concerned."

She smiled slightly and adjusted the blanket still wrapped around her shoulders. "All right. Well." She took a step back. "Drive safe. The road's really dark at night."

"Getting soft on me, Sophie?"

She snorted softly. "I don't want you driving off the cliff," she said. "How would I ever get my grandmother's plate back?"

He was still smiling when he reached his apartment on the far side of town.

The cheesecake was perfectly creamy. Just sweet enough with a hint of tart.

Pretty much like Sophie.

Chapter Seven

"Have you got everything?" Sophie blocked the doorway before Grange could bolt out of the house.

It was Tuesday morning, and she needed to get Grange and Leda delivered to school by way of Tanya's for a quick breakfast since the extra-large box of cereal had gone by the wayside after school the day before.

"*All* of your schoolbooks," she prompted, even though Grange was nodding. "What about the math book you were working on last—"

Grange whirled and ran back down the hall.

Leda rolled her eyes.

She, of course, had everything already tidily arranged inside her ridiculously heavy backpack. Her despair from Friday evening hadn't returned over the weekend, and she'd been her usual self when Sophie had dropped her off at school the day before.

"Looking forward to your mom being back?"

"Yeah." Leda scratched her arm. It was slightly pink

from all the time they'd spent out on the beach that weekend. "But it's been fun staying with you."

Sophie gave her a quick hug. "It's been fun for me, too."

"Got it!" Grange held the book over his head as he raced down the hall and pushed between them as he went out the door. "Shotgun!"

"No way!" Leda was after him in a flash. "You had shotgun yesterday."

Sophie pulled the door closed and hurried after them. "Maybe you *both* should sit in the back," she told them.

The idea was horrifying enough that Grange let Leda have the front seat.

Sophie tossed her own bag into the back, and then they headed into town.

The sunshine that had miraculously persisted throughout the weekend and yesterday was gone. In its place were heavy gray clouds. The wind had a bite to it that felt entirely like February and nothing like May, and when they reached Tanya's, it had started to rain.

They bustled inside, and Sophie contained a groan. She knew she should have gone to the grocery store the evening before. Tanya's was packed with a half dozen people already waiting for seats, and the final bell for the kids' first classes of the morning would be ringing in less than an hour.

She scanned the counter to see if any seats were available but only saw two, separated by several other customers.

"Guys, I think we'd better hit the drive-through," she said. "I don't think we have time to wait for a table."

"We don't need to wait," Leda said and plunged fearlessly through the cluster of people in front of them.

Grange, never one to be left behind, immediately followed.

"Sorry," Sophie muttered to the people they jostled as

she, too, slid between bodies in Leda's wake. "Excuse me. Sorry. Sor—" She finally saw what Leda had seen.

Meyer Cartell, sitting in a small booth all by his lonesome.

Great.

As if she hadn't heard enough of *Uncle Meyer this* and *Uncle Meyer that* all weekend long.

Leda and Grange had already piled into the booth across from Meyer, which left only *his* side when Sophie stopped next to the table. "Sorry," she told him, eyeing the kids. "They just—"

He raised his hand, cutting her off, and slid over a few inches. "Place filled up fast this morning." As if aware of her reluctance, he patted his hand on the yellow bench beside him.

Feeling cornered by the expectant looks on the two faces across from her, she steeled herself and sat next to him.

"That wasn't so bad, was it?" he murmured for her ears alone while he handed his oversized laminated menu across to Leda and Grange.

She ignored the comment.

"You'll probably need to share," she told the kids. "By the looks of things, Tanya's already got her hands full."

"You don't need a menu?" Meyer asked her.

"Except for the specials, I think I have it pretty well memorized."

He smiled slightly. "I can say the same. Surprising we haven't run into each other here before now."

"Not really. I'm more the Sunday-brunch type than Tuesday morning." She glanced around fruitlessly for the server, and when she looked back, Meyer was holding the thermal pot that had been sitting on the table in front of him.

"Coffee?"

She shook her head. "No, thanks. That is at least one

thing that I haven't run out of at home." Plus, there was only one mug on the table, and he was using it.

She finally spotted a waitress and waved her hand to catch her attention. "I don't want them to be late for school," she told Meyer. As if she needed to explain her hurry.

"I'm sure there's time."

She wished she shared his confidence.

The previous day, she'd barely gotten Leda and Grange to school on time, and there'd been no bad weather or empty pantry to contend with.

She'd thought she'd allowed enough time this morning to include breakfast, but now that she'd seen how busy the restaurant was, she was seriously second-guessing her fitness as a teenage-sitter.

"Heard from Meredith lately?"

"Not since Sunday." Sophie felt as nervous as a tick. No matter how hard she tried to keep to the narrowest slice of bench, she could still feel Meyer's broad shoulder beside her. Short of turning sideways with her feet sticking out of the booth, there was nothing she could do about it. "They're due back this morning, though. Meredith expects to pick up the kids from school like usual."

He'd begun shaking his head before she even finished speaking. "They're not getting close to the Portland airport in this soup," he told her. "Storm front reaches all the way across the state."

The menu across from them lowered to reveal Leda and Grange. "Mom's not getting back today?" Leda looked alarmed. "But I have a dance at school on Thursday!"

"We don't know for sure that she isn't getting back today," Sophie soothed just as a waitress stopped next to their table and set another saucer and mug in front of Sophie.

She was young and pretty with a cheerful smile. "Coffee's in the carafe, but can I get you something else to drink? Orange juice? Cranberry?"

"Milk for the kids," Sophie said. "And we're ready to order now, if you wouldn't mind. I need to get these two to school."

"You bet." The waitress pulled out her pencil and order pad, giving Grange and Leda an expectant look. "What can I get you?"

Grange ordered stuffed French toast, eggs and bacon. Leda, yogurt and granola.

"And for you?" The waitress looked at Sophie.

"Daybreaker," she ordered her favorite protein smoothie without delay. "Extra scoop of peanut butter powder."

"How about you, Meyer?"

"Same," he said. "Plus another stuffed French toast."

"The Meyer special." The waitress smiled at him before tucking her pencil behind her ear. She took the menu from the kids and left again.

Despite the nerves coiling inside her, Sophie glanced at Meyer. It had been plainly obvious the waitress knew him as more than an occasional patron. "Meyer special?"

"Uncle Meyer always orders that when he comes here," Leda said.

"And you always order yogurt and granola," Meyer pointed out. "Nothing wrong with knowing what we like."

She couldn't help herself. "How can you drink a Daybreaker *and* eat stuffed French toast?" She managed not to add the rest—*and look like you do?*

He shrugged, which just meant his shoulder brushed against her again. "Growing boy?"

She made a face and tried once more to shrink the space she occupied. Meyer was all man, but pointing it out was as unacceptable as acknowledging it in the first place.

"But what if she *doesn't* make it back," Leda persisted.

"I won't have anything to wear to the dance!" She looked like she was ready to cry. "She has to take me shopping."

Sophie tugged at her ear. "Your mom didn't mention you had a dance coming up."

"She doesn't know," Leda said. Her eyes were flooding. "We only just decided to go and—"

"Hold on," Sophie interrupted her. "Don't get upset. We can go shopping after school this afternoon and find a dress."

"It's a formal!"

Ouch. It was one thing to find a simple dress. Another to find a fancy dress. She'd spent countless hours during her adolescence being dragged by her mother to one shop after another trying to find the right gown. Unlike Corinne— who'd loved shopping in any and all forms—Sophie had endured.

"We'll figure it out," Sophie promised.

Leda looked somewhat mollified.

Thinking about Corinne while sitting next to Meyer felt disloyal, and she quickly flipped the mug right side up in the saucer and reached for the carafe.

Meyer beat her to it and filled her mug.

"Thank you," she murmured and wrapped her hands around it. The rain was sheeting against the window next to them. "What happens with JCS in weather like this?"

He lifted his own mug and looked at her over the rim. His eyes seemed exceptionally blue. "The boss gets to go have breakfast."

Grange was working the simple puzzles printed on his paper placemat even though he was years beyond the elementary level. The fact that his mom might not be back as scheduled or that he might be late for school didn't bother him one whit.

On the other hand, Leda was twisting a ringlet around her finger while she chewed her lip and stared out the window.

Sophie wished she could say something to alleviate the girl's worry, but all she could do was to try and act normal herself and hope it translated to the girl. "I'd have thought the boss could have breakfast any day that he wanted," she told Meyer.

"And you would be mistaken." He leisurely refilled his own mug. "Mornings are usually a busy time at the airfield."

"With what?" She set down her coffee and pulled out her cell phone. She didn't have any messages from Meredith, and she was reluctant to send one that might interrupt the last few hours of her friend's trip with Walker. So instead of messaging Meredith, she sent a text to the man sitting right next to her.

I don't want to upset Leda. Do you really think they won't make it back today?

"Charters mostly," Meyer answered. "Making sure—" He pulled his phone out and glanced at it. His brows pulled together in a quick twitch when he saw the text from her, but other than that, he didn't react, simply thumbed in a response while he spoke. "Making sure they're fueled up, flight plans are filed, all that kind of stuff."

Unless the gusts die down and fog lets up. Maybe tonight, but wouldn't count on it. Storm will move out of here but it's still heading toward them.

Sophie's phone buzzed with another message the second she'd finished reading his.

But it was only her dad, checking in as he often did, ever since her parents' divorce several years ago. She sent a quick reply that they were still on for dinner that evening but added that she would probably have company with her.

"How…how many charters do you usually have on a weekday? Aren't you busier on the weekends with vacation travelers?"

He gave a few absent-looking swipes on his phone. "Leisure travel has been increasing, but we still have more business charters than anything."

Leda's the most even-keeled kid I know. All this over a dance? Who's the boy?

She lifted her shoulders slightly.

You know exactly as much as I know.

"Who you going to the dance with, kiddo?"

She should have known he'd just ask. He was that sort of man.

"Just friends," Leda mumbled.

Meyer's gaze slid to Sophie.

She lifted her shoulders slightly again. If there was a boy that Leda was interested in, Meredith hadn't mentioned it.

The food came then. Between Grange's plates and Meyer's, the small square table was practically overflowing.

She glanced at her cell phone to check the time. "Eat quick," she told the kids. "We only have thirty minutes before your school bell rings."

"What if there're no good dresses left?" Leda asked, obviously *not* interested in her yogurt and granola. "I'll look like a geek!"

Sophie mentally cursed all junior high school dances. She'd hated them when she'd been a girl, and she hated them even more as a helpless adult. "You won't look like a geek," she assured.

"She always looks like a geek," Grange said around a mouthful of bacon.

Giving him a look, Meyer dumped the eggs from one plate onto the plate with his French toast and poured syrup over the whole lot. "You're as beautiful as your mom." His voice was matter-of-fact. "Whatever you wear, your date is gonna be lucky."

"We're not going with *dates*," Leda said.

"Yeah, you gotta go with your besties 'cause none of the guys asked you," Grange goaded.

"Shut up," Leda snapped.

"Why's the dance on a Thursday?" Meyer asked calmly.

"We always have our dances on Thursday. They start at *six*," Leda told him. "I think it's stupid. Like we're little kids or something."

"They did that when I was in school, too." Sophie unwrapped a straw and plunged it into her thick smoothie. "The senior high dances were always on Friday. Unless it was prom. That was always on the second Saturday in May." Pieces suddenly clicked into place. "Leda, is this your end of year dance?" For junior high kids, it was *the* dance of the year.

Leda nodded miserably.

It was no time to say how much she wished Leda would have just said so earlier. Instead, Sophie leaned across the table, trying to keep the arm of her sweater from falling into Meyer's plate, and squeezed Leda's hand. "I *promise* you, Leda, that we will have you ready for Thursday even if your mom can't make it back today."

"I'd rather not even *go*! But Danielle Dowling was all about it last week, and she's such a bi—" she broke off, her breath hitching. "And now if I don't, she's gonna say I chickened out and—"

"Leda." Sophie squeezed her fingers again around Leda's. "Take a breath."

Leda pulled in another jagged breath. Her wide eyes were fastened on Sophie's.

Sophie smiled gently. "One more. In—" she inhaled deeply herself for example "—and out." She exhaled slowly, and Leda emulated. "You trust me, right?"

Leda nodded. She was still plainly worried, but at least she'd stopped twisting her hair.

"Okay, then. Eat your yogurt. Let me worry about the dress. Right?"

"But—"

"Sophie's got you covered, squirt," Meyer said, shocking Sophie spitless with the arm that he circled around her shoulders. "And you know your mom isn't going to let a storm keep her down for long. It'll all work out. Right, Sophie?"

She hoped her bright smile didn't look as false as it felt. "Right."

But Leda's shoulders were finally going back down where they belonged and she picked up her spoon, stirring her granola into the yogurt. "Danielle Dowling needs to go soak her head," she muttered after a few bites. "D'you know that she'd be failing Biology if it weren't for me?"

Meyer caught Sophie's gaze, and he winked almost imperceptibly. She almost smiled, but it was more from relief that he'd pulled his arm away than the wink.

At least that was what she told herself.

Aware of the ticking time, Sophie went to find their waitress so she could pay their bill now. She grabbed a few take-out containers on the way back to the table.

Grange didn't need one. He'd wolfed his food as rapidly as ever. Leda dumped the contents of her parfait glass into a cup and switched to the plastic spoon that Sophie handed her. Since Sophie's smoothie was already in a take-out cup, she just added a lid as she began shooing the kids out of the booth.

"Thanks for sharing the table," she told Meyer.

He lifted his own smoothie in acknowledgment. "Thanks for the company." He, too, had already decimated the rest of his meal, and her gaze skittered again over his flat stomach.

Realizing it, she quickly grabbed her purse and hustled the kids through the busy restaurant.

It was still raining buckets, and she told them to wait under the awning while she got the SUV. She flipped up the sweater hood, but it didn't do much good as she ran to her SUV and threw herself behind the wheel.

She was pretty much soaked.

Fat lot of good it did to keep her umbrella in the door of her SUV if she didn't pull it out when it was pouring. Shivering a little, she shoved the key into the ignition, turned it and...

Nothing. Just three little ticks and then utter silence.

"Oh, come on," she muttered and turned the key again. Once more. Nothing. Not even the little ticks.

"Why?" She pressed her forehead to the steering wheel. "Why this morning?"

Not surprisingly, the SUV—dead battery and all—said nothing in return.

She reached into the back seat for Leda's and Grange's backpacks and almost staggered under their combined weight. There was no way she could manage the umbrella, too, so she just ran back to the restaurant, the heavy bags thumping against her ribs from both sides.

"My battery's dead," she told the kids and handed off the weighty backpacks. "I'll have to call for service." And much as she was loath to admit it, she was grateful that Meyer was still inside the restaurant. "I'm going to have to ask Meyer if he'll get you to school." She didn't wait for a response as she pulled open the door and hurried inside again.

Meyer was still at his table where the waitress was leaning against the booth, all smiles.

To her credit, she didn't seem overly annoyed by Sophie's return. "I'll talk to you later, hon," she told Meyer as she moved off.

Feeling like a drowned rat, Sophie couldn't make herself meet Meyer's eyes. "My battery's dead. Can you get the kids to school?"

He immediately pulled out his wallet and dropped some cash onto the table as he slid out of the booth. "When it rains, it pours, huh?"

She made a face. "Something like that. Feels more like a Monday than a Tuesday." She turned and started back toward the entrance and didn't *quite* jump out of her skin when she felt Meyer's hand on her elbow as they circled around the line that had once again formed near the door.

He reached around her to open the door, and once they were through, his hand was gone as if it had never been there. "I'll bring the truck around," he told Leda and Grange, who were both leaning back against the brick building, their backpacks propped on their feet.

Fortunately, Tanya's restaurant had an awning that stretched all the way across the front. It was more than ample to protect them from the rain, unless it was blowing vertically against the restaurant.

So far, it wasn't.

Sophie pulled out her cell phone again and called the Howell Elementary office to let them know she would in be late. By the time she was connected to an actual person, Meyer had driven up in his truck.

"If you don't see your mom after school, you'll see me," she told the kids as she dashed out from beneath the awning to pull open the back door of his truck for them. It was a nice truck, with a full-sized back seat.

Grange launched himself in with no hesitation, maneuvering his heavy backpack with ease. Leda, however, hung back. "What if your car's still not running?"

"It's just the battery," she assured and nudged her to move along. "Easy fix." The second Leda was inside, Sophie closed the door and moved back a few steps.

Meyer didn't drive off, though. He just rolled down his window. "I might as well drop you off at work, too," he said. "I'll send over someone from the airfield to change out your battery," he added almost carelessly.

Even though it was second nature to take the opposite position on anything where he was concerned, it was plainly obvious that he intended to wait until she got in the truck. She glanced at her phone again. The school was ten minutes away, the bell due to ring in eight.

She clenched her jaw slightly and ran around the truck to climb into the passenger seat. "I need my bag from my car," she told him.

He put the truck in gear and drove through the lot to where she'd parked in the corner. It only took a few seconds to retrieve her own satchel, and then they were finally off, heading toward the junior high school.

As soon as she fastened her seat belt, she began working the key fob to her vehicle off her key ring. She had other keys that she would need for the nurse's office at the elementary school.

"I can call for auto service," she told him. She paid for an annual membership for situations just like this.

"They'll be plenty busy enough on a day like today. Whereas my crew at JCS is twiddling their thumbs."

Expedience, she told herself and dropped her key into one of the empty cup holders in his console.

She realized, then, that she'd forgotten her Daybreaker smoothie back in the restaurant.

Par for the course.

She worked her fingers through her tangled hair, pushing it back from her forehead. It wasn't entirely wet, and the moisture was making her hair frizz in messy waves. She almost reached for the sun visor to look at herself in the mirror that was surely on the underside of it. "Thank you. I'll… I'll pay you whatever the battery costs." She realized he was taking the shortcut through the cemetery that she herself would have used and relaxed slightly. The route would shave several minutes off the trip. "You didn't grow up here, did you." It wasn't really a question.

"No. Why?"

She made herself stop fiddling with her hair. "Not many people know the cemetery shortcut."

"I spent a few summers with John when we were in college. He used to cut through here whenever he was picking up Meredith from school." He waited a beat while he navigated the roundabout in the center of the cemetery. "Now it's the place nobody can find me when I need to think."

She frowned slightly, watching him from the corner of her eye. "I guess it's quiet."

His lips twisted. "One way of putting it." He turned out of the cemetery gate and sailed through an intersection that deposited them only a few minutes away from the campus where both the junior and the senior high schools were located.

It was a good reminder of the past, she decided. It wouldn't do for her to get too accustomed to Meyer's helpfulness.

She swiped her damp palms down her thighs and looked out at the rain.

He soon turned into the long driveway that ran between the two schools and joined the line of vehicles and school buses dropping off youth. As soon as it was their turn, Leda and Grange hopped out and jogged toward the entrance.

Sophie sighed slightly and got out herself in order to close the truck door that Grange had left open. She climbed back inside, knowing that she was even wetter.

She focused on her hands as he followed the other vehicles back out of the parking lot again. "Thanks again for the lift. And—" she shrugged "—everything."

His silence went on just a little too long, and she finally looked up to find him watching her. "I don't see any obvious signs of pain," he said, "though I figure that had to hurt."

Heat ran into her cheeks. "You have no idea," she muttered.

She expected him to drop it, but he didn't. "How *is* Corinne?"

He might as well have knocked her sideways.

She looked out the side window. "Fine." Out of sight, she childishly crossed her fingers. "Why?"

"You're the one who mentioned her," he reminded.

"Don't pretend you care whether she is fine or not."

He stifled an oath. "Your sister and I went out a few times *twenty* years ago. If I've even talked to her twice in the time since, I'll eat my hat. So, what is supposed to be my crime that you have a grudge still to this day?"

Her temples tightened. She wished she'd never mentioned Corinne's name that one day on Bluff Road. She wished that Meredith and her kids weren't inextricably tied to Meyer because of John and JCS.

Most of all, she wished she had a knife that could lance her attraction to Meyer out of her veins once and for all.

"Maybe I should just call her myself," he said. "Have a drink for old time's sake. Where's she living these days?"

"That's foul, even for you."

He lifted his hands. "What?"

"You know she has a drinking problem!"

His gaze focused on her sharply. "Why would I know that? Hell, Sophie, I've known *you* twice as long as I ever knew your sister!"

"Meredith knows!"

"So? You think Meredith and I sit around talking about the good ol' days? Hate to enlighten you, sweetheart, but we have bigger fish to fry these days." The dark blue rim of his lighter blue eyes seemed almost black. Sucking her in. Making her want to believe every word that passed his perfectly shaped lips.

"Just—" She sliced her hand through the air between them. "Never mind."

He wrapped his fingers around her wrist, and the air seemed to evaporate from her lungs. "Sophie."

"Let me go," she said huskily.

He looked ready to argue, but he released her wrist and wrapped his fingers around his steering wheel instead. "All right, Nurse Lane." He turned out of the parking lot. "Howell Elementary?"

"How'd you know that?" There were several elementary schools in Cape Cardinale.

"My nefarious ways." His lips twisted. "You wore a school shirt on the airfield tour," he reminded.

She deliberately relaxed her shoulders. "I told you I was filling in for the school nurse," she said abruptly. As if she needed to provide a valid reason. "She's on maternity leave for the rest of the school year."

"Meredith mentioned Doc Hayes would be back in June." His voice had gone bland. As if, once again, they were still in the company of Grange and Leda.

If he could pretend, so could she.

"Middle of the month." She looked away from his hands on the steering wheel. "Unless I pick up a third gig, I'll have a couple weeks off before he gets back. Summer vacation."

"Doing anything special?"

"Nothing but surfing and lazing around on the beach." Her gaze kept bouncing back to him like he was a magnet. "One beach or another."

His lips twisted. "To each their own. You can sunbathe your sweet self all day long on Cardinale Beach if you want. Won't bother me any. I doubt it'll bother the others. Particularly Cutter."

She raised her brows. "Cutter?"

"My brother. We all—" He broke off, shaking his head.

She realized his fingers were curling around the steering wheel so tightly his knuckles were white.

"—have to live together in the house for twelve months," he finished flatly.

She blinked. The run-down house barely looked like it could accommodate one person, much less four. "Why?" As soon as the word escaped, she shook her head. "Never mind. None of my business."

"It'll get around soon enough. Terms of the old man's will."

She couldn't help herself. "Is that usual?"

"Nothing about Pietro Cardinale was usual. Starting the beginning of June, we'll be one cramped, miserable family." He turned another corner and stretched out his fingers on the steering wheel. "Maybe that was his plan."

"To make you all miserable?"

"Continuing the work he'd begun in life? Why not? He wasn't what you'd call a model parent."

She frowned. "I don't know what to say."

"There's nothing *to* say. Either we all agree to the sentence or we lose out on the house altogether." He turned into the elementary school parking lot. It was considerably smaller than Leda and Grange's present school, but there was a similar line of vehicles in front of the school building, letting off children.

He was inching along, his engine barely more than an idle, and she unfastened her seat belt and gathered up the long strap of her bag. "What about the rest of it?"

"The estate, you mean?" He grimaced. "There is no 'rest of' the estate. The beach property is all there is."

She felt her jaw loosen. "Does Meredith know?"

"You are the first person I've told." His smile was humorless. "Makes you feel really special, doesn't it?"

They'd reached the beginning of the line, and it was Sophie's turn to jump out of the vehicle.

His words had been facetious. But she really didn't know how Meyer's admission made her feel.

It was just one more item in the disturbing basket that was Meyer Cartell.

She pushed open the door.

"What time are you off?"

The question was unexpected. "Three."

"I'll pick you up then."

She frowned. "Why?"

"Take you back to your car? You have a dress to find for Leda, remember?"

She felt herself flush all over again. "I can get a ride back to my car."

"Don't want to be indebted? Or don't want to be indebted to me?"

She slid out of the truck. "Take your pick. They both work." Then she closed the door and hurried toward the school entrance.

She felt his eyes on her every step of the way.

Chapter Eight

"We're still in Colorado." The phone line crackled, making Meredith's voice sound even fainter. "Flights are being canceled all over the place. Can't even find a rental car."

Sophie tapped the end of her pen against the report that she'd been filling out on her lunch hour. "Are you guys okay there?"

"We're fine." More crackling. "I'm just ready to be home. Walker's—" Meredith's voice broke up again into incomprehensible gibberish. "—shouldn't have come," she finished.

Sophie propped her head on her hand, trying to decipher the broken call. "Sorry. You're breaking up a lot. You think you shouldn't have gone with Walker?"

"No…timing…"

Sophie moved to the window and pushed the bottom of it out, as if it would have some positive effect on the quality of the call. It didn't, but it did let in a rush of cool air that was welcome in the too-warm nurse's office.

She told Meredith about Leda and the dance. "Sounds

like Danielle Dowling is a thorn—" She realized the call
had cut out completely.

"—in her side," she finished to nobody but herself.

Hoping that a text would make it through to Meredith
better than a voice call, she started typing.

I'll make sure Leda has a dress one way or another, even if
I have to find one from my own closet. Don't worry about
anything but keeping warm with Walker. Hugs.

Meredith's response was quicker than Sophie had expected.

I checked weather. Storm is supposed to last until
Thursday. Airlines will be a mess. She'll never forgive me
if I miss her first formal dance.

She hesitated for a moment, then responded.

Maybe Meyer could fly over and get you.

She watched the three floating dots, feeling oddly tense.

Hadn't thought of that. Have to see if he can spare a
pilot and a plane.

The bell rang, and the corridor outside her office filled
with the sounds of children. She left the desk for a moment
and looked in on Teddy Dowling. He was still lying on the
narrow couch, snoring slightly. He'd come to her office
complaining of nausea, but she suspected it was more an
aversion to his impending vocabulary test than anything.
Nevertheless, she'd left a message for his mom, though Sophie was still waiting for a response.

She returned to her desk and her cell phone.

Why does he need a pilot? I thought he WAS a pilot.

"Nurse Lane?"

She guiltily dropped her phone into her desk drawer.

Howell Elementary had a strict rule about no cell phones for students as well as staff. But at least it wasn't a school administrator standing in her doorway, and unlike Gertrude Maitland, Becky Newberry wasn't likely to report her cell-phone infraction.

She approached the first-grade teacher who looked young enough to still be in high school. "Hi, Ms. Newberry." She had a tearful student with her, and Sophie crouched in front of the little girl. "Who do we have here?"

"Alicia Savage."

The little girl held up her index finger. Huge tears were welling on her long eyelashes. "I smashed it in the door."

"I bet that hurts a lot." She held out her palm. "Can I take a look?"

The girl nodded. Her lower lip was quivering. "It's broken in two. I know it is."

Cradling the girl's hand, Sophie solemnly looked at the slightly pink finger. "How about we put a cold pack on it and rest it for a little while? Maybe it won't feel so broken in two."

"Okay, but am I gonna need an ambulance? My brother had an ambulance last year."

"Oh, my." She straightened and gave a quick wink at the teacher, who nodded and turned to hurry back down the corridor that was nearly clear of children again. She pointed at the wooden chair pushed in the corner of her small office. "Have a seat there, Alicia." She pulled out a cold pack and shook it slightly to activate it. "Why did your brother need an ambulance last year?"

"He was climbing in our tree and fell out. He broke his leg."

Sophie slowly coaxed the child into allowing her to fold the cold wrap around her finger. "Is he all healed up now?"

"Yeah. I got to draw on his cast."

She wound adhesive gauze around the cold pack to hold it in place. "What did you draw?"

"Our cat. Whiskers. She's orange."

"I've heard that orange cats are some of the best cats." She settled a little pillow under Alicia's wrist. "Okay. Just sit there for a little while, and we'll see if we can avoid the ambulance."

"But will I have a cast?"

"Maybe not this time," Sophie feigned regret. "I'm sorry."

Alicia sighed hugely. Her tears had dried, and the quivering lip had steadied.

"On the bright side, though, casts can end up being *very* smelly by the time they get removed. And it's no fun going around with a smelly cast."

The girl suddenly wrinkled her nose. "Oh, yeah. Aidyn's cast smelled really *bad.*"

Sophie picked up the receiver on her desk phone. "Is your mom or dad at home? Do they work?"

"My mom works at home. My dad's gone. He's in the army. I miss him."

"I bet you do. Do you know your number at home?" She had a card file of every student's emergency information.

Alicia nodded proudly and reeled it off. Sophie dialed and soon had Alicia's mother on the line. She explained the situation before handing off the receiver to Alicia.

While they spoke, Sophie glanced in on the still-sleeping

Teddy, then returned to her desk and the report she was supposed to complete by that afternoon.

She added the day's activities to the report and, when the girl was done talking to her mom, escorted Alicia back to her classroom.

She finally reached Teddy's mother, who came to pick him up, and before she knew it, the release bell was ringing. She closed and latched the window, packed her bag and checked her reflection in the mirror on the back of her office door.

After her wet start to the day, she'd twisted her hair up in a knot, but it had still dried in messy twists around her face. It would just look like blond frizz if she tried brushing it.

Annoyed for caring, she locked the office and joined the orderly disorder making its way to the school entrance.

It was still raining, though not as heavily as it had been that morning, and children were lined up in groups as the monitors directed the pickup cars.

She worked her way around them, not entirely sure where Meyer would be. She didn't see his truck in the lot or in the line of vehicles stacked three-wide to pick up students.

She hovered under the awning for several minutes before pulling out her cell phone. "Should have expected him to forget me," she muttered.

"Nurse Lane!"

Sophie looked over her shoulder to see the school secretary waving something in her hand as she weaved around the milling children. "My student assistant was supposed to get this to you earlier," she said breathlessly and held out a small manila envelope.

"What—" As soon as Sophie took it, she realized what it contained and tore it open to shake her key fob into her hand. She looked at the secretary. "Who dropped it off?"

"You don't know? He didn't leave his name, but he was a good-looking one that one." The woman smiled. "All that auburn hair and intense blue eyes."

"Meyer." She couldn't believe he'd brought her SUV himself. She scanned the parking lot.

"He said he left it in the teacher's lot."

No wonder she couldn't see it. The teacher's lot was around the side of the building, accessible by a completely different door. "Thanks, Mrs. Crowe." She walked back with the older woman into the building.

"He said not to disturb you," Mrs. Crowe said, "when he brought the key. Such a nice young man."

Sophie couldn't help smiling at that, wondering how Meyer would like the description. She curled her fingers around the fob. "He's unexpected, that's for sure."

If he weren't, she'd have an easier time keeping the man slotted in the spot he'd held for over twenty years.

She and Mrs. Crowe parted company at the administration office, and Sophie headed for the building's side exit.

Sure enough, her SUV was parked beneath one of the covered spots, very close to the door.

She tossed her bag into the back and got behind the wheel. It started right up and she patted the steering wheel. "That's *much* better."

She had plenty of time left to pick up Leda and Grange.

She looked at her phone while she waited for the heater to warm and, before she could talk herself out of it, called Meyer.

He answered on the third ring, his voice sounding loud since the SUV's Bluetooth had taken control of the call.

"Engine start okay?" he greeted.

"Perfectly. I didn't expect you to bring the SUV here."

"Just worked out that way. You found it okay, obviously."

"Considering you parked in the assistant principal's spot? Found it right away."

"Spot was available," he said, as if that was all he needed to say.

She realized she was in danger of smiling and pinched her lips between her fingers to curb it. "How much do I owe you?"

"Receipt's behind your visor."

She reached up and lowered the visor. A small receipt slid free, and she caught it before it landed in her lap. She checked the amount, which was less than she'd expected. What wasn't expected, though, was the fact that the receipt was dated that morning from a local auto parts store.

"When you said you'd have someone from JCS take care of it, I didn't think that meant sending them out in the rain to buy the battery in the first place," she said. Just because she had an ax to grind where Meyer was concerned didn't mean she had one with the people who worked for the company that he ran for Meredith. "You'll have to give them my thanks."

"You're welcome," he said.

She pressed her tongue against the back of her teeth for a moment. "*You* replaced the battery," she concluded.

"Have a problem with that?"

She looked up at the visor. The small mirror on it reflected her uncertainty. She flipped up the visor, back where it belonged. "I'll pay you back tomorrow," she said briskly.

"No rush. I know where you live." Irony dripped from his voice. "And I can always hold your granny's plate for hostage."

She pinched her lips again until she conquered another temptation to smile. "Well, anyway. Thanks again. Oh, wait!" She scrolled her cell-phone screen to find her text conversation with Meredith. "If the weather's clear enough, couldn't *you* fly over to Colorado and retrieve Meredith and Walker? Sounds like the—"

Yeah, he's still a pilot, but he never flies anymore.

Meredith's response to Sophie's question earlier that afternoon stared up at her from the screen of her phone.

"Sounds like what?" he prompted.

She shook herself. What did it matter whether Meyer flew planes himself anymore or not? He *ran* JCS, which employed several other pilots. "The, um, the airlines are going to be a mess after all the flight cancellations," she finished.

"Yeah, they probably will be. But that's a good idea. Leda would certainly be relieved. I'll check the schedule."

"Great. I won't, um, mention anything to her or Grange until something is settled."

"I'll let you know."

She nodded as if he could see her. "Right," she said belatedly. "I'd better go. Don't want to be late picking them up." Not only did she have to fit in dress shopping, but the kids needed fresh clothes from their house. At least Grange wouldn't be in danger of starving since they'd be having dinner at her dad's.

"Let me know if you need anything," Meyer said.

"Just a pretty gown on no notice," she said wryly.

"Anything *besides* that," he amended. "Good luck."

"Thanks."

She ended the call, and since she still had a few minutes before she needed to be at the junior high school, she stopped at the grocery store and bought another box of cereal and two loaves of bread.

Dinner at her dad's was one thing. Breakfast for Grange's insatiable appetite, another.

She made it to the school and was actually one of the first cars in line and once her passengers were on board, made a beeline for the shopping mall.

Two and a half hours later, Grange had the new video game that she'd bought as a bribe for him to stop haranguing Leda while they shopped.

But they had no dress.

And they were in danger of being late for dinner at her dad's.

They let themselves in and found her dad in the front hallway. He'd obviously been watching for them.

She greeted him with a hug. "Sorry we cut it so close. You remember Meredith's kids, Dad?"

"Leda and Grange." Fitzgerald smiled. "Of course I do. It'll be a regular party this evening." He ushered them into the family room.

Sophie's steps faltered when she saw the stunning brunette already there.

"This is a friend of mine," Fitzgerald said. "Francesca Page."

Sophie recovered quickly and crossed the room, hand extended. "I'm—"

"Sophie," Francesca said, meeting her halfway. She had a faint accent that seemed entirely in keeping with her luxurious brown hair and extremely stylish white blazer and slacks. "Your dad's told me so much about you."

Sophie smiled. She couldn't say the same. But Francesca had a firm handshake—none of the limp fish fingers—and it was high time her dad started socializing. The divorce had been almost seven years ago, and Sophie considered her dad to still be a catch.

She gestured toward Leda and Grange, who were hovering in the doorway, looking uncertain, and introduced them. "They're staying with me for a few days while their mom is on a trip." She nodded toward the adjacent all-weather sunroom. "You guys can work on your homework in there. Wi-Fi password's *Lollipop5.*"

Grange gave a mumble and nod and crossed the room. Despite her nerves over the dress, Leda had a little more aplomb and offered a shy greeting before following her brother.

Fitzgerald clapped his hands together—a little too heartily. Proof that he wasn't quite as nonchalant about the evening as he appeared. "I was going to grill out, but this storm took care of that."

"Dad grills a mean lobster," Sophie told Francesca before looking toward her father. "What's on the menu instead?"

"Chicken piccata."

"Ah." She nodded. "Another specialty." No reason to voice the fact that they were the only two dishes he'd mastered. "And dessert?"

"I brought a chocolate torte," Francesca said. "My little contribution."

"Hardly little." Fitzgerald slid his arm around Francesca's shoulders, then quickly removed it again.

Sophie bit back a smile.

"Sounds wonderful." She finally dropped her purse onto a side table. "I'm just going to freshen up, and then I can pitch in with whatever needs to be done."

"We've got it taken care of," Fitzgerald assured.

She smiled again and impetuously reached up to give him another quick hug and a kiss.

"What's that for?"

She smiled into his face. Her mother's acrimonious departure had left its mark for too long. "Just happy to see you."

It seemed as if love was in the air for more than just Meredith.

* * *

"What about this one?" Sophie pulled another hanger from the crowded closet and held up a ruffled dress.

The entire meal had been a hit, and now both Leda and Francesca were sitting on Sophie's childhood bed as she rooted through her closet for old party dresses while—down the hall—Sophie's dad was entertaining Grange at the Ping-Pong table. It had been Fitzgerald Lane who'd suggested looking in Sophie's own closet for a gown for Leda.

"Paid for enough of them over the years," he'd added dryly.

Sophie fluffed a ruffle, coaxingly. "Yea? Nay?"

Francesca—who turned out to be an attorney like Sophie's dad—and Leda both tilted their heads to one side as if trying to envision the baby-blue dress on Leda.

Their expressions were mirrors of each other.

"Fine." Sophie tossed it aside where it joined the growing pile of discarded dresses. "Too dated." She propped her hands on her hips and turned to look at the other side of her walk-in closet.

Her room was like a time machine to the past.

Her parents—together or apart—hadn't changed a single thing in her room since she'd been a teenager. Which was all the more reason why it had been high time she'd bought her own place and lived like the adult that she was.

Leda flopped back onto the mattress. "Why can't I get the flu or something?"

"Oh, stop." Sophie wasn't sure if she preferred a teary Leda or a melodramatic one. She pursed her lips as she flipped through the hangers.

She had long dresses. Short dresses. Black dresses. Pink dresses. They ran the gamut from casual to formal, but there was no pretending that they weren't more than a decade old. Back then, Sophie's mother had been *all* about making sure that her daughters were properly attired for every little thing. At school. At the country club.

She'd cared far more about the way their appearance reflected on *her* than she had about what mattered to Sophie or Corinne.

"Would you mind if I…" Francesca raised her eyebrows slightly.

"Not in the least." Sophie stepped out of her closet and spread her arm gratefully. "When it comes to style, you're leaps and bounds ahead of me. These days, for me dressing up means not wearing scrubs."

Francesca laughed lightly as they exchanged places, and she took over the hanger-flipping. "You're young and beautiful," she dismissed blithely. "That trumps style every day of the week."

Sophie was pretty sure that wasn't true but wasn't going to debate it with a woman trained to argue.

While Francesca continued examining Sophie's old wardrobe with no more success than she'd had, she wondered if Meredith would care if she took Leda out of school to go to Corvallis, where they'd have a better chance of finding a proper dress on such short notice. They'd already combed through the local mall to no avail.

"This is nice." Francesca held up a long blush-pink gown with a layered chiffon skirt and a puffy-sleeved top.

Leda wrinkled her nose. "Those sleeves?"

"Well." Francesca angled her head. "Without them. Without the whole bodice, actually."

Sophie smiled reminiscently. "That was from a wedding I was in. My first time as a bridesmaid." She scooted off the bed and went to the built-in bookshelf that was crowded with textbooks and novels and a lifetime of memorabilia. She pulled off two different photo albums before she had the right one, and she carried it back to the bed, showing Leda and Francesca. "Corinne and I were both brides-maids." She showed them the photograph. Sophie, not yet eleven. Corinne, already nineteen. "It was our cousin's wedding, and I was thrilled."

"You were just little," Leda peered at the picture. "I'm almost fifteen!"

"And you're as thin as a runway model," Francesca said. "Imagine." She slipped the gown off the hanger and held it up by the waist, letting the overblown bodice fall behind the skirt. "The skirt alone is lovely. Add a little beaded belt? Very chic."

Sophie went back into her closet and pulled a shoebox off the shelf. She rummaged through it until she found the belt she remembered and dangled it in front of Francesca. "How about this?"

"Oh, pearls. Perfect." Francesca turned Leda so that she was facing the floor mirror tilted against the wall next to the bureau and held the dress in front of her.

"It's supposed to be a long dress, though," Leda protested. "It'll be too short on me."

"It would be interesting," Francesca insisted. "Add a silk T-shirt. Or a little cropped sweater. Pin up those glorious curls, and oh, you'll be the envy of your little friends."

Sophie could see the growing interest in Leda's eyes.

"You would need to find a seamstress to make the alterations, but—"

"Corinne sews," Sophie said abruptly. "She was always altering her clothes when we were younger." Mostly because their dad had often cut off her allowance in punishment for one stunt or another. "I… I've been meaning to call her for a while anyway." Now, at least, she'd have an excuse besides the "checking up" that Corinne typically objected to.

She nudged Leda toward the bedroom door. "Bathroom's

down the hall. Go try it on," she coaxed. "Just to get an idea of the skirt. If it doesn't fit at all, I'll call your mom and see if it's okay to take you to Corvallis tomorrow afternoon."

"I *can't* go to Corvallis tomorrow! I have a math test." She heaved a sigh and took the gown and belt, slumping out of the room.

Sophie reached out and touched Francesca's hand. "Thank you."

"I remember being a girl." Francesca smiled ruefully. "Though it's longer ago than I like to admit."

Sophie managed not to roll her eyes. She was going to have to ask her father just how old Francesca was because the woman's appearance was positively flawless.

She replaced the photo albums on the shelf and began hanging up the discarded dresses. From down the hall, they could hear the routine *thwop* of the Ping-Pong game.

"Will your sister be able to help, do you think?"

She could tell by Francesca's expression that her father had told Francesca all about his other daughter, too. "You mean will she be—" She broke off when Leda reappeared.

She had fastened the dress around her waist and tied on the belt but just held the bodice in front of her chest. The corkscrew hem swirled around her legs from her knees to her ankles.

The smile on Leda's face, though, was the first one Sophie had seen all day, and she put aside her doubts.

She'd sobered up her sister before.

If she needed to do it again, she would.

Chapter Nine

"Are you home?"

Sophie rubbed her eyes and sat up further on the couch as she held her cell phone to her ear. "Meyer?"

"Yeah. You home?"

"What time is it?" She realized she must have dozed off after getting the kids to bed.

"Almost eleven. I woke you, didn't I?"

"No," she lied on a huge yawn that had to be plainly audible. "What's wrong?"

"Nothing's wrong. I just realized I still had Grange's gear in my truck."

"Gear?" Something about hearing Meyer's deep voice was making her stupid. Obviously.

"Baseball gear. He has a game tomorrow after school."

She rubbed her hand down her face. Of course.

After dinner at her dad's, the dress and then Sophie's unexpectedly fruitful phone call with her sister, she hadn't been thinking about baseball at all.

"Right. Against Xavier," she said, if only to prove that she wasn't entirely oblivious of the details.

"I'm on your side of town. I can bring it by tonight. Leave it under the carport, but I didn't want to drop it off without letting you know it was there."

"You could have waited until tomorrow."

"I'm busy." His tone was short and so final that she automatically wanted to ask for details.

Instead, she padded barefoot down the hall, peeking through the ajar doors of the bedrooms Leda and Grange were using. They were both asleep. "Then I appreciate you bringing it by," she said, more hushed. "Grange would forget his nose if it weren't attached."

"Can't say I'm any better. I've forgotten about the gear twice," he admitted before disconnecting.

Whereas she hadn't thought about Grange's baseball gear at all. Instead, she'd been entirely preoccupied with Leda's concerns.

How did Meredith *do* it—manage the demands of her two children all at the same time? Sophie had only had the kids with her for five nights and she was exhausted.

As if to make up for her failings, she snuck into Grange's room and smoothed the blanket over his lanky shoulders. He snorted softly, turned over and kicked it off again.

She started to reach out again but stopped herself. Her guilty conscience wasn't going to be assuaged by waking him.

She left his room and went to her own. She slipped her feet into hard-soled slippers and returned to the living room to wait for Meyer. He'd said he was on her side of town. But even then, it took some time to traverse the switchbacks on Bluff Road. She curled up on the couch, listening for the sound of his truck engine beyond the rhythmic ebb and flow of the surf. When she realized she was in danger of dozing off again, she pulled on a sweater and walked out to her carport.

A duffel bag sat in front of her SUV.

She'd missed Meyer altogether.

She could *not* be disappointed.

Could she?

She transferred Grange's baseball gear to the back of her SUV and walked out to the end of her driveway.

The wind was damp, but the rain had finally passed and the sky was clear.

She looked to the left. The narrow road traveled into inky darkness. It was the same to the right. Up on the cliff, far above where the road ended, she could see a few pinpoints of light from the houses that existed up there.

More of the McMansions that Meyer had threatened. Fancy dwellings with spectacular views that were rarely occupied by the wealthy owners who built them.

She hugged her collar to her neck and went back inside. She sent the text before she could talk herself out of it.

I wanted to catch you.

The response didn't come for so long that she'd convinced herself it wouldn't come at all. And then when it did, she smiled despite herself.

We know you'd just throw me back if you did.

A picture of swimming fish accompanied the text.

She typed again.

Any progress on retrieving Meredith before Leda's dance?

His fish were followed up with a thumbs-up.

JCS to the rescue. Soon as storm over Colorado lets up.

Was that why he would be busy the next day? Picking
up Meredith and Walker? But Meredith had said he didn't
fly anymore. Was he accompanying the pilot, then?

Her blood seemed to suddenly pound in her ears.

You're a good friend to them.

She stared at the words she'd typed, her thumb hovering
over the Send key. But instead, she pressed the Delete key
until the words were erased altogether. She began again.

Thanks for bringing the gear. Good night.

Then she plugged the phone in to charge and closed it
in a drawer before going to bed.

"I can't believe how beautiful she looks," Meredith whispered. She clicked off another photo on her cell phone before reaching out to squeeze Sophie's hand.

Sophie smiled.

Leda *did* look beautiful. But it wasn't because of the
fluttering blush chiffon that swirled around her lithe legs
or the shimmering tank top that—surprisingly—had come
from Corinne.

It was because of the laughter on her face as she twirled
around the small living room with two of her girlfriends
who were dressed to the nines as well. With all the boister-
ous femininity, Grange had hastily taken refuge upstairs.

"She looks like *you*," Sophie said. "Of course she's beautiful."

"Sweet. But she's really a female version of her dad,"

Meredith said. "She and Grange both take after John." Her sigh sounded wistful.

Since Meredith had gotten back to town just that morning, Sophie hadn't had a good opportunity to find out how the weekend—that had turned into a week—had gone. And now, with the girls prancing and giggling around the living room while they waited for the rest of their group to pick them up before the dance, that discussion would still have to wait.

Meredith took another picture of the girls. "Can't believe that was an old bridesmaid dress of yours."

"Francesca was right about using only the skirt. Corinne had it fixed up in no time at all. We were only at her apartment for an hour. Took us longer driving back and forth to Lincoln City than it did for her to actually do the sewing."

Meredith gave her a sidelong look. "How was she?"

Sophie lifted her shoulder. "She seemed fine. We didn't talk about much actually, except her new job. Staff accountant with some new firm. Claims she's been sober now for three months."

"You don't believe her?"

Sophie sighed. Corinne's struggle for sobriety had been a roller coaster her entire adulthood. Her longest stretch had been a blessedly calm three years that had ended when their mother had walked out on their father.

In the time since, Corinne hadn't made it past twelve months without falling off the wagon. One lost job after another. One eviction after another. The hardest thing Sophie'd ever had to do was refuse to help Corinne the last time she'd come begging for money to tide her over.

"I want to believe it'll last this time," she admitted. "But…" She lifted her shoulder again. "I know that Corinne is the only one who can help herself, but I still live in hope, I guess."

"I remember when we were in high school," Meredith said. "Your sister was *the* queen of the school. Most likely to succeed. The whole bit." She smiled slightly. "She was a year ahead of me, but I was just as envious of her as everyone else was."

Sophie couldn't hide her surprise. "You've never said that before."

"You and I didn't even know each other back then."

True. Sophie had only been an elementary student when her sister had graduated from high school. And she hadn't met Meredith at all until Sophie'd started working for Doc. "I was guilty of my own heroine worship, too."

"She's your big sister," Meredith said, as if that explained everything. "And look, three months of sobriety is better than two," she said. "And there's nothing wrong with hope."

The teenagers' excitement suddenly ratcheted up a notch because their compatriots had arrived.

"Danielle brought a *limo*," Leda breathed, her nose pressed against the window that looked over the front of the house.

Meredith eyed Sophie and rolled her eyes. "Seems a bit much for a junior high dance," she told Leda, "but you still have to be home by eleven. Limo or not." She handed her daughter a fancy little purse that matched the little woven-pearl belt circling her waist. "You get my cell phone for tonight only." She picked up the cordless telephone from the table next to the couch and waved it at her daughter. "That's only so you call the house here if anything goes wrong. The ride home is late. Your friends start doing anything you shouldn't be doing, or you want to get out of a situation you're not comfortable with? Tell them it's not worth it when your mom will ruin your life for the next year, and call me."

"I know the rules," Leda said hurriedly and kissed her

mom. Then she twined her arms around Sophie's neck and squeezed tightly. "Thank you for the dress," she said fervently.

Sophie squeezed Leda in return. "Have fun."

"Just not *too* much fun," Meredith added and pulled open the door just as the other trio of girls landed on the doorstep.

More giggling and gushing ensued, and Meredith took several more pictures of the entire group before they climbed into the back of the long black limo. Even after the car doors closed on them, the sounds of their hilarity were still audible.

"You'd think it was their senior prom," Meredith said, exhaling. "Why do they have to grow up so fast?"

Sophie lifted her shoulders.

"Remember your first formal dance?"

Sophie made a face. "Unfortunately. Your daughter? She has the right idea. Just go out and have fun with your girlfriends. No worries about feckless guys."

"Don't kid yourself. Leda's going with her friends, but Grange clued me in that Danielle's brother is the real appeal where this sudden friendship of theirs is concerned. From the sounds of it, he's seventeen going on twenty." Meredith waved one last time at the girls who'd popped their heads through the moonroof of the limo and were waving their hands like they'd become members of the British monarchy. "Sit down and put on your seat belts," she yelled out the door.

A peal of laughter was her only response.

She immediately punched out a phone number on the cordless phone she was still holding.

A moment later, Sophie could see at least one head retreat into the limo.

Satisfied, Meredith ended the call without speaking and closed the front door. She threw herself down onto the couch with obvious relief. "She's not much younger than me when I met John. From then on, he was the only thing I could think about. And we know where *that* led."

"You didn't have a mother like Leda has," Sophie reminded. Meredith's mother had washed her hands of her parental duties the second Meredith had turned eighteen. "Does the brother have any interest in *Leda*?"

"Not that I've been able to tell. His name's Scott. Works at one of the surf shops down by Friars. Sounds like he's pretty busy. Hopefully too busy to become a problem."

"Leda has a good head on her shoulders."

"Which can go right out the window when hormones are involved." She huffed out a breath. "John used to tell me I worried about things too much."

Sophie silently noted yet another mention of John.

Grange was still taking refuge upstairs in his bedroom, and she refilled her coffee mug before taking the chair opposite the couch. "Not to change the subject, but to change the subject...long time to be cooped up with Walker."

The corners of Meredith's lips turned down. "That's for sure."

"Sorry things didn't live up to your expectations."

"That's what I said to *him*," Meredith admitted. She tossed the phone onto the cushion beside her. "The man's just...too perfect."

"I didn't know there was such a thing."

"Neither did I." Meredith's gaze went to the ceiling as if she were listening for Grange. But the only noise coming from upstairs was the faintly muffled sound of a television. "But Walker is proof otherwise. And yes—" Meredith's cheeks turned dusky "—the new undies were worth the expense."

"But...?" Because clearly there was a *but*.

Meredith closed her eyes. "I just felt like I was cheating on John," she admitted softly. "And the better the…the sex…the worse it got." She opened her eyes again. "And I know how…ridiculous that must sound, considering everything."

Considering Meredith and John's marriage had gone through more than one rocky stretch thanks to the man's penchant for infidelity, Sophie knew.

"I'm sorry. I was hoping that you were having an absolutely magnificent time."

"I'm sorry, too." Meredith's fingers toyed with the phone beside her. "If I hadn't gone, you wouldn't have had to deal with dresses and Meyer and—"

"I didn't mind any of it. I love your kids. You know that."

Meredith raised her eyebrows. "And Meyer?"

Sophie willed herself not to flush. "I don't know why everyone suddenly seems to think I have an issue with Meyer."

Silence followed her statement, and then Meredith shook her head. "There's no *suddenly* about it, Soph. But I am curious who else is pointing it out."

"Leda said something."

"Ah." Meredith nodded. "She's observant, that one. More than I ever was at her age, that's for sure." She made a face. "Or *any* age, when it comes to that."

"Meyer's a good friend to you," Sophie said. "I know that."

"And?"

"Well. Maybe the reason why things weren't marvelous with Walker is because you should have been with Meyer." The words, so long stoppered, came out in a blunt rush.

Meredith looked startled. She shook her head again and looked away. "*No.* No, no, no."

She sounded too vehement. Sophie studied her friend's downturned head. "Not even tempted?"

Meredith's laugh sounded forced. "You sound like Walker. He thinks men and women can never be just friends."

"I don't know that I think *that* but—"

"—I'll tell you what I told him. Kissing Meyer is like kissing my brother. If I had a brother."

She managed not to wince, as much for Walker as for herself. "You've kissed?"

"Ages and ages ago," Meredith dismissed almost curtly. "Before John and I were engaged."

"I didn't mean to bring up a touchy—"

"—you didn't," Meredith interrupted. She exhaled loudly. "Sorry. I'm just feeling sensitive because of Walker."

"Sure," Sophie said faintly. Even though she wasn't sure at all.

Meredith looked at her coffee mug and abruptly stood. "I want wine. What about you?"

Sophie nodded, but Meredith was already going into the kitchen.

She rubbed her forehead, wishing that she'd never opened what was obviously a can of worms. She hadn't figured out how to seal it up again when Meredith returned.

"I'd just graduated from high school." Meredith extended a glass of wine. "When I kissed him."

"*You*—" Sophie broke off and took the glass. By some miracle, she managed not to gulp down half of it.

"Yeah. Me." Meredith sat again and seemed to relax a little. "Meyer never would have made a move like that. He and John were too tight."

"Did he kiss you back?" She couldn't stop the question.

Meredith took a sip of wine. "I'd just graduated from high school. My mom had already taken off, and I was mad at John for some stupid reason that I can't even remember anymore."

Sophie couldn't help but notice that Meredith hadn't answered her. "What happened then?"

Meredith lifted her shoulder. "I got over being mad. Like I always did. And a few weeks later, everything was back to normal, except that John and I were engaged and Meyer was going out with your sister. Not that *that* lasted."

"Why didn't it?"

Something shifted in Meredith's gaze again before she focused on the golden wine she was swirling in her glass. "The only thing Meyer cared about was flying. The Air Force was his ticket to that. He never made any secret of it."

Sophie's fingers tightened around her glass. "And that's why they broke up? Meyer and Corinne?"

"I think the term 'broke up' implies more of a relationship than they had."

"Sure," Sophie said darkly. "They were just sleeping together."

"They were?"

Sophie frowned at Meredith. "Corinne got *pregnant*," she said.

Meredith's fingertips fluttered to her throat. She looked startled. "I had no idea."

"Yes, well, my mother made sure nobody knew." Sophie grimaced. "Hustled her off for an abortion, and that was that."

Meredith set her glass on the coffee table. "Corinne would have been twenty or so. She surely had a choice about it."

"Wouldn't say that if you'd ever met my mother." The one abiding thing that Sophie's mother had cared about was appearances, and neither one of her daughters had been up to snuff. "All I know is that nobody under our roof ever talked about it again."

"Did *Meyer* know?"

"Of course he knew. When Corinne told him, he said it didn't fit in with his *plans*."

"It just doesn't sound like him."

"Doesn't sound like the guy who only cared about being a pilot?" *And who may, or may not, have kissed his best friend's girl?*

Meredith sat forward on the couch. Her expression even more troubled. "And that's what's been behind your antipathy toward Meyer all these years?"

"He broke her heart."

Meredith didn't answer.

"What?"

Meredith sighed. "I always thought that Corinne was more in the business of breaking other people's hearts."

"Doesn't mean it didn't happen to her. I was there."

Meredith reached out and squeezed Sophie's hand. "Of course you were." She sat back again. "It just seems unfathomable that Meyer…" She spread her hands. "He *hated* the way his father showed so little concern about him. I've always figured that's why he's never gotten serious about anyone. He cared about the Air Force first, last and always. He didn't have the time or space to devote to anything else."

"He left the military when John died."

"He and John were best friends. Meyer knew we'd lost everything. He was doing what he thought was right, and I was such an emotional wreck that it didn't even occur to me at the time how much he was giving up for us."

And there they were. Full circle. Back to Saint Meyer. Who hadn't cared enough about Corinne but obviously did when it came to the family John had left behind. And Sophie was no more convinced that Meredith didn't have deeper feelings for Meyer than ever.

"Why haven't you ever mentioned Corinne's pregnancy before?"

Sophie spread her own hands. "Because you're *my* best friend."

They both exhaled. Then smiled, albeit more shakily than Sophie had expected. Which was exactly why she'd tried never to get into the issue of Meyer with Meredith. She didn't want it to ruin their friendship.

"So." She determinedly struck Meyer out of her thoughts. "*Walker.*" Who might be "too perfect" but apparently had his own issues regarding the closeness between Meredith and Meyer. "How'd you leave things with him?"

"He said he'd call. But after everything that happened, I know he won't. I can't blame him. I mean," she huffed and shook her head, "I still keep John's old Camaro in the garage even though it hasn't run in years. All because I can't bring myself to let it go. Walker's right to move on. He deserves more."

"Do you *want* him to call?"

"I want… I want things to be easy," Meredith admitted. "It's really all I've ever wanted. Which didn't exactly lead to perfection with John, either."

"Are you sure it isn't fear of getting hurt again that's holding you back?"

Meredith lifted her shoulder. "No, but it's moot because I don't—" She looked away and cleared her throat. "We had a good time in Colorado, and that'll be it." She let her head fall back on the sofa cushion.

"Do you know what he was doing today?"

"Walker?"

Sophie felt her face warm. She was pathetic. No willpower at all. "Meyer."

"No idea." Meredith lifted her head and studied her. "Why?"

"No reason."

"Sophie," she chided.

Sophie spread her fingers and examined her fingernails. "He just mentioned that he was busy, that's all."

"Probably JCS," Meredith said. "You can't imagine how much of his time it takes."

"Is that why he doesn't fly anymore? Because he's too busy?"

"I'm sure that's part of it, but maybe he doesn't want to fly if it's not with the Air Force. I'm telling you, Soph. The man was pretty committed."

"You never asked him?"

"I don't think I could bear it if he confirmed it. He's given up too much already for us. I told him years ago that he should own half the business, and he flatly refused." Meredith swirled her wine again. "If you're really curious, ask *him*."

"I'm not going to ask Meyer!"

"No. You'd just prefer to stew and speculate, apparently."

"I'm not stewing."

"But you're speculating." Meredith's expression finally lightened. "Interesting, considering how much you supposedly dislike him."

Meredith's words were still hanging in Sophie's mind that weekend when she drove home after her yoga class.

There was an unfamiliar truck parked down by the beach house when she passed it, and before her common sense kicked in, she turned and drove slowly down the steep, narrow drive.

The sand had been bulldozed away from the cracking pavement, creating a wall on one side of the drive. The bulldozer was still parked there with its sharp blade planted into the side of the mound, as if the work weren't yet finished.

Without a proper barrier, the sand would just blow back,

blocking off the driveway in the same way it had done for years.

A big white pickup truck was parked right up next to the rear of the house. The truck wasn't Meyer's, though the make was similar. Meyer's truck was dark gray.

She turned off her engine, and the ocean breeze tugged at her hair as soon as she stepped out of her vehicle. She glanced inside the truck window as she walked past. Nothing inside gave a hint to its owner.

The back door was standing open, and she stepped cautiously through the doorway. "Hello?"

A tall, good-looking guy with short brown hair stepped into view at the far end of the hall, and the corner of his lips lifted. "Hello."

"Who are you?"

He looked amused. "Who are *you*?"

"I know the owner of this place." She held up her cell phone. Meyer's number was already displayed. "So state your business, or clear out."

The man's smile widened. It was the kind of smile that said it had earned him plenty of leeway in the world. "And if I don't?" He took several long-legged steps toward her.

Though there wasn't anything particularly threatening in his manner or his expression, her thumb still hit the Dial button.

It only rang once before it was picked up.

"What's wrong?"

Aside from the shiver rippling down her spine at the first sound of Meyer's deep voice in three days? "There's a strange man in your beach house," she told him.

Said man extended his hand. "Let me talk to him."

She ignored him and his calloused hand. "Were you expecting someone," she asked Meyer, "or is he trespassing?"

"I wasn't expecting anyone."

"He's not expecting you," she relayed to the stranger and gestured toward the door behind them both. "Out."

"Oh, for—" The man pushed his fingers through his hair, leaving it mussed. "It's Cutter," he said loudly, obviously for Meyer's benefit. "And when you hire a guard dog, go for something bigger than a poodle."

"Poodle!" Sophie curled her fist. "You should know I'm a black belt—" She broke off on the lie, hearing a choked sort of laughing curse coming from Meyer on the phone.

"Cutter's my brother," he said. "And I'm on my way." He ended the call before she could.

"Want to put away the fist?" Cutter asked conversationally.

She narrowed her eyes. "Why didn't you just tell me you're Cutter Cartell?"

"Cardinale, actually. And I'm the one with a valid reason to be here," he reminded. "And I still don't know who you are. I mean, I can call you Fifi. That was the name of the poodle my mom had when I was a kid."

She exhaled and finally pocketed her phone. She stuck out her hand. "Sophie Lane."

"Any connection to Lawyer Lane?"

"If you mean Fitzgerald Lane, he is my father."

"Are you here on his behalf?"

She shook her head and gestured in the direction of her house. "I'm the neighbor."

"Well, well." He grinned and took her hand in his. "Suddenly, Fifi my friend, things are looking up."

Chapter Ten

Meyer followed the sound of laughter around to the front of the beach house.

Sophie and Cutter were sitting on the edge of the cedar deck, looking more comfortable than Meyer liked.

"You're early," he told Cutter when they finally stopped laughing long enough to realize they weren't alone.

Cutter's gaze cut from the woman beside him to Meyer and back again. "Figured I'd stake out my territory while I could."

Meyer ignored the innuendo and looked away from Sophie, who'd risen to her feet and was swiping the sand from the backside of her yoga pants.

"Cutter was telling me he's just come back from Dubai," she said.

Meyer looked over her head at his brother. "Surprised you want to start slumming sooner than you need."

Cutter shrugged. "Told you before that I can work from anywhere, but I also need to make sure I have some basic necessities in place." He smiled at Sophie with frank appreciation. "Good neighbors being a primary necessity," he added.

She laughed lightly, but the pink color on her cheeks didn't thrill Meyer any.

"How'd the dance go?" he asked her.

"Great." She was avoiding his eyes. "No shocker that Leda looked spectacular."

"That's your business partner's kid, isn't it?" Cutter asked. "Leda?"

Meyer nodded. His nerves continued tightening. "Thanks for the watchdog duty, but I'm sure you have better things to do."

Sophie's squint against the sun narrowed even more. "I suppose I do." She focused on his brother. "Nice to meet you, Cutter."

"Nice to meet you too, Fifi."

She laughed softly and stepped around Meyer with barely a nod. "I still need my grandmother's plate."

"I still need the money for the battery," he returned.

She huffed slightly and walked quickly around the house until she was out of sight. A minute later, they heard an engine start.

He looked back at Cutter. "Dubai?"

His brother shrugged. "Business takes me all over. What's going on between you and Fifi?"

"What the hell is this Fifi business about?"

Cutter was obviously enjoying himself. "One thing I can say for sure is that she's got *your* shorts in a knot."

"Is this what I can look forward to for the next year?"

"Gives you all the warm and fuzzies, doesn't it, bro?"

Meyer sat beside Cutter. "What're you really doing here?"

Cutter shifted and pulled a folded paper out of the back pocket of his jeans. He handed it to Meyer.

"What is it?" Meyer began unfolding it. When he recognized Lotus's writing, he grimaced. When he'd finished reading the brief letter, he'd graduated to swearing.

He folded the letter back on its lines and reinforced the creases between his thumb and forefinger. He handed it back to Cutter. "Not a chance in hell."

"It's going to get a lot of publicity." Cutter spread his hand in the air, like a marquee. "Pietro Cardinale's final photo honored by the President."

"Vice President," Meyer corrected. "And I'm still not going."

"Lotus's not going to let it go."

"Is that why she sent you? You always were a soft touch where Step-Mama is concerned."

"Lotus isn't so bad." Cutter pocketed the letter again. "Old man left her out in the cold even more than he did us. The only thing she has left is whatever profits she can make keeping his website alive."

"I'm still not going to some dog-and-pony show while people praise the photographic genius of the great Pietro."

"Here." Sophie reappeared around the house, a wad of cash in her hands. "Battery."

He didn't give two flips about the cost of the battery. He took the cash anyway. "I'll get the plate to you."

She nodded and turned on her heel, striding away again, her sandals sliding slightly in the sand.

When Meyer realized his brother was watching her retreat with as much interest as he was, he elbowed him. "Put your eyes back in your head."

"Could say the same to you."

"She's off-limits."

"Says who? Would make the foreseeable future a lot more appealing."

"Says me." The only thing that *was* appealing was knowing that Sophie Lane was practically within shouting distance, but that didn't mean Meyer wanted his brother getting near her. "Have you told Alexa and Dana about the presidential thing?"

"Vice presidential," Cutter reminded dryly. "Their reactions were slightly less polite than yours. I'll tell you the same thing I told them—right now, Lotus is satisfied with the presentation happening in Washington. If she doesn't think she's getting the appropriate amount of attention, she could end up bringing her caterwauling back to Cape Cardinale."

The memory of their father's funeral was all too fresh. "There's nothing here for Lotus. She's gotta know that."

"Like it or not—like *her* or not—Lotus loved the old man." Cutter's tone was matter-of-fact. "She has a right to her grief."

Meyer pinched the bridge of his nose. "All of his wives loved him. God knows why. The man was a total—" He broke off when a flock of squawking seagulls dove, en mass, toward the water's edge. "When's the thing again?"

"Week from tomorrow." Cutter waited a beat. "Wondered if JCS could spare a plane. We could pick up Dana. Then Alexa. Simpler than coordinating a bunch of commercial flights."

"JCS isn't my personal charter service, you know."

Cutter snorted. "JCS would've been defunct by now if not for you."

"And it's hard to spare a pilot when I'm already down one. All I've been doing the last few days is interview replacements."

"So?"

He swallowed an oath and watched the seagulls chasing each other over whatever morsels the low tide had revealed. "I'll see what I can arrange," he said wearily.

Cutter nodded and pushed to his feet. "I got a room at the Highland," he said. "Be there a couple days."

"Thought you were getting an early start on making this place workable."

Cutter made a face. "The only thing that'll make this place workable is the wrecking ball before a total rebuild." He gestured at the other side of the deck, where it was falling down.

"You agree with me, then. We need to unload the place the second we can legally do so."

"I didn't say that."

Meyer eyed his brother. "*What* is the point of keeping it? To do what? Vacation rentals? I counted the number of short-term rentals registered with the town and checked the occupancy rates. They're lower than anywhere else on the coast."

Cutter sat back down again and stretched out his long legs. "The old man left it to us."

"All the more reason to dump it. Would you rather have your share of the profits now or wait who knows how long? Five years? Ten?"

"Profits don't interest me."

"Bull. Your business makes a profit, or you wouldn't still be doing it."

"Profits where the *house* is concerned," Cutter amended. He leaned back on his hands, and they were silent for a while, just watching the surf. Eventually, a trio of surfers—gleaming in their wet suits—appeared among the waves. This group seemed more skilled at the sport than usual.

"Never could surf for squat," Cutter finally said.

"Me, either. Spent more time chewing sand." Sophie'd said she surfed. He didn't know why that had surprised him.

"You remember living here?"

Meyer envisioned her in a wet suit, running into the waves. "Not really," he said absently.

"You remember him being around?"

"Him?" He shook himself when Cutter gave him a look. "I remember his departures more than his presence," Meyer said. "And my mother telling me not to blame him for having itchy feet."

Some people are meant to wander. That was what Sandra Cartell had told Meyer.

By the time he'd been a teenager, he'd known he'd inherited the trait. The desire to see the world had been all-consuming. The only reason he'd been in Cape Cardinale this long now was because of a promise to John Skinner long ago.

Hell. He couldn't even bring himself to sign a lease on his apartment for longer than six months at a time.

"Itchy feet." Cutter's smile was humorless. "Until they split up, my mother continued to believe that she'd cured him of his wandering spirit. Gotta be genetic, though. He wasn't around enough to rub off on me, either, but the same spirit's in here." He thumped his chest with the pad of his thumb.

"That particular gene missed the girls," Meyer said.

Cutter made a face. "Wouldn't be so sure about that. At least where Dana's concerned. Alexa? Think that divorce of hers clipped her wings. Only thing she can think about these days is security."

"Can't blame her for that. And Dana's been in one place with Ty since college."

"Come on, man. How many houses do they own? How often do you think they're actually in the same one at the same time?"

Meyer squinted at his brother. "You saying there's trouble in the Mercer paradise? Has Dana said something to you?"

"Dana's as closemouthed as always. But how would *you* feel if your supposedly devoted spouse didn't give a flip if you were gone for twelve months at a time?"

"She had a reasonable explanation. The investment of time—"

"Is worth a higher profit?" Cutter shook his head. "I don't buy it. That's all I'm saying." He pushed off the deck to stand on the sand. "I've got work to do. Let me know if you want to grab a beer later. The pub at the hotel has a decent chowder, too."

Meyer nodded and watched his brother walk around the house before he looked back out at the surfers. He had work to do also. He'd bartered the use of the bulldozer for the weekend from a contractor friend in exchange for a few hours of flight simulator time out at JCS, and the sand he'd moved so far was only a drop in the bucket of what needed to be relocated back to the base of the seawall where the sand had been eroding for decades.

He had about as much desire to sit in a tractor and push sand around as he did to have a hole drilled in his head, but the work had to be done.

And at least this way there wouldn't be any financial cost.

He walked around to the back of the house and went inside. He'd been there several times now. The interior never got any better, though the stale air had cleared once he'd pulled out the ancient green carpet. He'd also added a small mini refrigerator that he'd brought over from JCS where it had been sitting unused in storage.

It was too small to hold anything but a few necessities, but it was better than dealing with an ice chest just to have something cold to drink. He pulled out a jug of water and thought about the fridge in Sophie's kitchen. They'd need a similar size.

But mostly, he thought about Sophie. And realizing it, he shoved the water back into the fridge and pulled out his cell phone to call Hannah. He told her about the trip to Washington, and she confirmed what he'd already suspected.

"Yes, 902 is available." It was Hannah's shorthand for the tail number of their oldest and smallest jet. "We just don't have a pilot. Everyone but Jason is scheduled, and he'll be up in Montana by then for his sister's wedding." She waited a beat. "Of course, if *you*—"

"No."

He heard her sigh. "You haven't logged any hours since your last flight review. That was almost two years ago."

Twenty-one months and twelve days.

"I'll deal with it."

"Just not now," she concluded before he could say the words.

Not surprising. She'd heard them often enough over the last few years. He'd only endured the last flight review because he'd had no choice. Regulations and insurance requirements demanded it. Now he had two and a half months before the next one.

"Cast a wider net with the job advertisement" was all he said.

"Nothing gets better by ignoring it," she said waspishly and hung up on him.

That wasn't surprising, either.

Hannah would give her eyeteeth to still have her commercial ticket. She was great at what she did around JCS and she could still fly for pleasure, but she couldn't fly JCS passengers. Not at her age.

Whereas Meyer—in all respects—was current on all of

his certifications and—in Hannah's opinion—was letting them go to waste.

She had no use for waste.

Generally speaking, neither did he. But he had no desire to tell her that every time he climbed into a cockpit, the only thing he could think of was John Skinner deliberately flying into the side of a mountain during a bad thunderstorm.

The official story had attributed it to pilot error.

Meyer didn't buy the story, though.

John had been the best pilot Meyer had ever known. He didn't make mistakes in the cockpit. Not minor ones. And definitely not fatal ones. It had only been outside of flying that John faltered. And maybe, if Meyer had joined him in the business like they'd planned all those years ago, John would still be alive today.

Meyer roughly shoved the water jug back into the refrigerator and left the house again.

Hopefully, the noisy bulldozer would be enough to drown out the noise of the past at least for a little while.

He knew better than to think it could ever be totally silenced.

Some punishments weren't meant to end.

Sophie leaned as far over the top of the plexi-deck wall as she dared and held the tiny pair of binoculars to her eyes again.

She still couldn't see well enough through the tree branches to make out the identity of the person operating the bulldozer. The low growl of it had been a constant hum for more than an hour now, making it impossible to concentrate on the report she was writing up about Otto Nash for Cardinal Cares.

One bulldozer, running for an hour, and she was ready to tear out her hair.

What was it going to be like if Meyer sold off the property to real estate developers? She'd be listening to the sounds of construction day in and day out for who knew how long.

She stepped off the chair she'd been standing on and tossed down the binoculars before stomping into the house.

Even if Meyer *wasn't* behind the bulldozer noise, she still blamed him.

She'd cleaned her house. Done her laundry. She had no other plans until later that day when she'd be seeing Otto.

But until then, that still left Sophie's afternoon empty. She knew Meredith was busy with the kids. She sent a text to her dad to see if he was up for a game of tennis. His response was decidedly belated—he and Francesca were spending the afternoon together.

"More than the afternoon, I'll bet," she murmured to the seagull that was slowly bouncing his way closer to her opened patio door.

She got a handful of birdseed from the container she kept on the fireplace mantle and went back out onto the deck. The bird immediately flew off but didn't go far. Just perched on a branch and dove as soon as she tossed the seeds into the air.

And then, like magic, the growling buzz ceased.

She closed her eyes, breathing a sigh of relief. Silence. Blessed silence.

Only the pulse of surf. The caw of birds.

She went back inside, sat down with her notes, but even under the best of circumstances it wasn't exactly riveting stuff to write reports.

She returned to the deck and her binoculars. The tide was out, and the waves were as calm as they ever were. There were nearly a dozen surfers out on the water.

She'd much rather be out there with them, and when

the engine of the bulldozer started up again, she decided it was a sign.

She went inside and changed, retrieved her surfboard and carried it all the way down to the beach. There, she pulled off the striped board sock, weighted it down with her shoes and pulled up the zip of her wet suit. Then, carrying the board, she headed out into the water. As soon as it reached her waist, she began paddling. And after that, it no longer mattered what was happening back on shore. The sun was bright. The waves were good.

She just needed them to be good enough to finally, *finally* wash Meyer Cartell out of her brain.

Chapter Eleven

"Cheers." Cutter tapped the base of his beer bottle against Meyer's and scooped up a handful of peanuts from the brown plastic bowl the bartender had set in front of them. "Didn't think you were gonna show."

"Wasn't sure I would, either." Meyer straddled the barstool and folded his arms on the top of the bar. He looked around the pub. It was small and aging in a comfortable way. A dozen booths upholstered in worn red leather lined the perimeter of the room. Another half dozen tables were scattered around a lone pool table that nobody was using. "Used to come here twenty years ago." He tapped the peanut bowl. "Looks like nothing's changed since."

"Not a routine patron, I take it."

Meyer smiled faintly and spun his stool around until his back was to the bar top. He lifted the beer bottle and took a long drink. "Plenty of bars closer to the airfield," he finally said. And none of them came with memories of him and John, young and full of plans for a future that never was.

"Speaking of airfields." Cutter turned, too, mimicking his position. "Decide anything about the charter to DC?"

"Unless something on the schedule gets canceled before Saturday, we'll have to go commercial." That was true enough. Just not the entire truth.

"But you'll *go*."

Meyer exhaled. "I'll go," he muttered.

"Get you boys anything from the menu?"

Meyer looked over his shoulder at the bartender. She was middle-aged, with unnaturally red hair. But her smile was friendly as she plucked a laminated menu from the mouth of a plastic whale standing on its tail.

He turned his stool around again but didn't take the menu. "My brother recommends the chowder. What do you like?"

"Chowder's the best on the coast," she assured confidently. "But we've got a killer burger, too."

"Bring both of 'em, then." He'd worked up an appetite dozing half of Cardinale Beach back where it belonged. "Medium rare on the burger."

"All the fixings?"

"No onions."

She nodded and looked to Cutter, who ordered exactly the same thing.

"Like two peas in a pod," she said.

Cutter laughed shortly. "I'll claim him as a brother, but I draw the line at pods."

The bartender tucked the menu back into the whale's mouth and pulled down three wineglasses from the rack over her head. "I was guessing you were related," she said. "Got the look about you. I'll get your order in. If you need anything else, just yell. I'm Donna." With the glasses in one hand, she plucked a wine bottle from the mirror-backed shelf behind the bar and carried it around to one of the tables on the far side of the room.

The place was steadily filling. He didn't remember it being so popular, but a lot could happen in twenty years.

A lot could happen in six.

He lifted his beer to his lips again and pushed the thought out of his mind. He chased the draft of beer with a handful of peanuts and eyed his half brother. "Pool?"

Cutter shrugged. "Why not?" He pulled off the jacket he'd been wearing and tossed it over the stool before following Meyer over to the pool table.

He racked the balls, and Cutter grabbed a couple cues from the selection on a wall. He won the coin toss for the break, and Meyer stepped back, giving Cutter room as he bent over the table.

The *thwack* of balls breaking apart added to the rising noise in the pub. If he closed his eyes, he could have been in any number of officers' clubs. He scratched his cheek. Back in those days, he'd never gone unshaven. But now, he couldn't remember the last time he'd bothered with a razor. At least a week.

He'd shaved the day he'd dropped off Grange and Leda at Sophie's and stayed for lasagna.

He rubbed his jaw again, mind wandering while Cutter rapidly cleared the table, and glanced at the door when it opened yet again, letting in a trio of newcomers. They weren't together, though. The couple turned one way, heading toward a booth occupied by another couple, and the lone woman aimed directly for the bar, where she took up a stool at the end of the bar. Her hair reminded him of Sophie's. It was just as blond. Just as wavy, but longer, stretching almost down to the middle of her back. This woman, though, was tall. Almost statuesque in comparison to Sophie's small frame.

"Your shot."

He looked back at the table. Cutter had nearly cleared the table already. "What're you doing? Taking pity on me?"

Cutter smiled faintly. He nodded toward the brunette half of the couple who'd just entered. "Got distracted."

Meyer lined up his own shot. "Know her?"

"Wouldn't mind if I did." His brother was giving the woman in question a frankly appreciative look.

From the corner of his eye, Meyer saw Donna talking to the newcomer at the end of the bar. "Guy she's with might not agree." He sank another ball.

Cutter smirked. "I don't see a ring on her finger."

Meyer shook his head and chuckled softly. "At least you observe *some* boundaries."

"Unlike the old man?"

Meyer shrugged and sank two more balls in short order. "You said it, not me." He kept his attention from straying to the bar and the blonde again. Her hair was like Sophie's, but she was *not* Sophie.

What would he do if it were?

"You were thinking it, though."

Meyer was distracted enough that it took him a second to catch up to his brother's comment. The old man and his extramarital proclivities. "Some things are too obvious to bother with." He studied the table for a moment. He'd made all the easy shots. He lined up a jump shot but missed. Not surprising. He'd never been interested enough in billiards to learn more than the basic skills.

He suspected the same couldn't be said for his brother. By the time Cutter had cleared the table a few minutes later, Donna had delivered their food, and they returned to the bar.

The blonde at the end was watching them. She had a faint frown on her face, and when their eyes met briefly, she offered a stony smile before turning her attention to the peanut bowl directly in front of her.

He studied her profile for another second, debating internally, then left his barstool. He heard Cutter ask where he was going but didn't respond. He stopped behind the woman.

She was focused hard—too hard—on the peanuts.

"Corinne?"

Her shoulders stiffened, but she slowly angled her chin over her shoulder as if she were looking back at him, though she really wasn't. "Long time, Meyer."

The bar stool next to her was occupied by a beefy guy who was neck deep in a bowl of chili. Meyer moved to the other side of her. "Twenty years," he agreed. "How are you?"

"Peachy. And it's twenty-one. Not that anyone's counting." She rotated her coffee mug between her fingers. It looked like it only contained coffee, but who came to a bar to order coffee when there was a coffeehouse on nearly every corner?

"Twenty-one, then," he said. "I'm surprised we haven't run into each other before now."

She lifted her shoulder, looking supremely disinterested. "I moved up to Lincoln City a long time ago. I only stopped here because it's on my way home. I've been in Eureka on a job." She lifted the coffee mug. Her nails were unvarnished and cut short. Neat.

Like Sophie's.

"A happy coincidence, then, our paths crossing like this now."

She didn't look at him. "If you want to see it that way."

It was a good thing his ego wasn't dependent on this. He forged ahead anyway. "I heard about you fixing Leda's dress."

She had faint lines around her eyes. They seemed to deepen a little. "Yeah."

As conversations went, this one felt like pulling teeth. If she were anyone besides Sophie's sister, he wouldn't bother with the effort. But she *was* Sophie's sister.

And he couldn't forget what she'd told him—that Corinne had a drinking problem.

If he was being too quick to judge, too damn bad.

They *were* in a pub—the primary point of which was to serve alcohol in one form or another.

Even though he was pretty sure the only thing in Corinne's mug was coffee, he felt an uneasy compulsion to make sure it stayed that way.

He took out his cell phone and found the photo of Leda in all her finery with Grange standing next to her looking pained. "Meredith sent this to me the evening of the dance." He showed it to Corinne. "Leda was all smiles," he told her.

Her expression finally softened. Their fingers brushed when she took the phone from him to look at the photo more closely. She smoothed her thumb gently over the image. "Grange looks like John," she murmured before handing him back the phone. "So does Leda."

Everyone, including Meredith, always said how much the kids took after their father. But Meyer saw an equal measure of Meredith in them. "So what're you doing these days besides last-minute dress alterations?"

"I'm an accountant."

He was genuinely surprised. The Corinne of old had never seemed particularly studious. According to John—who'd known her since high school—she'd been more interested in maintaining her social calendar than maintaining her grades. "No kidding. My mom's an accountant." She'd gone back to school after Meyer's father had defected to another woman. "She's a CPA with a firm in Seattle."

"Good for her." Corinne's words were fine. The tone, however, plainly stated she wasn't the least interested.

From his position, he could easily reach the coffee carafe that sat on a warmer behind the bar. He picked it up. "Want a top off?"

She eyed him for a moment, and he figured he'd been too obvious. Not that he cared all that much. He was less interested in Corinne than the effect she had on her sister.

But Corinne shrugged and nudged the coffee mug toward him. "Thanks."

He refilled the cup and stuck the carafe back on the warmer. "I'd better get back to my dinner. You look good, Corinne." That much was true. Aside from the hair that he remembered being lighter and a few lines on her face, she hadn't changed much. He was surprised he hadn't recognized her right off the bat. "It was nice seeing you." That much was not so true.

Her lips twisted, and he knew she felt the same way.

"You too, Meyer."

He went back to his seat next to Cutter. His brother had already finished his soup and was halfway through his burger. "Old girlfriend?" he asked.

Did you categorize a girl that you'd dated only a handful of times as a girlfriend? They'd never even gone beyond a good-night kiss. "Something like that," Meyer answered. He picked up his spoon and dipped it into the thick chowder. "She's Sophie's sister."

"Oh yeah?" Cutter looked past Meyer toward the end of the bar. "I guess I can sort of see a resemblance."

"Sort of," he agreed. He was less interested in their resemblance than what his great sin had been where Corinne was concerned that it colored Sophie's opinion of him to this day.

The picture of Leda and Grange was still on his cell phone screen. He swiped it away and texted Sophie.

I'm at the Highland Pub.

He'd finished his chowder and half his hamburger by the time she finally responded.

And that's relevant because...?

Good thing his ego didn't depend on her, either.

I have your grandmother's plate with me.

A total fabrication. Her grandmother's plate was still sitting on the breakfast counter in his apartment. He looked at it every morning, debated whether to put it in his truck so he could get it back to her the next time he saw her.

And every morning, he left it right where it was.

A man had to use what tools he had available, and where Sophie was concerned, his tools were minimal. Granny's plate. And nothing.

If you want to come and get it, I'll buy you dinner.

Again, her answer seemed slow in coming.

I've already had dinner.

Did he have to beg? He glanced at the end of the bar where Corinne still sat, nursing her coffee mug. Even if she weren't tempted to have something stronger, she seemed very alone. Weren't sisters supposed to lean on each other?

He didn't have any personal evidence of that in *his* family, but that didn't mean anything.

Dessert, then.

He waited a beat. Then typed another line.

Your sister can join us. Right now she's all alone.

Sophie's response was almost instantaneous.

Is this your subtle way of saying Corinne is at the pub?

Cutter leaned toward Meyer, peering at the text bubbles on the phone screen. He made a face and snatched the phone right out of Meyer's loose grip.

Meyer swore and tried to grab it back, but Cutter turned his back and, short of wrestling his brother for it, couldn't do a damn thing but wait for Cutter to return the phone. Which he did a few seconds later after he'd sent off his own text message.

Meyer looked at the screen.

Hey, Fifi. Cutter here. That was Big Brother's pathetic attempt of making you think he intends to "renew" old acquaintance with your sis. Ignore him. Ignore her. But come and save me from his belated adolescence. I beg you.

"You're an ass," he told Cutter.

"Undoubtedly," Cutter agreed, and his smirk widened when they both heard the soft whistle of another text message.

On my way.

"You're welcome." Cutter flagged down Donna. "Cash me out, would you, darlin'?"

"Sure thing, but it's a shame." Donna gave him a wink and turned away to the register. "Night's still young."

Meyer dragged a french fry through his ketchup. "Thought you wanted Sophie to save you."

"Nah." Cutter glanced at the check that Donna had slid in front of him and pulled cash from his wallet. "That was all so she could save you." He dropped the cash onto the bar and left before Meyer could respond.

Save *him*?

He shook his head and attended to his cold fries before they got any more inedible but still found his gaze getting tangled with Corinne's in the mirror behind the liquor bottles.

She looked away when she slid off her barstool. He watched her reflection as she worked her way between the patrons and disappeared down the hallway where the restrooms were located.

He turned his attention back to his meal. Several people had taken over the pool table, and the music had gone up several decibels. He decided the fries were a lost cause, and he let one of the servers take the plate away while he read through the dessert specials also stuck in the whale's mouth.

Despite the noise around him, he felt a shift in the air and looked up at the mirror again to see Sophie standing just inside the entrance.

She was wearing a pair of green scrubs and seemed to steel herself as she glanced around. He stifled a sigh. She'd have no reason to gird herself where her sister was concerned. So it was probably the prospect of *him* that made her lips set just so and her shoulders align even more precisely than usual.

He stuffed the dessert specials back in with the dinner

menu and shook his head when Donna asked if he wanted to order anything more. "Just the check."

He was pulling cash from his wallet when Sophie stopped next to him, her eyes narrowed. "I thought you said my sister was here."

"She was." He nodded toward the end of the bar where Corinne's coffee cup was still sitting. "Think she went to the restroom."

"And Cutter? Were you pretending to be him or something?"

Annoyance drizzled through him. "You think I couldn't get your attention without pretending to be him?"

Her eyebrows rose slightly and her cheeks seemed to flush. She crossed her arms over her chest. "Don't see my grandmother's plate, either."

"It's in my truck."

Her eyes narrowed even more. "No, it isn't."

He looked at the amount on the check Donna had given him and dropped a twenty on top of it. "Okay." He stood and pocketed his wallet again. "It isn't. It's still sitting on the counter at my place." Over her head, he saw Corinne reappear. "There's your sister."

She seemed to tense again before she looked over her shoulder. So maybe the tenseness *wasn't* entirely about him.

She hitched the woven strap of her purse higher on her shoulder and looked up at him through her lashes. "I appreciate you letting me know she's here."

Judging by the expression on Corinne's face when she spotted her little sister standing there with him, he was pretty sure Corinne didn't share the sentiment. "If it's any comfort, I think she's only had coffee since she came in."

Sophie nodded wordlessly and aimed toward the end of the bar, and he headed toward the exit. Being curious at all about Sophie and her sister was pointless—staying there to indulge his curiosity even more so.

Knowing so didn't stop him from looking back toward Sophie before he walked out of the pub, though.

Last thing he expected was to find her watching him, too, and the impact of her gaze stayed with him long after he let the door swing shut behind him.

"What're you doing here, Soph?"

Sophie finally dragged her eyes away from the pub door. Meyer had left. He wasn't going to come back. Why would he?

She was assigning way too much thought to the man. So what if she'd had another dream about him the night before? Dreams about sex weren't necessarily about sex at all. Just because she'd—

"*Sophie!*"

She yanked her attention back to her sister, who was giving her a skeptical look. "I thought I'd come for some fish 'n' chips," she lied. She and Olivia had grabbed salads at their favorite salad bar after they'd finished with Otto Nash. But Corinne would never buy a story that Sophie'd come to the pub only for a drink.

The stool next to her sister was occupied by a burly guy, but the one on the other side of him was empty. She set her purse on the bar next to Corinne's coffee cup, hoping that he would offer to move over one stool, but he didn't. "What're *you* doing here?"

Corinne's lips twisted. "Don't worry. I still have to drive home yet tonight." She lifted her coffee cup. "Caffeine only. No booze." She held up her hand, oath-like. "Promise."

Corinne had made that promise more times than Sophie could count.

"Did you...talk to Meyer?" Just saying his name caused heat to collect inside her.

But if she'd expected a reaction from Corinne, she didn't get one. "Briefly." Corinne was eyeing Sophie up and down. "Are shapeless scrubs your fashion du jour now?"

Familiar ground was a relief, and Sophie plucked at the green top. "Don't knock 'em. Comfortable. Easy to take care of. Lots of pockets." As far as she was concerned, women had been strongly shortchanged in that department.

Corinne reached out and pinched the fabric near Sophie's waist. "If they'd just use a few darts, you'd actually have a figure." She let go and picked up her coffee again.

"That's the last thing I need to be showing off," she said wryly. "Particularly with the home-health client I have. Despite his age, he considers himself quite the lothario."

"Thought you were playing school nurse while Doc was on sabbatical."

"Doing that, too. But school ends in a few weeks. And I'm only doing the home-health thing on the weekends."

"Can't believe Doc Hayes is still practicing."

"He's only sixty. He has lots of years left."

The big guy next to Corinne tossed some cash onto the bar and left. Sophie immediately confiscated the spot and arched her tired back a little. Surfing that morning and trying to avoid tussling with Otto Nash had left a mark. "How long's it been since you've seen him?"

"Doc Hayes?"

Sophie curled her fingers against her thigh. "Meyer."

Corinne gave her a curious look. "I don't know. A long time. He showed me pictures of Grange and Leda. Her outfit looked good."

"It did. She was very happy." She flagged down Donna long enough to order her meal and then propped her elbows on the bar, studying her sister. "I appreciate you helping her out like that."

"Why wouldn't I?"

She lifted her shoulders slightly. "I don't know."

"Walking on eggshells around me doesn't help anything, Sophie."

"Dad know you're in town?"

Corinne shook her head. "I didn't expect to be in town at all. I've been in Eureka. Thought I'd drive straight home, but—" She shrugged. "Old habits, I guess." She toyed with her coffee cup. "Used to come here back in the day all the time." Her lips twisted. "Even before I was legal to drink."

Reminders of the past made Sophie feel even more guilty about the present, and she was grateful when a server came by, delivering a glass of water and a small dinner salad in a bowl. She had forgotten the fish 'n' chips came with a salad, and she nudged it toward her sister. "Want it?"

She thought Corinne was going to decline, but instead she picked up a fork and jabbed it into the lettuce that had also already been copiously dressed with oil and vinegar. "What's Meredith doing these days?"

The question surprised her. "Keeping up with her kids, mostly."

Corinne nodded slightly, still focused on the salad. "I'd forgotten how grown up they'd be by now. My head still thinks of them as children. As if they would be stuck there forever after John died. But time trucks on."

"Leda's graduating soon from junior high and Grange turns thirteen in a few weeks. Boy eats like a horse."

"Like his dad. John always had a huge appetite. I heard he left Meredith hanging, too. If not for Meyer…" Corinne made a face and reached for her coffee cup, but it was already empty.

Sophie pushed her water glass toward her, and Corinne

drank half of it down before she set the glass back on the bar top. "Tell me about Francesca," she said abruptly.

Clearly Corinne wanted to get off the topic of Meyer.

"I don't know a whole lot except that she's an attorney, too. And Dad is very taken with her. I see him for dinner nearly every week. Come with me next time. I'll tell him you want to meet her."

"Didn't say I wanted to meet her. Much less have dinner with Dad."

Sophie let it drop, knowing better than to push. If her hunch was correct, she imagined there would be plenty of opportunities involving Francesca in the future if Corinne ever softened up about it.

"Mom doesn't know about her?"

Sophie shrugged. "No idea. I haven't talked to Mom in months."

"Lucky you. She calls me constantly." Corinne made a face. "Checking to make sure I'm not on the verge of embarrassing her. As if anyone in Portland cares what's going on over here."

"I'm sure that's not—" She swallowed the platitude when Corinne gave her a sidelong look.

"She needs a fling of her own," Corinne muttered. "Some eligible guy to keep her focus on something more interesting than her failure of a daughter."

"You're not a failure," Sophie chided. "Repeat it until you believe it."

"There's not enough time in the day." Then Corinne rolled her eyes at Sophie's continued stare. "I am not a failure," she repeated.

"That's a start." Sophie smiled her thanks to the server who was delivering a hot plate loaded with crispy deep-fried fish and french fries and a second glass of water.

"And what about you? Any eligible guys distracting you these days?"

Corinne immediately reached over and took several fries. "Oooh. Hot." She took another sip of water. "I've been sober three months. Until I'm stronger I can't even think about romance."

"And you have a new job to focus on as well."

"A new job that's boring as hell, but sure." She took one of the fish fillets as well.

"We *can* have them bring you out a dinner plate," Sophie said.

"I'm not hungry enough."

Sophie gave a pointed look at the pile of food that Corinne had transferred to the dinky salad bowl. *Sophie* was the one who'd already eaten dinner, but she wasn't about to admit that lie now. "Let me know if you change your mind. I'll never finish all of this anyway." She broke off a chunk of fish and watched the steam rise from it before gingerly taking a bite. She had to chase the blistering hit with a hasty sip of water.

"Yeah, you will," Corinne said. "You always had a huge appetite." She gave Sophie a sideways look. "And you're still annoyingly skinny under that birth control of an outfit. You still running? Yoga? Surfing? What?"

"Surfed this morning actually, but the real workout I had was with my client." She shifted on the barstool again. From the get-go, she'd told Otto that she had a boyfriend, but the lie had never made a dent in the man's innuendoes. "Guy lives in a gigantic house up on Seaview Drive."

"Didn't used to be anything up on Seaview except parking," Corinne recalled. "Everyone used to go up there at night."

"It has the best viewpoint in all of Cape Cardinale."

Corinne snorted. "In those days nobody was looking out their windshields. They were making out."

"Didn't Dad go up there once to find you?"

"Oh yeah. He dragged me out of the back seat of some guy's car more than once."

"When'd you stop going up there?"

"Not until after I was old enough that Dad couldn't ground me anymore," Corinne's voice had gone mocking.

It wasn't the answer Sophie'd wanted. She didn't want to imagine Corinne and Meyer in a car with steamed-up windows any more than she wanted to imagine a youthful Meredith kissing him "Well, there's no place to park and make out anymore. Now it's all fancy houses with million-dollar views. The place I was at today has three floors. Several wings. There's even an actual elevator. Client has a broken leg, and I think I pulled something helping him in and out of his wheelchair."

"So much for the yoga."

"You kidding? Yoga is the reason it's not worse," she countered.

"If you say so." Corinne finished the last of the fries she'd filched and started on the fish. "Get a massage. Better yet, get a man and work out the pains that way. When's the last time you had a date, anyway?"

Sophie coughed on a bit of french fry, thinking again of Meyer. "A massage is a lot less trouble." She didn't realize how grumpy she sounded until Corinne laughed.

It had been so long since Sophie'd heard her sister laugh that she reached across and squeezed Corinne's hand. "I miss times like this."

"Me, too," Corinne said softly. She squeezed back before helping herself to another handful of Sophie's french fries. "And you're right—I learned a long time ago that the only thing men are good at is causing heartache."

Strictly speaking, that wasn't what Sophie had said. But there was no point in belaboring the point.

Particularly when the only man Sophie seemed able to think about these days was the very man who'd taught Corinne that lesson in heartbreak in the first place.

"Hey," she forced brightly. "How about we hit Parnells after you finish eating my fish 'n' chips? They still make the best hot fudge sundae in the world."

Corinne smiled faintly. "Is that your tactful way of making sure I leave the pub tonight without falling off the wagon?"

"Maybe. But it's also my way of spending a little more time with my sister, whom I love very much," she said honestly. "You could even spend the night at my place if you wanted. Make the rest of your drive home in the morning."

Corinne looked like she might argue, but in the end, she shrugged. "Maybe I'll think about it."

It wasn't the most enthusiastic of responses, but where her sister was concerned, Sophie knew enough to take anything positive as a success.

And in a contest between her sister and the stupid preoccupation Sophie was developing toward Meyer, family came first.

Chapter Twelve

"Hi, Otto." Sophie set her case on the floor near the wall of windows where Otto Nash sat in his wheelchair, his attention fixed on the eyepiece of his fancy spotting scope. His chair was angled to accommodate his long cast around the tripod stand. "Not much to see out there today, is there?"

Otto didn't look at her. "You'd be surprised, my dear." His long fingers slowly turned a knob on the side of the scope. The wall of windows afforded the patient a panoramic view of the Pacific Ocean whether he was using his scope or the other variety of binoculars and telescopes that were placed all throughout the massive house.

She glanced over his bent head at the sky outside as she flipped open her case. Despite the fog she'd awakened to that morning that hadn't entirely burned off, the roof of her house almost directly below his hillside location was plainly visible. The water beyond was gray, reflecting the still-cloudy sky. "Whales?"

"Not yet." He continued adjusting the scope. "Better."

She used her hand sanitizer and tugged fresh gloves out of the box inside her case. "What's better than whales?"

He finally lifted his head. "Take a look."

She smiled faintly and, careful not to jar his injured leg, obediently leaned over to look through the eyepiece. A trio of women were strolling on the sand. They were clad in bikinis and obviously didn't care in the least whether it was cloudy or not. She laughed slightly and straightened to eye him. "Should have known."

Even at seventy-five years of age, Otto Nash had copious amounts of unruly white hair that tended to remind her of old black and white photographs of Einstein. The similarity ended there, though. Since she'd started seeing him, he always looked like an explosion of color, and today—clad in an unbuttoned purple-and-blue shirt that exposed a tanned and hairy chest and a pair of turquoise sweatpants with one leg cut off to accommodate his cast—was no exception.

He shrugged. "What else do I have to keep me entertained?"

She pulled on her gloves. "Well, you could try forgetting the scope for a while and actually leave this very fine, very beautiful room." His room was on the third floor of his opulent mansion and opened onto a wide, fully furnished veranda that she and Olivia had both been trying to get him to go out and enjoy.

Otto wasn't confined to his chair if he didn't want to be, though he did need to be careful maneuvering. He still preferred using the motorized chair with its elevated leg support for his cast to the walker that usually sat abandoned on the far side of the room. And even though his chair could easily navigate most of the areas of his mansion, he chose to remain holed up in his bedroom. Admittedly, it was a large and incredibly well-appointed bedroom, but they still wanted to see him expand his orbit.

So far, he'd been uncooperative on that front.

"Any pain today?"

He shrugged again.

"Scale of one to ten?"

"Five."

Better than six, which it had been the day before. His coloring was good, and his eyes looked clear. He didn't really *look* like a man experiencing that much pain, but everyone had their own threshold.

"Mind if I take—" She broke off when he lifted one hand and bent his head again to the scope. He made a slight adjustment to the scope with his other hand while she checked his pulse and respiration, both of which were within normal limits. She released his wrist and took out her thermometer. "Can you describe the pain?"

"Vividly." He lightly knocked his knuckles against the cast that encased his leg from above his knee nearly to his toes. He straightened again and eyed her. "We always talk about the same thing, beautiful. Let's talk about something more interesting."

"Like what?" She aimed the thermometer at his forehead until it offered a soft beep. "Your normal temp?" She set the thermometer aside and placed the pulse ox on his index finger.

"You wound me. I've always prided myself on running hot." He waggled his eyebrows at her.

She rolled her eyes and removed the device from his finger, making a note of the results. Aside from his healing fractures caused by a car accident, he was in pretty good shape. She cleaned the pulse ox with an antiseptic wipe and tucked it back into her case and pulled out her blood pressure cuff. "What would *you* consider interesting, then?"

He extended his arm without her prompting. "Anything other than the dullness of my vital signs."

She adjusted her stethoscope and took his blood pressure. "One-twenty over seventy. Excellent."

"I'm excellent in many ways, my dear. If I didn't have this cast, I'd turn your world sideways showing you."

"Don't excite yourself, cowboy. My world is just fine facing the direction it is," she assured. "I'm going to turn your chair, okay?"

"If you must."

"I must," she said wryly. By now, he knew the drill very well. She put away her equipment, adjusted his wheelchair and moved a slightly ornate side chair away from the wall until it was positioned directly in front of him. Not only was she checking his general health, but she handled his physical therapy on the days that Olivia had off. "Want to keep you strong, right?" She sat and handed him the end of a long stretchy band and wrapped the other end around her own hand. "Got to be able to keep up with those pretty girls you want to chase."

He sort of grunted in reply but didn't put up any resistance as she worked with him through the set of mild exercises prescribed by his medical team over in Portland.

"It's Sunday, isn't it?" He finally asked when they were through and she was moving the chair back to its spot on the wall near the wide bed.

"All day long." She propped her hands on her hips, turning to face him. "How about a sponge bath?" She knew Olivia had done the honors the day before yesterday.

She was surprised when he shook his head and wielded the joystick on his chair, making it turn on a silent dime until he was facing the windows again. But he didn't make any effort to get closer to the spotting scope.

She chewed the inside of her cheek. He'd been injured

more than two months ago, but Cardinale Cares hadn't gotten involved until the beginning of May after his hospitalization. She'd never known him to be so quiet or preoccupied. And he'd *never* turned down the sponge bath. If anything, he'd relished them, flirting his way through every moment.

So far, he hadn't even managed a really good leer at her, which was definitely unusual.

"How about a fresh shirt?" He had a closet bigger than her living room, and it was full of clothes just as bright as the wrinkled one he'd also been wearing when she'd checked on him the day before.

"Saying I stink?"

"Not at all." She moved across the room to stand in front of the windows, well within his range of vision where it would be hard to ignore her. "But a change of clothes is good for the spirit."

"Nothing wrong with my spirit that some spirits wouldn't take care of."

She lifted her hands. "Sorry. No alcohol or tobacco. Doctor's orders."

He grunted again. "What the doc doesn't know won't hurt him."

"No, it'll only hurt you." And truthfully, if he felt so compelled, he could go down to his first floor where she knew there was a fully stocked liquor cabinet. As far as she could tell, the bottles hadn't been touched since she'd started seeing him. And even though his bedroom possessed an actual wet bar, the shelves were empty and the only thing in the small built-in fridge were bottles of water and orange juice. "What's that pain level again?"

His lip curled. "Too damn high." He patted his thigh. "Wanna come sit here and make it better?"

She just shook her head. That was more like his normal self. "Nope, and not sorry."

He grunted, but the suggestive grin was back on his craggy face. "That boyfriend of yours keeping you satisfied?"

"Immensely," she lied and damned the warmth that she could feel collecting in her cheeks.

She looked over her shoulder out the windows. His spectacular view—particularly with the aid of his powerful scopes—encompassed both Cardinale Beach and Friars. It was probably one of the finest views that any home possessed up and down the coastline. She absently tracked the path of a plane far out in the sky. One of the major airlines, no doubt. It looked too big to be one of Meyer's jets.

She swatted away the thought like a fly and turned back to Otto. "How long have you lived here, Otto?"

"Bought it a while back on a whim." He rubbed his cheek that was slightly hazy with white stubble. "Never really lived here, though." He moved his toes beneath the cast. "Until this thing happened."

"Must have been quite an accident." She only knew what the notes in his file said since he'd never spoken about it with her or Olivia.

"One way of putting it." He turned his chair again obviously no more inclined to expound now than before. "Turn on the television, would you, dear? Remote is next to the bed."

She walked across the room and found the remote, though she wasn't sure where the television was, since there wasn't one in sight. But she pushed the button that said Power and wasn't entirely surprised when a large seascape painting on the wall slid up to expose an equally large flatscreen television. "Nice touch." She moved over to him.

"Can't abide televisions."

She raised her eyebrows as she handed him the remote. "With a view like you have, I wouldn't be inclined to watch much television, either." She also knew he was an avid reader. The stack of books on his bedside table changed each weekend. He definitely had a liking for suspense thrillers.

He turned the TV to a cable news station, muted the volume and dropped the remote into the pocket on the side of his chair designed to hold exactly that sort of item. "You do have a view," he said. "From that blue house of yours."

She'd already decided there was nothing she could do about his vantage point that also included her house, so there was no point in dwelling on it. Aside from her roof, there wasn't much else he could see no matter how powerful his scopes were. She'd looked herself, just to make sure. "True."

"Must have cost you a fair amount."

"Not like this place," she countered, smiling. "And I'd been saving up for quite a while."

"When I was young, nurses didn't make enough to afford a pot to pee in. Wouldn't have mattered how long they saved."

"Well, fortunately that's changed slightly. We can't all be tech geniuses like you." Otto had designed some revolutionary computer component when he'd been young and had been profiting ever since. "Anything else I can do for you while I'm here? How about another game of chess?" She was nowhere as good as Leda was, but she hadn't been an entire pushover the last time they'd used his granite chessboard with the crystal playing pieces. It was heavy as all get-out, but since it was positioned on its own custom table with gold wheels that she wasn't entirely certain weren't *real* gold, she'd been able to move it in the elevator from the first floor up to his room where it had stayed.

"Not today." He exhaled, looking suddenly weary. "Go on and turn your boyfriend's world sideways."

"He can wait," she said. She crouched next to his chair. "What do you have on order for dinner today?" He had a deal with several of the local restaurants, who delivered him fresh meals every morning and every evening. Olivia regularly tossed out the leftovers, but it was obvious that he consumed at least some of his food.

"Chowder from the Highland Pub."

It had been a week since Meyer had called Sophie about Corinne being at the pub. The darned fly was persistent. She swatted at it again. "Want some company?"

Otto patted her arm. "*Now* you want more time with me?" He arched a brow. "Don't feel sorry for an old man who's getting bored with his circumstances."

"If you're bored, then get out of this room," she chided gently. "For goodness' sake, we could *go* to the pub and have chowder together there." He still had several months of convalescence to get through before that tibia would be healed.

"I knew it would only be a matter of time before you'd start chasing me. My burden in life—the lovelies never can resist for long."

"Whew. I'm glad to know your ego is alive and well."

His lips twitched, and he pushed the chair's joystick with a finger, directing it smoothly across the gleaming marble floor toward his massively wide bed. When he reached the side, he lifted his cast from the chair's elevated support, propped his hands on the side of the mattress and stood on his good foot long enough to pivot and transfer himself onto the bed.

Even though it went against the grain, she let him do it unaided and waited until he'd adjusted his position to his satisfaction. By which time, a faint sheen of sweat was on his forehead, and he leaned back against his pillows with obvious relief.

She went over to the bed and carefully tucked one of the many spare pillows under his cast. Then she refilled the oversized plastic pink cup that was obviously hospital-issue with water from the mini fridge, recapped it and made sure it was within easy reach on his bedside table, along with his phone and the latest three-high stack of suspense novels.

"Olivia will be here tomorrow as usual," she said. "But you can call any time, day or—"

"Night, yada yada. Just push number two on speed dial. I remember." He opened one eye to look at her, aging rock star à la Einstein, sprawled amid his satin pillows and silk sheets. "Stop looking so concerned, beautiful. I'll croak soon enough, but not tonight."

"Not tomorrow or the next day, either." She pulled the television remote out of the pocket on the wheelchair and dropped it onto the mattress next to his lax fingertips. "You have lots of days and lots years to go, Otto."

"God help me."

"Ah, now." She set her fingers on his wrist, discreetly checking his pulse again. "Don't say that. Think of all the girls you have yet to chase."

"Chasing gets old when you're too old to catch."

His pulse was a little rapid, but not unduly so. "Then maybe you should try chasing someone who has slowed down a little too," she suggested. "Improve your odds."

He gave a sudden bark of laughter and deftly turned his hand, catching her wrist. "Who wants an old lady?"

"Oh, Otto." She rolled her eyes and easily broke out of his grasp. "Consistent as always."

"Maybe I'll have that sponge bath after all."

She looked at her watch. "Sorry. Time's up."

"And boyfriend's waiting. What'd you say his name was?"

Damned fly.

She fired a mental shotgun at it as she crossed the room to pick up her case. "See you next weekend, Otto."

The sound of his chuckling followed her until the mirrored elevator doors closed between them.

When she reached the main floor, her tennis shoes squeaked slightly in the yawning silence as she walked through the house to the massive front doors. They opened easily at her touch and closed soundlessly after her.

She knew if she tried to open them again, they'd be locked.

Otto had a security system that he could control from anywhere in his house, including his bed.

She looked up at the security camera and gave a little wave.

A slight metallic hum sounded beneath the voice that crackled out. "Be careful driving down those hairpin turns on Bluff Road, Sophie."

She smiled. "Have a good night, Otto."

There was another little crackle and then silence.

She crossed the dark red brick driveway and stored her case in the back seat of her SUV.

It had been a long week, but she didn't feel like going straight home.

Maybe because the silence of Otto's big empty house reminded her too much of the silence in her own little place.

There hadn't even been any loud activity going on all week down at Meyer's beach house for her to grumble over.

It was pointless. She wasn't going to get rid of that pesky fly even with all of her car windows rolled down.

She exhaled and called Olivia. "Just leaving Otto," she told her. "Think he was having a hard day."

"Pain?"

She turned the car around in the spacious drive. "His discomfort is apparent, but I don't think that's it." She glanced at the rambling wings of the house in her rearview mirror. "I'll enter all my notes online when I get home, but Cardinale Cares isn't interested in whether I think he needs more social interaction."

"Right. But he has no family," Olivia said. "Says he has no friends in Cape Cardinale. Nobody visits him except us. We need to get him out of that room."

"That's exactly what I was thinking. But what's enough to entice him?"

"A twenty-three-year-old in a string bikini?" Olivia laughed. "Old lech." There was no heat in her words. They'd both realized there was some odd appeal where Otto Nash was concerned. "The last thing we want is depression settling in. Dr. Westerbock'll just write a script like he always does."

That was true. Otto's doctor in Portland would rather err on the side of prescription medicine than some other more natural course. Sometimes that was fine. Sometimes not so much.

"Otto hasn't taken any of the pain meds he has. I doubt he'd be interested in antidepressants."

"Because he doesn't really need one. At least in my opinion."

"Not yet," Sophie agreed. Otto had no issues of depression in his health history, and she wanted to keep it that way. But there was no denying it was a real possibility when patients were faced with long recovery periods. Particularly when they had no discernable support from family and friends. "Have you had dinner yet?"

"Was just trying to decide between frozen this and frozen that."

"Appealing." Otto had cautioned Sophie about the hairpin turns on the road down to her house, but his long driveway had one of its own, and she slowed practically to a stop to navigate it. "I have the very same things at my place. Want to meet somewhere? Otto's having chowder from the Highland delivered, and it's made me want some."

"You want to head there now?"

"Might as well."

In typical Olivia fashion, she didn't waste words or time. "Meet you there," she said and ended the call.

Even though it only took Sophie about ten minutes to drive from Otto's place to the Highland Hotel, Olivia still beat her there and was sitting at one of the high-top tables.

Aside from them and one other couple occupying a booth, the place was empty, which left Donna—on duty behind the bar—plenty of time to watch the television that hung high in the corner of the bar. She left her post long enough to bring them glasses of water. "Want menus?"

"I just want the chowder," Sophie said. "Plenty of crackers and coffee, please."

"Same," Olivia said.

"You girls are too easy to please." Donna went back behind the bar and punched in their order before resuming her position, watching her game show while she polished glasses with a white towel.

Within a few minutes, a teenaged boy came out with their soup and coffees. His hand hovered over a little bowl filled with plastic cups of artificial creamer. "Cream and sugar?"

"Both," Olivia said. "But real cream."

He nodded, left the sugar dispenser on their table and disappeared again.

Sophie peeled open the cellophane wrapper on the crackers and crumbled them into the steaming chowder. "I agree about the girl in the bikini, but since that's probably unethical, what other ideas do you have?"

"We can't force him to do anything. What else does he like besides the ladies?"

"Who knows? His books." Sophie stirred the crumbled crackers into the chowder, making it even thicker. She peppered it thoroughly before lifting a spoonful to blow on. "Maybe a trip to the library?"

"He buys all those books online." Olivia shook her head. "I swear, we're living in a science-fiction novel," Olivia said. "The pandemic just made it more so. Person doesn't have to leave their house to work, to shop, to eat." She leaned forward, her voice lowering. "Take that couple over there. The more ways we have to communicate, the less we actually communicate."

She sat back while Sophie glanced over at the lone couple occupying a booth. The way they sat on the same side of the table implied some sort of closeness. But they both had their attention fixed on their own cell phones.

"Virtual reality," Olivia went on. "Artificial intelligence. Cars that drive without drivers. Before we know it, we'll have planes that fly without pilots."

Sophie coughed a little, a piece of pepper sticking in her throat. "Hopefully not any time soon," she managed and chased the peppery speck down with a drink of water. "But what are we going to do about Otto?"

A different teenager returned with a pitcher of cream that Olivia immediately picked up. She poured so much cream into her coffee cup that it overflowed the brim slightly.

"D'you know anything about his life before his accident?"

Olivia shook her head. "Not really. He told me he's lived all over and his closest 'friend'—" she air-quoted the word "—is his investment broker who watches over what Otto doesn't. Which leaves Otto to watch whales and planets and girls. He's clearly well off. If there's something he wants, it seems obvious that he can afford it."

"Yeah. He watches. If we could just get him to watch something from beyond the walls of his darned bedroom. I told you he can see my house, right?"

Olivia nodded. "He's mentioned it. But I don't think he means it in a stalker-sort of way."

"Yeah, I realized that."

"He can see Cardinale Beach way better than your place. And it isn't all girls for him. He was watching some beach volleyball tournament on TV the other day." Olivia scooped up more chowder. "So good, even if I've already singed off a layer of my tongue." That didn't stop her from swallowing down the spoonful, though.

"You're made of sterner stuff than I am." Sophie fished an ice cube out of her water glass and stirred it into her bowl. "What happens when Doc Hayes gets back? I'll still be able to see Otto on the weekends, but you're his physical therapist."

Olivia chewed her cheek. "I've been thinking about that, actually. I'm not sure I'll go back to the office."

Sophie set down her spoon, staring at her friend. "Seriously?"

"I've liked the home-health thing," Olivia said. Unlike Sophie, Olivia was working full-time for Cardinale Cares. "The money's decent, and there's such a variety of cases. There's just something more satisfying to me about it than being limited to Doc's patients. No offense," she added quickly. "I know you thrive with private practice."

"Don't worry," Sophie said wryly. "I'm not offended."

Olivia grinned. She dashed her mouth with her napkin. "Be back in a sec." She slipped off the stool and quickly headed toward the restroom.

Sophie stirred another package of saltines into her soup

and imagined what the doctor's office would be like without Olivia.

Doc had a total staff of nine. But it had been the three of them who kept it all organized. Meredith running the front. Olivia and Sophie running the back.

She realized she was staring at the cell-phone couple who still hadn't noticeably exchanged a single word with one another. Her own cell phone was sitting face down on the table next to her coffee.

Maybe the couple was sending texts to each other the way that she and Meyer had that morning at Tanya's restaurant.

Sophie actually turned her phone over and looked at her message threads. Meyer's was toward the bottom. She hadn't deleted any of his text messages.

She wasn't sure why.

Olivia returned. "Did you see they're talking about Meredith's partner on TV?"

"What?" She quickly turned her phone face down again. "Why?"

Olivia jerked her head toward the corner television, and Sophie squinted at the screen that had a grainy picture at the best of times.

The game show was done. Local news was on.

"He's in Washington," Donna said from behind the bar. "The rest of his family, too. At the capitol."

The image behind the newscasters was of the White House, but Sophie didn't bother correcting Donna. The picture changed to a garden, where Meyer and his siblings stood alongside a diminutive woman who was shaking hands with the Vice President. The chyron at the bottom of the screen was too small for Sophie to read from their table, and the volume was too low to hear. "What're they doing there?"

"Getting some posthumous award for their father." Donna pointed the glass she'd been polishing at the television. "That's the widow shaking hands with the Veep. Don't know why they're putting it on the news here." She sniffed. "Like Pietro ever did anything for *us*."

"They say his final photograph is going to earn a Pulitzer."

Olivia raised her eyebrows, turning in surprise toward the cell-phone couple. "They speak," she said under her breath.

Sophie bit her lip to keep from smiling.

"You can order a print online at his website," the female-half of the couple added. "I'm getting one for my mother. She *adores* Pietro Cardinale."

Donna harrumphed again. "*Adore-duh*," she emphasized the tense. "No accounting for taste, I s'pose."

"Oh, come on." Olivia's attention went to the bartender. "You have to admit the guy's photography was spectacular."

"He traveled around the world taking pictures of the sky. Big whoop." Donna pointed her glass in their direction. "Did he do a thing for this town? No, he just stole the name from here and never looked back."

Sophie frowned slightly. "Did you know him, Donna?"

"Nah." Donna picked up another glass. "Heard tell he left Meyer and the others high and dry, too. 'Cept for that hovel down on Cardinale Beach. Prob'ly have to pay for tearing it down outta their own pockets, poor souls."

Sophie knew better, but she wasn't about to tell that to Donna. The bartender spread gossip like it was fertilizer. But she didn't have it entirely wrong. Meyer had said his father hadn't given them much attention while he'd been alive. And the only thing the house on the beach had going for it was location. It wasn't a hovel, but it definitely needed work.

"Well, I still think his photos are—were—amazing," the woman from the booth insisted.

Sophie was barely listening. The picture behind the newscasters had switched from Washington to Cape Cardinale and the airfield, focusing on a sleek blue-striped JCS jet as its wheels left the runway. In the upper right corner of the screen was a headshot of Meyer, clean-shaven and looking particularly intense staring out from beneath the brim of a military cap.

"What if we could get Otto and his scope on a plane?" Sophie asked. "JCS does scenic tours. It'd give Otto something else to watch, at least for a little while. Think that'd be enough to whet his interest?"

"Won't hurt to try," Olivia said thoughtfully. "What can he say besides no?"

"Exactly." Sophie was still watching the corner television where the newscasters had already moved on from the story.

The image of Meyer in her mind, though, seemed permanently fixed. What else could *he* say besides no?

Chapter Thirteen

"No. No and hell no." Meyer stared across his office at Hannah. It was Wednesday morning. He was short of sleep and coffee, and it was a toss-up to know which one was darkening his mood the most.

"Why not?" Hannah waggled the inexpensive copy of *Pietro's Last* at him.

Since the trip to Washington three days earlier, the name had been seemingly bestowed on his father's final photograph by public consensus because Meyer doubted the old man would have been thinking it in those moments before he'd died.

"Because I don't want to make JCS about my old man," he said testily.

"Displaying some of his prints for sale in the passenger lounge is hardly turning JCS into a memorial." She tossed the copy onto his desk, and the slick paper slid until it hit his knuckles.

He eyed the sheet of paper. Since his father hadn't survived the boating accident, he'd never been able to develop the original. But the digital file had already been transmitted to wherever it was that digital files went.

Lotus claimed it had gone to her first, and Meyer had no reason to believe otherwise. She was already making money on it, and even though Meyer had detested the dog-and-pony show in Washington, he knew that his father hadn't really left her with many options.

The house they'd shared in New York had been summarily sold, which displaced Lotus to what she'd bitterly described as commonplace. The fact that the New York City apartment was located in one of the most expensive zip codes in the galaxy was apparently beside the point.

"I bootlegged that copy off the internet, but there are prints for sale all over town." Hannah's voice accosted his aching head. "Seems stupid not to get in on the profits, particularly when the man was your *father*!"

He squinted at her. "I said no."

She smirked. "Meredith's already okayed it."

He muttered an oath. "Then why the hell are you bothering me with it?"

"Because I didn't want you figuring I broke the chain of command!"

"Even though you did?" He shoved his fingers through his hair. He honestly didn't give a damn about the photograph—bootlegged or not. He was just sick to death of feeling like a marionette with his strings being yanked about by his dead father. They had to move into the beach house in ten days. Even since before going to Washington, Dana had been sending emails with pictures of the furnishings that she was arranging to be moved in, Alexa was sending sarcastic texts over what she considered Dana's highhand-edness and since they'd left Washington, Cutter had seemingly disappeared off the face of the planet.

If Meyer could do the same just to avoid the continuous stream of annoyance coming from his sisters, he would.

"Sell whatever you want," he told Hannah wearily. "Just don't bother me about it."

He expected her to leave, but she didn't, and he sighed anew. "What else?"

She pulled an envelope from her back pocket and tossed it onto his desk. It didn't slide the way the slippery photo paper had, and he leaned over to grab it.

The return address in Portland was enough to make him grimace even before he tore open the envelope to pull out an advertisement from one of the flight schools there. *Schedule your flight review now!*

He wadded up the flier and pitched it into the trash. "I'm not going to Portland for an instructor to sign me off," he said.

"Since it's required, I hope you're planning on *some* instructor. You've already nixed the idea of Jason—" She lifted her hands quickly in surrender. "Just saying."

"Well, don't say."

"I also hope you plan on having a better mood when you meet with the mayor this afternoon." She pressed her shoulder against the doorjamb as she pivoted out of his office doorway and left.

He waited until he could no longer hear her work boots on the metal stairs before leaning over to pluck the wrinkled ball out of his trash can and spreading it open on his desk.

Going to Portland wasn't the worst idea on the planet.

If he lost his nerve there, at least there would be some hope of word not getting back to JCS.

"Who're you kidding," he muttered to himself.

The pilot community was surprisingly small.

Word *always* got around.

He balled up the flier again and threw it once more into

the trash. Leaning back in his chair, he scrubbed his hands down his face. He had too much to do and too little time to do it. He had the meeting with the mayor that had taken six months to schedule. Plus all the details for the Memorial Day events. Not only was Jason taking up Ollie for a demonstration flight in the afternoon as part of the town's Memorial Day festivities, but JCS was hosting a public remembrance ceremony first thing in the morning that also included a pancake breakfast. He had some friends bringing in a few other vintage warplanes plus a crew of volunteers on Saturday to set up a display of more than two hundred US flags that he had yet to pick up from the vendor—

His cell phone pinged, three times in rapid succession.

More texts.

Dana.

Alexa.

Dana.

He was tempted to toss his phone into the trash after the stupid flier, but instead he shoved it into his metal desk drawer and slammed it shut.

When the desk phone jangled a few seconds later, he snatched it up with a snarl. "*What?*"

"Wow. Coax a lot of business with that greeting, do you?"

His shoulders came down, and he shook his head slightly. "Sophie? What's wrong?"

"Nothing's wrong."

"But you're calling me."

"Actually, I'm calling *JCS*," she corrected. "I didn't expect *you* to answer the phone."

That made a lot more sense.

He really needed more coffee. And fewer nights disturbed by tangled-up dreams in which she frequently had the lead. "What can JCS do for you?"

"I want to know what your rates are for a scenic flight."

He snorted. "Meredith would hang me up by my thumbs if she found out we charged *you* anything at all."

"It's not *for* me," she corrected. "Well, not specifically anyway."

He propped his elbow on his desk and pinched the bridge of his nose. "Who specifically, then?"

"Just a man I know."

The hair on the back of his neck bristled slightly, and he reeled off the rates. High-season rates. No discount. No deals.

"Not so fast. I'm writing this down."

He repeated the spiel, adding on twenty percent just for the hell of it. Then his conscience got the better of him. "That's for the whole group. Five passengers max for three hours."

"There will only be two passengers."

His hackles quivered a little more. "Two. Five. All the same."

"I don't know if he can last for three hours."

Meyer pressed his fingers into his eye sockets again. His imagination was having a field day. "How long *can* he last?" His voice tasted like acid.

"Probably an hour. To start anyway."

Meyer tortured himself a little more. "Guess you've been busy since the last time I saw you at the pub." Meeting superheroes who could last an hour.

To start.

"Busy enough. Tomorrow's the last day of school for the summer."

He swore again, remembering. "Leda has her graduation thing tonight." He spun his desk chair around and hunted for his calendar under the mess of flight charts, job applications and financial statements.

"Moving on to senior high school, yes. It's at seven, in case you've forgotten."

"I didn't forget," he lied. He finally found the corner of the calendar and snatched it free. Right there the date was circled, though his chicken scratch in the square was illegible even to him. "And Grange's birthday party is a week from Sunday." The day after they were all supposed to move into the beach house, he realized. "I suppose I need to get a gift for Leda, too." What would John have done?

A fresh pain joined the party going on behind his forehead. He'd already made plans to take Grange ax throwing before his birthday, but what was a guy supposed to do for a girl's ninth-grade graduation?

"I'm sure flowers or something simple will be fine."

"She's my goddaughter. Carnations aren't going to cut it. Did you get her something?"

"Of course."

He waited for her to elaborate. "And?"

"And what?"

"What'd you get her?"

"A pair of earrings that matches the necklace Meredith is giving her. Good grief, Meyer. You're even less pleasant than usual. Do you need a laxative or something?"

Despite himself, a snort of laughter rose in his throat. He turned it into a cough. "You going to Grange's birthday party?"

"Naturally."

"Gonna bring your new last-an-hour friend?"

"So what if I do?" He could hear the mockery in her voice. "Lots of people keep telling me I need more excitement in my life."

"Excitement's overrated," he muttered.

"Boy, you really did wake up on the wrong side of the bed, didn't you?"

It was true enough. "You want to book the flight or not? Schedule fills up fast in the summer months. Payment in full up front." That part wasn't so true at all.

"I'm not ready to commit just yet. But I appreciate the information."

His conscience nipped at his heels. "If the cost's prohibitive—"

"It's not."

"That's for the Cessna." What was wrong with him? Giving her more choices. More options to spend time with the superhero. "Could also do a hot-air balloon—" she'd said she'd go up in one again in a heartbeat "—or take up Ollie." That was even better. No room for Sophie to go with the guy since the plane had only been built for a crew of two.

"Oh, right! That blue-and-yellow biplane. I'll bet he'd love that. He's stuck in a long leg cast, though. I'm not sure he'd be able to navigate it well. What's the space like where he'd actually be sitting?"

Meyer revised the images inside his head, but that didn't alleviate the overall problem. He'd had a long leg cast once and it hadn't stopped him from having plenty of sex with his nurse's aide.

Admittedly, he didn't think he'd have been able to climb into confines like the Stearman cockpit with that cast. Not even with some assistance. But that didn't stop him from suggesting that she come out to the airfield anyway. "Look at the plane. You can climb in and out." He pulled up the schedule on his computer. "Judge for yourself." He didn't know if it was his imagination or not, but her silence felt as though she was considering it. "We're getting the plane ready for Monday's events, but that won't hinder you seeing her before that."

"What about this afternoon?"

He might as well have been a gawky teenager with his

first crush, considering the zap of electricity that jolted through him. "What time are you finished at school?"

"It's a half-day schedule today and tomorrow. So, I'm free by noon."

"Then come when you're free." He tucked the receiver between his shoulder and ear and began typing rapidly on his keyboard. "Plane will be here. Just go to the executive terminal."

"And you?"

Zap.

"I'll be here." As soon as he said it, he wished he could retract it.

But she surprised him. "Thanks, Meyer."

A zap accompanied by a hell of a lot of other mushy crap he didn't welcome in the least. "Yeah," he said gruffly and hung up the phone.

He looked at the computer screen and the email he'd rapidly composed.

So what if it had taken him six months to get this meeting scheduled with the mayor?

Hannah would have his head on a plate, but he guessed he'd survive.

He hit one more key on the keyboard.

Message sent.

Sophie nervously drummed the steering wheel as she turned into the parking lot of the terminal at the airfield. She'd have been smarter to leave all of this up to Olivia. Let *her* figure out how to coordinate things with JCS.

But no, they'd decided that Sophie could get things set up with JCS and Olivia would work on getting Otto to agree, and maybe through their combined efforts, they'd accomplish something beneficial for their mutual patient.

She parked between two dusty pickups and turned off

her engine, staring at the building through her windshield. It had been naive of her to think she could get through this by dealing only with Hannah. How many times had Meredith told her that Meyer was involved in every facet of JCS?

She smeared lip balm over her lips, pushed her sunglasses onto her nose and forced herself out of the car.

One of the JCS jets was just taking off, the engine noise almost loud enough to drown out the nervous thoughts going around inside her head.

She hadn't seen Meyer since the evening he'd called about Corinne from the pub.

She hoped to heaven that it wouldn't show on her face just how much she'd thought about him, though.

He was still the same old, irritating Meyer who'd broken her sister's heart. Who, it also turned out, had some kind of kissing history with Meredith. Didn't matter how many… decent…things he might have done in the years since.

Mentally girded, she straightened her shoulders, tugged on the hem of her purple school shirt and marched through the entrance.

Unlike the last time she'd been here with the school tour, the terminal lobby was quiet and empty. She walked over to the long counter and slowly tapped her fingertips on it as she looked around and waited. Her heartbeat was loud inside her ears by the time she heard a soft noise, and she turned, braced for the sight of Meyer.

But it was Hannah smiling at her with a hand extended. "Sophie. Meyer told me you were coming by to see Ollie."

It was relief flooding through her. Not disappointment. Had to be.

She met Hannah halfway and shook her hand. "Yes. I have a client I'm hoping to talk into taking a ride."

"A client," Hannah repeated. Her friendly expression

didn't change, but there was a hint of something in her voice that Sophie couldn't quite identify.

"I think it'll be good for his morale," she added.

"Sure, sure." Hannah nodded. "Ollie brightens everyone's day. Come on with me. She's out back."

She followed Hannah through the office behind the counter and down a hall, then out a back door that took a keypad code to open and into the sunshine.

The brilliant blue-and-yellow plane sat alone on the grass. A popup awning had been placed over the tail and the two people who were busily polishing the bright blue body with cloths.

Sophie wasn't quite sure why. The plane looked like it was spotlessly ready for a museum display.

"Meyer said you were getting the plane ready for Memorial Day?"

Hannah nodded as they walked toward the plane. "Jason's going to do a flyover to kick off the parade in the afternoon. With the parade ending here at the airfield, we've got a bunch of vendors coming in to sell food and whatnot. Then Jason'll take Ollie up again for a small exhibition along with a few other historic aircraft that Meyer's arranged to be here."

"Going to be a busy day here, then—what with the ceremony in the morning on top of all that. I had no idea about the exhibition, too."

"It should be entertaining. Won't be a proper airshow or anything, but they'll do some rolls and loops, dives. Things that show off the capabilities of the aircraft."

Sophie didn't have a clue what constituted a proper airshow, but evidently a handful of airplanes missed the cut. "Do you get to fly often?"

Hannah made a face. "Meyer lets me take up the Cessna or Ollie now and then for my own pleasure. But otherwise,

I'm too *old* to be trusted to pilot around passengers anymore."

Sophie stared. "Meyer told you that?"

Hannah laughed. "Not Meyer. But we have federal regulations to follow. Some are harder to swallow than others. *Anyway*, it should be a good time on Monday. You'll have to be sure to come out."

"I'm working one of the first aid stations during the parade, but I will after that."

"And maybe, one day, Meyer will succeed in getting a longer runway—" Hannah waved a hand, taking in the two runways. "Not only could we have a real airshow, but we'd be able to see some real growth."

"Is that what he's trying to do? Build another runway?" From her perspective, the two landing strips set at an angle to each other already looked extremely long, while the turf running adjacent to them had always reminded her of a nice golf course fairway.

"If he can get the city on board with annexing more space, yeah."

"Just for an airshow?"

"Airshows can bring in a lot of money. But no—to attract regional carriers."

"Wouldn't that cut into JCS's business?"

Hannah shook her head. "Not really. JCS and a regional carrier serve two different needs. A regional airline would have routinely scheduled flights. Our charters serve a different niche, but overall, JCS would still run the base ops." The other woman stopped next to Ollie, cupping her fingers around one of the struts that ran from the lower wing to the upper wing almost as if she were cupping a child's cheek.

"More business. More profits," Sophie said.

"Sure. But it's not just about our profits. It's about the rest of the town, too. Events like we're doing on Memorial Day not only bring more revenue to the town as a whole, but it shows that we care about the reason for holidays like this in the first place. Lost my dad and my grandfather in service."

"I'm sorry."

Hannah's lined face creased. "It was a long time ago. I can celebrate the lives they lived now."

John Skinner had already left the military before he'd died. But Sophie still wondered if the day would be harder for Meredith than she let on.

And Meyer?

She pushed the thought away as she stood on her toes, trying to see into the rear cockpit of the plane. "How hard is it to get the annexation?"

"So far, it's been almost impossible. But the land is here. It's just a matter of time before Meyer gets everyone on board with the vision he has." Hannah smirked. "Man could be mayor himself if he wanted."

"Mayor Meyer." Sophie smiled at the sound of it. "Is he interested in politics?"

"Hell no."

She spun around at the deep voice to see Meyer standing there not even ten feet away. He wasn't as clean-shaven as he'd been in that military headshot she'd seen on the local news that weekend, and a navy blue JCS ball cap had replaced the Air Force lid, but the level gaze beneath was just as intense. "I… I didn't think you were here."

"Told you I would be, didn't I?"

It was a pretty futile effort trying to swallow with her mouth going dry the way it had, but that didn't stop her trying. Fortunately, he didn't wait around for her to answer but just joined her next to the plane.

He ran his hand tenderly over a strut the same way that Hannah had, and she finally regained her powers of speech. "Do you all have a crush on her?"

He smiled. "Hard not to. She's old, but she's a beaut. Get in yourself and see." He shrugged out of the leather flight jacket he wore and tossed it over the lower wing before stepping slightly to the side of Sophie. He pointed at the black strip on the wing next to the fuselage. "Put your foot there on the wing walk. Just keep on the black strip—you'll be fine." He grabbed the corner of the rear cockpit. "This is a good spot to hold on either cockpit. Handholds are up there on the wing. Swing your leg in, stand on the seat with both feet, then slide down. Passenger in the front. Pilot in the back. Give it a try."

"Now?"

"You want to know how hard it is to get in and out, don't you?"

"What about the ramp—"

"I got this, Hannah," Meyer said, cutting off the other woman.

Rather than look annoyed, though, the older woman just grinned and strolled over to the two people working near the tail. She said something, and they all laughed before heading back toward the terminal building.

Nothing to do with her, Sophie told herself. Nothing to do with her and Meyer at all.

So why did she feel like the two of them had been left alone quite deliberately?

Corinne, she thought. *Meredith*.

"Sophie?" Meyer's voice was deep, her name sounding almost like a caress and usurping every other thought inside her head.

She was losing it. Well and truly.

Even though she already could tell that Otto would never be able to maneuver getting into this particular plane just yet, she abruptly lifted her foot onto the black tread that ran from the back of the wing to the front right alongside the body of the plane and grabbed hold of the corner of the cockpit to pull herself up. It was a bit of a reach, but she managed. She carefully inched forward, half-afraid that her feet would suddenly go rogue and step where they shouldn't.

"You have at least six inches to spare." Meyer sounded amused, as if he knew exactly what was going through her head, and she looked back only to find that he'd stepped up onto the wing walk behind her.

She felt an extra thump in her chest that was totally unwarranted, and she quickly turned back to the plane, sliding her hand forward until she could grab the corner of the front cockpit and hoped like fury that her visibly shaking hand was only because of the unfamiliar territory.

"You've got it," he said. "You're not going to fall or anything, so just reach up with your left hand for the handle up there on the wing." He moved slightly, reaching around her, and tapped the upper wing where it indented above the cockpit.

She reached up and curled her fingers around the handle.

He didn't touch her, but she still felt surrounded by him. And sucking in a deep breath didn't help any. Instead of fresh oxygen to quell her stupid shakiness, she just ended up wondering if that was aftershave he used or soap that smelled so stupidly good.

His head leaned forward over her shoulder. "You all right?"

"Mmm-hmm." She was losing her mind was what she was doing. She dragged her gaze from the bulge of his biceps beneath his navy T-shirt and abruptly reached her right hand up and grabbed the other handle before turning slightly to swing her leg over the side. Her toe found the seat, and she lifted her other leg in as well, having to hop a little to keep her balance on the seat. "Not very graceful here," she muttered.

"Pretty sure they had a taller pilot than you in mind when the plane was designed. And you're doing fine. I've seen guys with hundreds of flight hours in this very plane fall on their asses maneuvering in and out of it. Particularly getting off the wing."

She looked up at him. The sun was almost directly above them, sending sparks of fire through the rusty hair just visible beneath his ball cap. "Have you?"

"Fallen on my ass?" His lips quirked. "More than once. Just not while navigating an aircraft."

She couldn't seem to look away from his lips. "Why don't you fly anymore?" The words came out entirely without intention.

He jerked slightly, his eyebrows pulling together. She could see each individual eyelash as he squinted. "Where'd you get that idea?"

She shook her head, flushing. "I… Meredith mentioned it, I guess."

"You guess."

"She, uh, she said you're too busy with other things."

"Did she." A strange expression flitted over his face, but he resumed his usual resting stoic look before she could really pin it down.

"And that—" she moistened her lips "—that maybe you'd left that part of things behind when you got out of the military."

The quirk of a smile disappeared as quickly as it had appeared. Now his lips were compressed slightly.

Didn't make them any less perfectly shaped.

"None of my business," she said abruptly and slid down into the cockpit until she was sitting rather than standing on the seat. "It's like sinking into another era, isn't it?" She wanted to get off the subject of him flying, but the words were true.

The cockpit was entirely spare. Simple gauges were located on a panel in front of her. The seat was too far back to reach the pedals with her feet, but there was a long stick that rose straight up from the floor between her knees.

"A lot of World War Two pilots were trained in her," he said after a moment. He tapped a slightly pitted metal sign affixed to the panel with the words *Olive Oil* engraved in script on it. "She wasn't considered fancy, but she was a great trainer. Military scrapped all these planes from use after the war. A lot of them, like Ollie here, ended up being used as crop dusters."

Sophie studied the switches and the levers. They all looked much too rudimentary to be able to control something as complicated as an airplane. "Where did you get her?"

"From my first commanding officer. After he retired, he began collecting old girls like Ollie and restoring them. I talked him into selling her."

"Sounds like you talk a lot of people into a lot of things."

"We got a good deal because the restoration work wasn't finished. Our guys here did that. Hannah was the one who flew her over here from Ohio." He looked at the wing and ran his hand over it. "They did a good job," he added, sounding suddenly brusque. "Have you seen enough yet? Want to book a flight for your boyfriend or not?"

She raised her eyebrows. "I never said he was my boyfriend. Though he'd probably get quite a kick out of thinking it." She pushed herself up until she was able to stand on the seat again.

"Then who is he?"

She was almost eye level with him, and she went oddly breathless again. "Why do you care?"

"I don't."

"Liar," she whispered, shocking herself.

"Who is he, Sophie?"

She tightened her fingers over the binding that edged the cockpit until they hurt, and still couldn't quite shake his mesmerizing spell. "A patient I've met since I've started working with Cardinale Cares," she admitted.

"Patient, huh? Thought they frowned on that sort of thing."

"What sort of thing?"

"Sleeping with your patients."

She nearly choked. "He's seventy-five!" She shook her head sharply. "And it wouldn't matter if he were your age." Not the brightest choice of words, she decided swiftly. "I would *never* sleep with a patient."

"Then what're you here for?"

"Because he's alone and cooped up in a huge old house up on Seaview!" She was telling him details she had no right to share.

"If he lives up on Seaview, the guy is probably loaded. I should have hiked the rate three times."

"It doesn't matter if he's loaded or not. He's still alone, always watching the world outside his windows. I thought watching from a different viewpoint might be healthy. Get him out. Remind him that life is to be lived, not *watched*."

"Should have told me from the get-go about his age."

She lifted her chin. "Why? I suspect he's ordinarily very spry for his age." She suddenly shoved at his shoulder. "Now, move so I can get out of this thing. I have things I need to do yet today."

He moved, stepping easily off the wing and extending a hand to help her once she'd climbed out.

She ignored it and jumped unaided to the ground. It wasn't that far—less than two feet, probably—and the only thing that made it awkward was the slight angle. She still landed a little harder than she'd expected and was grateful when she managed not to face-plant right into the blue shirt covering his chest.

She carefully sidled a few inches away from the plane and away from the heady warmth of him.

"We have a ramp," he said abruptly.

"Pardon?"

"A ramp," he repeated, gesturing his hand toward Ollie. "A thing we can roll up next to the plane. It goes over the wing. Protects it while making it easier for people to get into the cockpit."

Her lips parted. Had *that* been what he'd stopped Hannah from saying?

"He'd still have to be able to support himself dropping down onto the seat, but he wouldn't have to climb over the edge. We had an Army vet celebrate his ninetieth by taking a ride a few months ago. Man could hardly get out of his wheelchair, but we managed to get him in and out of the cockpit. Had the time of his life."

Her chest squeezed. "I'll ask him. Thanks."

He wrapped his fingers around his jacket. "Thank Meredith," he said gruffly. "She's the one who'd insist on it."

He was probably right. But Sophie was also realizing that Meyer—*this* Meyer—would have made the offer anyway. "I, um, I saw the thing on the news about your father's award in Washington. Must have been something, going to the White House like that."

He shrugged. "Been there before."

"You're kidding! You've been invited there twice. That's… impressive."

He shrugged again, looking like he'd rather talk about bat guano. "My entire unit was recognized," he corrected. "Wasn't anything *I* did alone."

"Well, still, it's impressive." She wondered what he'd done—correct that, what his unit had done. She could ask Meredith, but that would only invite more comments from her friend.

She chewed the inside of her cheek. "So. I guess I'll see you this evening, then."

His eyebrows twitched, and he looked blank for a fraction of a second. Then he swore. "Leda's junior high graduation."

The laugh that rose in her came out of nowhere. It felt light and bubbly and dangerously intoxicating. "How could you forget it when we just talked about it on the phone!"

He lifted his arms. "I have stuff on my mind, Sophie!" He turned toward the terminal, muttering under his breath.

She trotted after him. "I told you flowers would be fine."

"It's not enough. John would've—"

She caught his arm, and he stopped walking so abruptly that she almost bumped into him all over again.

His gaze dropped from her face to her hand, and she belatedly released him. "I knew John, too. And he would've left the gift buying to Meredith the way he always did." She lifted her shoulders. "Sometimes simple things are the sweetest, Meyer. And every girl that I've ever known loves getting flowers from a man they adore."

A muscle was ticking in his sharp jaw, and she was appalled at her own desire to soothe it with her palm.

She balled her hand and pushed it into her pocket. "But if it bothers you so much, there's a bracelet at the jeweler on Beach Road that matches the necklace and earrings. The mannequin in the window is wearing it. White gold with little fairy wings on it. It's probably still there."

"Thanks."

She could see her SUV parked to one side of the terminal building. "I'll see you later, then."

She had only taken a few steps when he spoke again.

"What the hell is Cardinale Cares?"

That bubbly feeling rose again, and she turned, still walking backward. "A company that provides home health care," she told him. "I signed on with them to fill my weekends with something *other* than listening to that bulldozer down at your beach house."

"Bulldozing's done."

"Great! Peace and quiet can once again reign."

He rolled his eyes. "You haven't heard my sisters argue. You'll end up wishing for a whole fleet of bulldozers!"

She laughed and turned again to watch where she was going.

"Yeah, you laugh now," he called after her. "Just wait until we're neighbors. Then you'll see."

She didn't know what disturbed her most. The prospect of it, which had been an irritation for weeks now.

Or the fact that it suddenly...wasn't.

Chapter Fourteen

"Impressive display, isn't it?" Meredith greeted, spreading her arm to encompass the row of flags that lined the entire length of Perimeter Road leading to the airfield.

"I'll say." Sophie plucked at the lightweight dress she'd changed into after finishing her stint at the first aid station. They'd had two on the parade route manned by volunteers like her and one here at the airfield manned by the fire department. "For an unofficial start to summer, it's already crazy hot. There were already two cases of heat exhaustion at the parade. Hope you're pushing everyone here to drink plenty of water."

"We are. Fire brought by their ladder truck. They're going to hook up the hose and run it after the exhibition is over. More entertainment for the kids. They'll love running through the water."

"Entertainment for everyone," Sophie said with feeling. "I had to park in the edges of the galaxy, and I'm sweating like a rabid dog. I can't believe how many people are here!" She thought about Otto. He'd turned down the idea of the scenic flight, but he'd have had quite a field day with this crowd where there were as many bikini tops in use as there were at the beach.

Meredith was beaming. "It's great, isn't it? I'm so proud of Meyer." She propped her hands on the hips of her cutoff shorts and looked around.

Hundreds of people milled around the tented booths that had been set up near the executive building. Several planes that looked as vintage as Ollie were parked at the opposite end nearer to the huge hangar. They appeared to be drawing as much attention as the very modern, very powerful– looking JCS jet that was also parked there with its doors open and welcoming.

"Be proud of yourself, too," Sophie reminded. "JCS *is* yours."

"JCS is *all* Meyer," Meredith said dryly. "Let's not pretend otherwise."

Sophie could have argued. Yes, JCS wouldn't be where it was without Meyer, but if not for Meredith, he wouldn't even be there.

"Mom." Leda ran up to them, breathless and pink-cheeked in her JCS tank top and miniskirt. "Danielle's family's going to Friars Beach as soon as the exhibition is done. Can I go with them?"

Meredith adjusted the fairy wings on Leda's necklace. "Are you going for Danielle's company or for Scott's?"

Leda huffed. "Scott's not even going to be there. He's up at Cannon Beach all week." The popular town was several hours north of Cape Cardinale.

"Do you have sunblock?"

"In my bag." Leda gestured randomly at the mass of humanity spread out on blankets and lawn chairs.

"Swimsuit?"

"Duh." Leda plucked the pink strip showing beneath the tank top. "Plus a towel. Also in my bag."

"Her parents going to be there?"

Leda rolled her eyes. "Yeah. You want to talk to them and verify it?"

Meredith chucked her lightly under the chin. "Don't roll your eyes at me, miss. You know very well I have their number in my phone and can call them any time I want. But yes, you can go."

"Great." Leda gave her mom a fast hug, and the bracelet on her wrist that she'd gotten from Meyer winked in the sunlight.

"Where's Grange?" Meredith called after her.

Leda didn't slow her roll. "How should I know? Being annoying somewhere, like usual!"

Meredith exhaled and looked back at Sophie. "Does it make me a bad mother to have agreed she could miss Grange's birthday party next weekend so she can go camping for a week with the Dowlings up at Cape Disappointment?"

Sophie bumped her. "That's not even four hours away. Why would that make you a bad mother? Are you worried about Scott?"

"Oh, I made sure that Scott wasn't going to be on the campout. But I agreed just to have a few hours free of her and Grange's bickering."

"You could never be a bad mother," Sophie assured. "Whether Leda is there or not, Grange is going to have a great party."

"I hope so." Meredith adjusted her wide-brimmed hat. "Considering how much time I've spent planning it. His entire class from school is coming. I must have been insane to agree to that many kids. What was I thinking?"

"That you only turn thirteen once?"

Meredith's lips curved. "I suppose so. He wants a birthday cake that looks like Yankee Stadium. *And* he wants me to make it." She flopped her arms. "Can't just go to Tanya and ask her to do it."

"That's what you get for being supermom."

"Yeah. That's me, all right." Meredith snorted. "What say we find something cold to drink?"

"Please," Sophie said feelingly, and they headed toward the tented booths. "Saw my dad earlier. He and Francesca were here this morning for the memorial ceremony. Said you had a nice turnout."

"We did." Meredith turned up one palm with three bandage strips on it. "Meyer expected about fifty families, but we ended up closer to eighty. Earned myself blisters flipping pancakes, but it was worth it."

"I should've been here to help."

"We had plenty of volunteers. Besides, you were already doing your duty at the parade." She stopped in front of the first booth they came to that—according to the sign—was hosted by the Church of Sunshine and Harmony. They collected two huge cups of the ice water they were handing out for free, and it was all Sophie could do not to pour it down her back.

"It's at least ten degrees cooler in town," she said.

"It's the pavement," Meredith said after chugging half of her water. "Adds heat. But I will be glad if the forecast is right and we get some rain before next weekend. Cool things off a little." She slowly turned in a circle, taking in the activity. "If only John could see all this now."

Sophie tucked her arm through Meredith's. "Don't you think he is somewhere watching?"

Meredith rested her hatted head briefly against Sophie's. "Have I told you lately how sweet you are?"

"There's a pretty sight."

Meredith straightened and whirled. "Walker!"

Sophie hid a smile at how clearly flustered Meredith was by the sight of the man who'd appeared behind them.

"Think I'll head over and peek in the JCS jet," she said.

"Tell them hello," Meredith said somewhat nonsensically.

Sophie tucked her tongue into her cheek and nodded at the tall attorney. "Good to see you, Walker."

"You, too." But his eyes never strayed from Meredith.

Sophie managed to wait until she'd moved a few feet away from them before letting her smile have reign.

Meredith might have thought Walker had lost interest after their trip to Colorado, but Sophie was willing to bet the man had just been biding his time.

She stopped again at the Sunshine and Harmony booth to top off her cup and snuck a look back at the two of them.

Walker was standing even closer to Meredith, and Sophie could tell by the way Meredith kept fussing with her hat that she wasn't unaffected.

And she'd never seen Meredith look that way with Meyer.

The thought slipped in without invitation. She didn't want to think she was happy to see Walker and Meredith together just because it meant Meredith's friendship with Meyer really was just destined to remain friendship. She wasn't the jealous type, was she?

Particularly about *Meyer*.

She shook it off and decided she really would go see the planes. She had never seen the inside of one of the JCS jets before, and now seemed like the perfect opportunity to indulge her curiosity without witnesses. She and Olivia weren't giving up on getting Otto out of his house. He'd turned down the biplane idea, but maybe a private jet would be more his style.

Everyone she passed seemed in an excellent mood despite the record-breaking temperature.

Meyer really *had* outdone himself.

She'd almost reached the airplanes when her cell phone buzzed, and she pulled it from the hidden side pocket on her dress. The sight of her sister's name was a surprise. Aside from a couple of text messages, she hadn't talked to Corinne since that night at the pub two weeks ago. "Hey there. Happy Memorial Day."

"Baby sister! How're you doing?"

Sophie's stomach sank. Corinne's voice was abnormally high and bright. "Fine," she said cautiously. "How're you?"

"Fine, fine. Peachy."

Sophie's stomach sank further. Three and a half months this time. "Where are you? What're you doing?"

"You sound exactly like Mom."

Sophie winced. That was the last thing she wanted. "Sorry. Would you like some company? I could drive up."

"I could drive down," Corinne said.

"No!" The slur in Corinne's voice was more than enough evidence that wasn't a good idea. "Traffic's really heavy on Memorial Day," Sophie added quickly. "You'd waste more time sitting still."

"So would *you*," Corinne countered.

Sophie didn't already have one drunk driving conviction under her belt, either. But she didn't say so.

She ducked into a wedge of shade on the side of the hangar. "How much have you had to drink?"

"Spoilsport."

"You called me, remember? Pardon me if that feels like a sign that you *want* me to know."

"Just some beer. Work had a picnic."

Great. "You were drinking at a *work* event?"

"*Everyone* was drinking," Corinne said testily. "And I got a rideshare. So stop being such a goody-goody."

She felt a pain unfurling in her forehead. "You're home, then? At your apartment?"

"I'm not an idiot. Yes, I'm home."

"No," Sophie said quietly. "You're not an idiot. You're a woman who can't tolerate even an ounce of beer. I love you. Make some coffee. Sober up and find a meeting."

"I know." In typical fashion, in a flash Corinne went from too happy to weeping. "I will. I promise. I just—"

Sophie squeezed her eyes shut, but they still stung with tears. "Just what?"

"Just want to be happy," her sister whispered.

"Everyone wants to be happy, Corinne."

"But it's *hard*. It's not hard for you! Perfect beach house. Perfect life. Perfect daughter."

"Nothing about me is perfect. But I know I'm not going to find any secrets to happiness at the bottom of a whisky glass."

"Shows what you know. I was drinking *beer*."

Sophie sighed again. "Call me again after you've been to a meeting."

"Priss." Corinne hissed and hung up.

Sophie pressed the edge of the cell phone against the pain in her forehead. Her sister had certainly called her much, much worse.

"Sophie!"

She was so startled she dropped her cup, and water spilled over her white tennis shoes.

At least her *feet* would be cool for a few minutes.

She focused on Grange, who was running toward her. His face was flushed. "Hey there. Your mom's—"

"You're a nurse, right?"

"Most days," she quipped a little wearily.

He grabbed her arm. "You gotta come and see Uncle Meyer."

Of all the people that she should not want to see, particularly after talking to Corinne, it was Meyer. "Why?"

"'Cause I think he's sick." Grange dragged on her harder.

She snatched up the cup she'd dropped and followed him around the hangar. "Where is he? Why do you think he's sick?"

"Because he's sweating and puking in his trash can! He's in his office." He pulled her toward the open bays of the enormous hangar.

When it rained it poured.

"Do you know where the first aid station is?"

He shook his head.

"Okay, go and find your mom. She's with Walker over by the terminal building and the booths. First aid's over there, too. Meyer's probably just overdone it in this heat, but they should be alerted."

"He looks really bad, though."

"Heat exhaustion does look bad, honey. But let's not worry too much until I've seen him, okay? Meanwhile, get yourself some water to drink, too, and cool down yourself. Last thing we need is for you to get dehydrated." She pointed at the metal staircase visible at the very back of the hangar. "Up there, right?"

Grange nodded.

"Okay." She tossed her empty cup into a trash can and started toward it, walking between a small airplane with a propeller and another JCS jet. "Remember. Drink your own water, Grange."

He ran off, and she quickened her pace to the stairs, squishing slightly in her wet shoes. There was only one way to go at the top of the stairs, and she jogged along the catwalk until she reached an open doorway.

She looked in cautiously, taking in an enormous metal desk that looked like it had come from Ollie's era, two tall filing cabinets standing in opposite corners and a shelf that was crammed with notebooks. "Meyer?"

"Yeah." His voice sounded rough, and she stepped around the desk to see him flat on his back on the floor between the desk and the shelf, his arm circled around a round metal trash can.

Alarm was swift, but she hadn't been a nurse for ten years for nothing.

She crouched next to his side, pressing the back of her hand to his cheeks. His forehead. He was flushed and sweating, just as Grange had said, but his skin felt cool and clammy. Classic symptom of heat exhaustion. "Did you fall? Pass out?"

"No."

"Vomit?"

He shoved the trash can a few inches away from his side. "Not yet."

"Grange said you were."

He didn't open his eyes. "'Cause Grange caught me with my head in the can, hoping I would."

"What were you doing before it came on? Leda said you were doing something with the kids. Outside?"

"That was earlier."

"So were you up here?"

"I'm up here now, aren't I?"

"Good to know your crank level is normal." She grabbed several thick books off the shelf and stacked them on the floor. "I'm going to raise your legs a little," she warned before sliding her hand beneath his jean-clad knee.

He jerked as if she'd poked him with a cattle prod. "I don't need that."

"Humor me." Instead of touching him directly, she nudged the stack of books against his leg.

He muttered under his breath but raised his knees. She tucked the books under them and then slid another stack beneath his ankles. Then she crawled around in the tight space until she could reach his shirt buttons. "I'm going to loosen your clothes."

He swore again, finally opening his eyes a slit. "This is *not* how I've imagined that."

She made a face, looking away from the thin slice of blue staring up at her from between thick eyelashes. It wouldn't exactly do to tell him this wasn't how she'd imagined it, either.

The top two collar buttons were already undone, and she unfastened the rest, tugging his shirttails free from his belt. Then she spread the fabric wide to expose his chest and pretended that the only reason she felt too warm was because of the temperature outside.

The hangar was air-conditioned, but heat did rise, which made his office warmer than it had been down below.

In her case, though, it was still a thin excuse.

She popped her head up long enough to find something suitable among the mess of items on his desk. A large manila envelope sitting under a pair of reading glasses suited the bill, and she waved it over him like a fan. "Do you have any water up here?"

"Bottom drawer." He'd closed his eyes again. "It's not heat exhaustion."

"It's doing a good imitation of it, then." Which bottom drawer? She opened the one on the desk. It was full of folded maps. She tried the filing cabinet in the corner of the room near her feet and struck gold. She pushed aside a ball cap with *PILOT* printed on the front and pulled out a tall bottle of electrolyte water. "Can you drink?"

"If I want to puke. Sure."

She glanced around the office again and spotted a JCS T-shirt hanging on the back of the office door. She got up and retrieved it, soaking one part of it with water before draping it around his neck. Then she cupped her hand next to his head and wet his hair, running her fingers through it to keep the water from dripping in his face.

She picked up the envelope again and fanned it vigorously. The air movement didn't help her in the least. "Feeling a little cooler?"

"Yes, but I told you. Not heat exhaustion."

"Did you eat something bad?"

"No."

She pressed the backs of her fingers again against his forehead. The clamminess was already better. Now his skin just felt cool because of the water and the fanning.

She didn't stop waving the envelope even while she found the pulse in his wrist with her other hand. It was steady and not the least rapid. "Headache? Dizzy?" She mentally ran through the other symptoms of heat exhaustion. "When's the last time you peed?"

"Jesus, Sophie."

"I'm a nurse."

"You're a woman to me, not a damn nurse."

She pressed her lips together, torn between a shiver and a smile.

"I peed the last time I needed to." He yanked away the wet shirt draped around his neck and pushed himself up on one hand, dislodging the books under his legs.

She grabbed his shoulders. "Hold on there, cowboy. Just go slow."

He gave her a look. "Cowboy?"

She felt her cheeks flush. "Shut up. Don't move too quickly. I don't want you getting dizzy and falling."

"I'm not gonna get dizzy and fall." He sat up further, his head hanging between his shoulders, looking to her exactly like a man who could get dizzy and fall.

"Are you on any medications?"

He shook his head.

"Does this happen often?"

"Having a freaking panic attack?" His voice was low.

She sat back on her heels, frowning at the top of his head where his unevenly wet hair stood up in spikes. "Has it happened before?"

He looked at her from beneath his lashes.

"How often?" she repeated quietly.

"Too often."

He sounded so hollow that she had to catch herself from wrapping her arms around him. "Have you talked to anyone about it?"

"Don't need to."

She linked her fingers together just to keep them under control and in her lap. "Do you know what triggers them?"

He scattered the books even further while turning onto his knee and then pushing to his feet.

She braced herself, hoping that she wouldn't have to catch him. She wasn't exactly in the best of positions, and he outsized her by a lot.

But all he did was slump into the rolling chair that she'd pushed out of her way. "Flying," he said so quietly she would have missed it had her attention not been solely focused on him.

She remained exactly where she was, fearing that if she moved at all, he'd spook like a wounded animal.

He spread his palms, looking down at them. "Not flying in general. Me flying, specifically." His fingers curled into fists.

She did move then, pushing to her own feet and moving instead to kneel next to his chair. "Anxiety can be treated."

"I don't need drugs."

"I wasn't saying anything about drugs. Counseling can be—"

"I don't need counseling, either."

"It's okay to need help. If one of your airplanes doesn't operate properly, you'd call in a mechanic, wouldn't you? Have you tried just sitting in a plane without trying to fly it?" She remembered that he hadn't sat in Ollie when she'd first checked out the plane. But he certainly hadn't shown any anxiety being around the plane in general. "Sometimes it helps to take small steps that don't feel threatening—"

"There's no help for this, Sophie, so just forget it, would you?"

She touched his arm. "Meyer—"

He grabbed her wrist, pulling it away from him but not letting go, either. "I appreciate you thinking you can help." The glint in his eyes was fiercely pained. "But you can't. Tell Grange it was the heat. Tell him whatever you want. But I'm *fine*."

"That's certainly plain as day." She waited a beat. "Meredith doesn't know about this, does she." It wasn't a question.

"No, and the last thing she needs to know about is me imagining her husband's plane crashing every time I get in the cockpit."

"Oh, Meyer." She exhaled. "I'm so sorry."

"I don't want your pity, either."

"It's not pity to acknowledge someone's pain. How long has—"

"Too damn long." He glared at her as if the situation were somehow her fault. "I know you two tell each other everything, so just figure out a way to keep your mouth shut this time."

Not everything, she thought.

She finally wiggled her fingers. "Can I have my hand back, please?"

He released her, and she rocked to her feet. Her wrist still tingled. "What'll happen when you have a panic attack while," she managed a careless shrug, "I don't know. Driving Grange home from a baseball game? Or Leda from a chess tournament?"

"They don't come on unexpectedly like that."

She spread her arms to encompass his office. She knew there wasn't a lot of time before Meredith and the first aid crew would get there. She could already hear a commotion from downstairs. "Just unexpectedly right here in your own office?"

"Jason's got a ruptured eardrum."

She frowned, not following. "What?"

"Jason. The pilot who's supposed to fly Ollie this afternoon." Meyer pinched the bridge of his nose. "He's had an ear infection. But after the flyover for the parade, the pain got worse. He went to urgent care. There's no way he can get through the exhibition. Not today. I was up here in the office because he was calling me from the doctor. There's nobody else to do the show except me." He leaned over suddenly and grabbed the trash can.

And this time, it wasn't just a precaution.

She waited until he'd finished retching and silently pushed the water bottle into his hand. He swigged some, then spit it out into the can just in time before they heard footsteps pounding on the metal stairs.

In a matter of seconds, Meredith rushed through the doorway, her gaze taking in Meyer sitting in his desk chair, his hair wet and his shirt still undone.

She looked toward Sophie, who was leaning against one of the corner filing cabinets. The plastic trash bag that she'd tied off in a knot was inside the trash can, hidden behind her legs.

"What's going on?"

"Heat," Sophie said before Meyer could. She looked at the paramedic who'd come up behind Meredith, and Walker, who'd brought up the rear.

Gang's all here. Under other circumstances, the thought that raced through her mind might have been funny.

"Hi, Ricky," she addressed the paramedic first. "Think everything here's going to be fine."

"Soph." Ricky greeted with a nod. "You sure?"

She smiled at him. He was a good guy, even if he had dumped her to marry one of her friends. Now he and Becca were expecting their first baby. The same could be said for Chris and his wife. And Kyle and Bree before him.

So far, she was batting three for three when it came to inspiring marriage proposals. Just none of them had been made to her.

She'd finally learned her lesson, though. Don't fall for guys and she wouldn't have to worry about them falling for someone else.

"I'll stay up here with Meyer for a little while for good measure," she told Ricky. "But—" she held up the water bottle as evidence "—he's already getting some fluids and his symptoms have pretty well abated."

Ricky nodded. "Let us know if you need anything." He sidled around Walker, and his sturdy boots clumped noisily back down the catwalk.

Meredith's gaze was bouncing between Sophie and Meyer. "What's really going on here?"

"Nothing," Meyer said tiredly. "Nothing for you to worry about."

Meredith's hands went to her hips. "Of *course* I worry about you, you dolt! You know I love you!"

Sophie's hand tightened spasmodically on the plastic water bottle. It crinkled, making more noise than Walker did, who turned silently and disappeared from the doorway.

The man had the right idea, she decided.

She picked up the T-shirt that she'd doused with water and dropped it over the top of the trash can. "I'll just go wring this out," she said and followed after him, the trash can tucked under her arm.

When she reached the bottom of the stairs, Walker was nowhere in sight.

Not surprising.

If Sophie hadn't been expecting this very thing, she would have disappeared, too.

But Meredith was still her best friend. Just because she'd finally admitted her real feelings where Meyer was concerned didn't mean that changed.

Her eyes were stinging, and she went into the bathroom near the stairs.

She threw away the trash bag and washed her hands. The shirt had been an excuse more than a fact. Wringing it out produced only a few drops of water. She shook the wrinkles out of it as well as she could, then leaned her hands against the sink and eyed her reflection in the mirror.

"You're an idiot, Sophie Lane," she whispered. "The man broke your sister's heart. Your best friend is in love with him. *Stop* thinking any of that will change."

Then she turned away from the red-rimmed eyes looking back at her and pressed Meyer's shirt against her face.

"Tell me the truth," Meredith said. "You pissed off Sophie, and she dumped water over your head. Is that what really happened?"

Meyer raked his fingers through his wet hair. "I didn't piss her off, but yeah, she poured water over my head. Only because she thought I was having heat exhaustion. So, cool your jets. She doesn't need your protection."

Meredith leaned her hip against the desk and glanced around. "Your office is a mess."

"You're welcome to take it over."

She made a face. "We both know I couldn't run this place even if I wanted to. And I don't." She leaned toward him, her gaze searching. "Why won't you just let me sign it over to you? You've sacrificed more for me and the kids than anyone should ever do."

"John—"

"Is gone." She pushed off the desk and paced in front of the window overlooking the hangar below. "I know it. You know it."

"So why don't you move on?"

She spread her hands. "Why don't *you*?"

He couldn't answer that. If he did, he'd lose the only family he'd ever cared about—her and the kids.

"John made this business for you," he finally said.

"Which means it is mine to give."

"You'd better go after Walker. You know he misinterpreted what you said."

"Walker's..." She sighed, shaking her head. "He's got an issue when it comes to you and me. But even if he didn't, he's too good for me."

"Bullshit."

"Ever the hero, aren't you, Meyer?"

"Not even on my best day. I love you, too, by the way. But—"

"Not like that," she finished before he could. "Thank God. Marrying one jet jockey was enough to last me a lifetime, and I'm way too wishy-washy for the likes of you.

Path of least resistance—that's me. You'd be bored to tears."
She turned to look out the window again. "You knew he
cheated on me, didn't you?"

Meyer winced. "No. Not for sure," he added carefully.

"Then you suspected."

He didn't answer, and she gave him a baleful look.

He still didn't answer.

"I warned him that I wouldn't tolerate it again. *Third
strike, you're out*, right? I told him I'd go. Take the kids
and leave this place forever."

Meyer had gone still.

Third?

"Pretty sure that's why he killed himself," she murmured.
"He knew I found out he'd done it again."

He stood so fast the chair shot out and slammed against
the shelf behind him. "No."

"Come on, Meyer. Even you always said he was the best
pilot around."

He rounded the desk. "Accidents still happen." *Third*.
The word kept circling inside his head.

"Grange and Leda can never know," she said abruptly.

On that, they agreed. "Does Sophie?"

Meredith nodded.

"She never said—" He broke off when Meredith frowned
slightly, looking up at him again. Why *would* Sophie say
anything to him about it?

"She also knows I loved him despite it all," Meredith
said with a sigh. She raked her fingers through her hair,
looking like she wanted to pull it out by the roots. "Women
are stupid where men are concerned, Meyer."

"Whereas men are stupid all the way around."

She gave a laugh that held no humor and wrapped her
arms around his shoulders, resting her head against his
chest. "Maybe that's what makes us so well suited."

A soft sound at the doorway made Meyer want to swear all over again.

Sophie entered the office, looking everywhere but at them.

She returned the T-shirt to the peg on the back of his office door and set his empty trash can on the floor next to the desk. "Looks like you're in good hands, and I... I told Corinne I'd drive up and see her."

Meyer figured it was an excuse, and the surprised look she got from Meredith as she moved away from him clinched it.

"I thought you were going to be around for the exhibition." Meredith looked at her watch and then Meyer. "Which should have gotten started by now. Were you planning to kick it off with an announcement or anything? I could do it if you tell me what to say."

Sophie was inching her way back to the doorway.

No matter how hard he willed it, she didn't look his way.

"There's no announcement," he told Meredith. "Except that Ollie won't be going up after all. But we've got three others that will."

"What's wrong with Ollie?"

Finally, finally, Sophie's gaze slid his way.

"She needs a mechanic."

Despite everything, Sophie's lips softened, and he imagined they held the faintest of smiles before she turned and walked away.

Chapter Fifteen

"That's the last of it." Cutter stacked an enormous box on top of another enormous box and dusted his hands together, looking around the crowded living area of the beach house. Between the stacks of boxes and the sectional couch that had been delivered earlier that week along with a truckload of furnishings for the bedrooms, there was barely any room to move inside the place. "Whose idea was this again?"

Meyer hadn't needed to cart in stacks of his own boxes for the simple reason that he'd only brought one. But he'd done his own share of unloading the piles of stuff the girls had brought and was presently sprawled on the couch, a beer balanced on his belly. "Blame the guy who gave us that." He jerked his thumb at the large glossy framed photograph that Lotus had sent to them "celebrating" what she was calling their new family adventure.

Pietro's Last was a sea of blues. Ocean to galaxies, and Meyer wasn't sure where one ended and the other began.

Whether he wanted to admit it or not, the photograph was startlingly beautiful.

But it also just meant the old man was even more of an intrusive presence in their cramped dwelling than they'd expected.

He glanced at Cutter. Since the girls had gone into town to pick up groceries, it was just the two of them there. "You actually setting up a tent outside?" It wasn't a metaphor. Cutter really had dumped a long bag that contained a tent on the deck when he'd arrived.

"Maybe. Depends how loud you snore."

"If *you* snore, I'll put up the tent *for* you."

Cutter smiled faintly. Then he blew out a long breath. "This is totally fu—"

"We're *ba-ack*." The rear door opened, and Alexa's sandals clattered on the linoleum as she and Dana came inside.

Meyer set aside his beer and got up. "Need help with anything?"

"I think we have all the bags." Dana's tennis shoes were as silent as Alexa's weren't. "But we saw a grill on sale. It's in the back of the SUV." She set her recycled-fabric bags on the kitchen floor and winced a little as she straightened. She rubbed her back. "We bought steaks for dinner."

"She—" Alexa jerked her head "—bought steaks for dinner."

Dana sighed. "Alexa—"

"I'd have been happy with hot dogs and coleslaw, but whatever."

"I'll get the grill." Cutter escaped.

"We don't have to share every meal," Dana told Alexa. Her gaze flicked to Meyer. "But I thought it might be nice to spend the first night having dinner together. *My* treat," she added before Alexa could open her mouth again. "We can figure out how to split expenses later."

"Won't be splitting any fifty-dollar steaks," Alexa grumbled. She yanked open the small refrigerator that had replaced the mini-fridge and stuck a gallon of milk on the shelf. "This thing isn't going to cut it. We'll have to go to the store every time we turn around."

"Look at the bright side." Dana's tone was tight. "It'll give you somewhere to go every time we turn around."

Meyer grabbed his beer. There was something to be said for all of them having been raised in different households. "We'll make a schedule. Assign duties."

"Aren't you Mister Military."

"Give it a rest, Alexa," Dana snapped. "We're all in the same boat here, so stop acting like you're the only one whose life's been derailed." She set two bottles of wine on the counter.

"Poor Dana. No local gourmet-food shop. How *will* you manage?"

Dana threw up her hands and left the kitchen, brushing past Meyer. "I'm going to see how Cutter is doing." She sidled around a stack of boxes and went out the front door that Meyer had gotten replaced just the week before and slammed it closed behind her so hard it was a wonder the glass door lights on the upper quarter didn't shatter.

Meyer looked at Alexa, who was pinching her eyes closed as if she were in pain. "She's right, Alexa. We're gonna sink or swim together."

"I know." She dropped her hand wearily. "I *know*. What was he thinking?" She gestured at the incongruously modern frame that sat on the boxes stacked in front of the fireplace. "A couple months ago, it was easy to decide that all of this would be worth the bank deposit at the end, but now that I'm here?" She shook her head. "I don't know."

"None of us do," Meyer said quietly.

She made a face and silently finished emptying the fabric

bags. Then she yanked open one of the drawers, which stuck after only a few inches. She muttered an oath and shoved it shut again. The second drawer opened, but it was equally empty. "There's got to be a wine opener somewhere."

"Check Dana's boxes. They're labeled with the contents."

"Of course they are."

She left the kitchen, and Meyer drained the rest of his beer. Then he went out the back door, only to stop short at the sight of Cutter sitting on the ground surrounded by metal parts.

"She neglected to say the grill had to be *assembled*. I brought a crapload of stuff," Cutter wagged a thin paper packet in Meyer's direction, "but I didn't bring a freaking screwdriver. You have any tools?"

"At my apartment," Meyer said dryly.

"Couldn't bring yourself to give up the place, huh?"

"Keeping it as a bolt hole," Meyer admitted. "Not against the rules. We don't have to live in each other's pocket twenty-four seven." Just part of every twenty-four.

"Thank God." Cutter looked skyward as raised voices filled the air again. "Let's go now. I think it'll take two of us."

"Hardware store's a lot closer than my place."

"Forget that. I say drag the trip out as long as possible. Maybe they'll exhaust themselves."

Meyer looked back through the doorway toward the front of the house. The passage was almost blocked off by boxes. "I should tell them we're leaving."

"And chance either one of 'em wanting to come along?" Cutter tucked the assembly instructions under a piece of metal and pushed to his feet. "No way."

Meyer decided Cutter was right. The girls probably wouldn't stop warring long enough to even notice their absence. "I'll drive."

* * *

The collection of vehicles parked down at the beach house had grown since that afternoon when Sophie had gone out to see Otto Nash.

She hadn't seen either Meyer or Meredith since the beginning of the week. But judging by the activity at the beach house, it was safe to assume that he and his siblings must have all moved in.

She carried the dry cleaning that she'd picked up on her way home from Otto's into her house, put it away and changed out of her scrubs and into a pair of shorts and a T-shirt. The heat wave that had engulfed them the weekend before had passed thanks to two solid days of rain, and she was once again able to leave the doors open to enjoy the ocean breeze.

She fixed some iced coffee and carried her laptop out onto the deck to work on her notes from her session with Otto.

She'd made herself revisit the scenic flight proposal even though she'd have preferred to forget it entirely. But that would have meant explaining why she'd given up so easily to Olivia. Sophie was already avoiding questions she didn't want to answer from Meredith. The last thing she wanted was to do the same with Olivia.

But Otto had remained steadfast regardless of what sort of plane she proposed.

I have plenty to look at already, he'd said, his attention never leaving the scope focused out the window. *Beach volleyball tournament at Friars.*

She rolled her eyes at the memory of his comment, then completed entering her notes, set aside her laptop and called Olivia. "Still a no-go on the flight," she said as soon as her friend answered. "But there's a volleyball tournament going on through tomorrow afternoon at Friars. I'm going to see if I can talk him into at least driving down there. Even if all I accomplish is getting him in the car for a drive, it's at least a step in the right direction."

"Good luck. I'd go with you, but I have a new client to evaluate tomorrow. Had to tell Meredith I wasn't going to make it to Grange's birthday party, too."

Sophie didn't need the reminder about the party. She'd debated with herself fifty times about going, even though she knew she'd have to do so in the end.

But if Sophie had to congratulate her and Meyer for finally realizing they were meant to be together, she wanted to be able to do it convincingly.

So far, her practice attempts had been abysmal.

"I'll let you know what happens," she told Olivia.

"Thanks. Meredith says Doc's coming back a week early?"

"She texted me a few days ago about it. He wants to open the practice as soon as he's back, too, so she's been busy getting everything back in place."

"Can't believe it's been six months already."

"Did you tell her you've decided to stay with Cardinale Cares?"

"I'm having lunch with her on Monday. I'll tell her then. Want to join us?"

"I can't." Sophie was glad she didn't have to make up something. "Already have plans meeting my dad and Francesca. We're having lunch at the Cliff." Even her sister had agreed to be there.

"Ooh. Hoity-toity time. Special occasion?"

"I'm not ruling it out," Sophie admitted. The Cliff was that sort of place. "We usually go places that are a lot more casual. But I'm not about to turn up my nose at their scallops."

Olivia chuckled. "Smart. Another time, then. I know we

won't be working together at Doc's, but that's no reason to stop our usual trips to Tanya's. Right?"

"Right," Sophie echoed. Then Olivia hung up, and Sophie dropped the phone onto the cushion beside her.

She shouldn't have avoided Meredith's calls all week. It just made the prospect of going to Grange's birthday party the following afternoon even more awkward.

"Get over it," she murmured. "There's nothing that's actually changed." Meredith was still her dearest friend. They'd be seeing each other nearly every day when Sophie went back to Doc's office.

She had a sudden vision of Meredith and Meyer standing in front of a church, hands clasped, vows on their lips, and she squeezed her eyes tight. Which only served to sear the image into her mind even more.

"Hello?"

She jerked, and her iced coffee tipped over onto the table. She stifled a curse, swiping at the liquid with her hand as she looked over to the source of the voice.

A slender blonde was peeking around the top of the stairs to her deck. "I'm so sorry," she said. "I didn't mean to startle you."

"It's okay." Sophie rolled off the chaise and dried her hand on her cutoffs. Obviously the No Trespassing sign at the bottom of her stairs had meant nothing. "Can I help you?"

"I'm Dana Mercer." The woman tilted her head to one side. "Staying down at the—"

"You're one of Meyer's sisters!" Sophie exclaimed, too surprised to control herself.

The woman smiled faintly. "Yes. Again, so sorry to intrude, but you wouldn't happen to have a wine opener we could borrow, would you?"

It was such an unexpected request that Sophie was momentarily bemused. She stopped trying to see some family resemblance to Meyer and beckoned. "Sure. Come on up."

Dana came up the rest of the steps and onto the deck. She wore shorts and a T-shirt, too, but in comparison to Sophie's ancient ones, the tall, slender woman's ensemble seemed more fitting for a day on a yacht.

It would definitely have earned a stamp of approval from Sophie's mother. But Sophie just ended up feeling under-dressed. She nodded toward Meyer's sister as she turned to go inside the house. "I like your necklace."

Dana's hand went to the pale blue spiral shell hanging from the long chain around her neck. "Thank you. My husband gave it to me a couple hundred years ago." She stopped shy of following Sophie through the opened slider and looked back over the deck. "You have a beautiful location."

"It's the same location as your beach house." Sophie grabbed two different wine openers from her kitchen and returned to the doorway. "But thank you. I'm rather fond of it."

"I'll bet." Dana looked at the openers that Sophie offered. "This one's fine." She chose the smaller waiter's corkscrew. "I'll bring it right back."

Sophie shook her head. "No worries." She held up the other electric one. "I have a spare."

Dana's lips curved. "I thought I did, too. Of all the things I packed—" She broke off, shaking her head. "Would you like to come down and have a glass? Our deck is almost falling down at the moment, but if you know Meyer at all, then you probably know that we'll be neighbors for a while."

Sophie felt a pinch inside her chest. "It's your first night here. I wouldn't want to intrude."

"Believe me, you wouldn't be. I don't know *where* Meyer and Cutter got off to. They left hours ago. I was going to grill steaks, but the barbecue's still in pieces in the box, so

Alexa and I may just be drinking our dinner." She waggled the corkscrew.

"I've got a grill," Sophie said before she could stop herself. She gestured at her gas grill, currently protected by a beige heat-resistant cover. "It's built in, but you're welcome to come up here and use it."

"Oh. We couldn't possibly—"

"What're neighbors for? Besides," she thought about her sister, "nobody should just drink wine for dinner."

Dana's smooth forehead wrinkled slightly. Her gaze moved over the deck, and Sophie was pretty sure she didn't imagine the hint of longing in it. "Are you sure?"

She wasn't, but that seemed to be the state of her life lately. "Absolutely."

"Well, then, yes." Dana smiled with barely veiled relief. "Thank you. I'll just…just run down and get our stuff."

"No rush. I'll be here. You might want to drive over, though. If you have a vehicle, I mean. Tide's supposed to be really high tonight, and sometimes it cuts off the walkway. It'll be a longer trek back to your place if you have to go by the road instead."

"Good to know." Dana lifted her hand in a little wave. "See you in a bit." She hurried back to the stairs and disappeared.

Sophie exhaled. Then, spurred into motion, she quickly cleaned up the rest of the spilled coffee and put her laptop away. She repositioned the patio table farther beneath the covered awning to avoid the late afternoon sun. Then she pulled out several wineglasses, double-checked that they were free of water spots and set them out on the table.

She was just unwrapping some crackers and cheese when she noticed another person on her deck. Much shorter than Dana, but still blonde.

Sophie quickly went to the slider. "Alexa?"

"Guilty." The woman seemed like a burst of contained energy in comparison to Dana's almost languid elegance, and her combination of lime-green capris with an orange-and-pink shirt was eye-popping. "You were at the lawyer's office back in April."

"I'm Sophie. He's my father. Come on in. I was just putting together a few nibbles." She waited a beat. "Your brothers show up?"

"Nope. Can't blame 'em, really. It's been a bit of a day. Not helped by the fact that Dana and I pretty much detest each other, and I can't keep my mouth shut for love nor money."

Sophie managed to keep her jaw from dropping a little.

"Don't worry. We've agreed to a truce. Turns out keeping up the vitriol for more than an hour is actually exhausting. She's bringing her Escalade around with the grub." Alexa held up two bottles of wine. "I have the important stuff. Red and white, just to cover our bases."

Feeling even more bemused, Sophie extended the electric wine-bottle opener that she hadn't yet put away.

"Perfect." Alexa, clearly practiced, tore off the foil and fit the corkscrew over the end of one of the bottles. "I love these things. So fast." She pressed the button and in seconds had removed the cork. "So, are you a lawyer like your dad? I've always thought lawyers were mostly devils, but your dad seemed a good enough sort."

Sophie shook her head. "I'm a nurse."

"Oh." Alexa beamed at her. "Well, then. Nurses are angels." She uncorked the other bottle and held it out. "Want to stick the white on ice?"

The beach house was dark when Meyer and Cutter finally returned.

Dana's fancy SUV was gone. Alexa's ancient Volkswagen was not.

"Hope we're not going to find Alexa's body in there," Cutter said. He was weaving slightly, courtesy of the bourbon he'd moved on to at the Highland Pub. They'd holed up there for as long as Meyer had dared, but Cutter still managed to navigate around the grill parts that were still spread out over half the carport without disturbing them. He tried to open the back door and grunted. "Locked."

Meyer produced a key and unlocked it.

The house inside was dark.

He flipped on a switch.

A few of the boxes had been moved around, but they still nearly blocked off the hallway.

"Bet she went to a hotel."

"Possible." But Meyer doubted it. He made no claims to knowing either one of their sisters very well. But even as fragmented as their family was, Dana had shown the most tenacity over acting like they were a family at all.

He wasn't confident that they could all make it through an entire year together, but he doubted she'd be one to actually wash out.

He glanced into the bedrooms on the right, not surprised to find them empty.

"No body," Cutter said, looking in the room across the hall. He accidentally knocked into a box and impatiently shoved it aside with his foot. "How much freaking stuff do they need?"

"Not everyone can live out of a ditty bag like you." He flipped on another light and unlocked the front door, leaving it wide. The breeze coming off the ocean was stiff and cool and welcoming after the crowded pub.

"*You* can."

"I didn't bring all my gear. The advantage of having an apartment nearby." Unlike Cutter, he hadn't been drinking all afternoon, and he pulled a beer out of the fridge before going back out front.

Cutter was unfolding one of the sand chairs that constituted the only furniture he'd brought, save his tent and some computer equipment. "I smell steak."

So did Meyer. He looked toward Sophie's place. A few lights were flickering beyond the wind-tossed trees. "There weren't any in the fridge."

Cutter flopped down onto the low-slung chair and stretched out his legs. "Should have eaten more at the pub."

"Probably." The place had been crowded as all hell with players from some volleyball tournament going on over at Friars. Except for a beer, Meyer had left the imbibing to Cutter. But he wished he'd eaten more, too. His stomach was growling.

He peered again at the flickering light from Sophie's place. "Come on." He kicked the base of Cutter's chair.

"Back to the pub? Don't blame you. That chick who was hitting on you is probably still there."

The last thing Meyer was interested in was the brittle, overly tanned woman who'd cornered him at the pub. "We're not going there."

Cutter rolled out of the chair and pushed himself up from the sand. "Then where?"

He pointed. "To find our steaks."

Chapter Sixteen

"I *love* this one." Dana carefully picked up a sand dollar from the felt-lined box. "It's real?" She held it up to the light streaming from inside the house, peering at it.

They'd eaten their steak and killed one bottle of wine already. Now it was dark and the sea spray had chased them as close to the house as they could get without pushing them inside. But none of them seemed ready to give in to that, even though it was getting progressively cooler.

"I found three of them right here on Cardinale Beach not long after I bought this place." Sophie tucked her leg beneath her and adjusted the woven throw over her lap. "King tide had washed them past your seawall."

Alexa was sitting cross-legged on the lounge, her blanket pulled up to her chin. "Our seawall?" She looked a little startled. "The water gets that close to the house?"

"Not often. A couple times a year at most."

"Do I need to learn how to swim?" She didn't sound like she was entirely joking.

Dana gave her a sideways look. "You grew up in California. How can you not know how to swim?"

"I grew up in the middle of the city! Not everyone had country club memberships like you did!"

"I'm sorry," Sophie interjected. "I know it's none of my business, but *how* can you all be Pietro Cardinale's kids and have had such different childhoods?"

"The only thing consistent about Pietro was his wham-bam style when it came to marriage," Dana said. She, too, had taken the offer of a throw, but it was draped around her shoulders like a scarf. "The longest he was married to anyone was Sandra. Meyer's mother. When my mother got pregnant, he divorced Sandra and married her."

"And changed his name to *Pietro*," Alexa sniffed.

"Don't blame that on my mother," Dana said swiftly. "That's the name he was already using by then." She looked at Sophie. "As if his artwork had more élan with a more exotic name."

"He was a regular hit-and-runner," Alexa said. "Knock 'em up, marry 'em and move on to the next. Why any of them grieved his death is beyond me. Far as I'm concerned, he lived the life of a schmuck and died as one, too." She plucked a tiny orangish whorl from the case. "Can you really make earrings out of these?"

"Yeah." Corinne was the seamstress, but Sophie was the one who'd learned how to make jewelry. Nothing as fancy as what she'd bought Leda for her junior high graduation but enough to suit herself and make an occasional gift. "I have a really fine drill that can make the tiniest of holes. Add a little wire. Voilà." She tucked her hair behind her ear to show the small dangling earrings she was wearing. "Just like these. But what about child support and that sort of thing? Was he really that uninvolved in your lives after—"

"He moved on to the next shiny object?" Dana nodded.

"He couldn't avoid the child support, and no matter what Alexa's implied, he did pay it. That, plus spousal maintenance—"

"Unlike my beloved rotten ex-spouse," Alexa muttered.

"—but he really *was* that uninvolved," Dana said as if Alexa hadn't said a thing. She replaced the sand dollar on the felt. "What did we spend, three—" she looked to Alexa "—Christmases together?"

Alexa nodded. "They were awful."

"Really dreadful," Dana concluded. "Whoops." She turned the wine bottle she'd reached for upside down. Not even a drop remained. "That's two down," she said regretfully.

"I can open another," Sophie offered.

"If you do, I'll fall asleep right here and sleep on your deck," Dana said.

"Can't do that," Alexa said, yawning right on cue. "What if her father—" she jerked her head in Sophie's direction "—does a bed check just to see if we're following the letter of the law?"

Sophie couldn't imagine her dad doing anything of the sort, but she also wasn't privy to the finer details of Pietro Cardinale's will.

"Well, first, I can say that sleeping on my deck is a sure way to wake up very cold and very wet. So no matter how bad the conditions are down at the beach house, you'll at least be warm and dry there. But," she added, "I do have peanut butter cookies."

Alexa's hand went up. "Count me in."

Sophie smiled and pushed aside her throw and went inside. The evening had been much more entertaining than she'd expected. Meyer had complained about the way his sisters argued, but they hadn't done much of it in front of Sophie.

Humming under her breath along with the music on the radio, she took several cookies out of the sealed jar where she kept them and placed them on a plate.

Then she grabbed three clean glasses and carried everything out to the patio. "I have milk if…" She trailed off at the sight of Meyer and Cutter. "Where'd you come from?"

Cutter homed in on the plate of cookies like a hound dog. "Homemade?"

She nodded, still watching Meyer. He'd placed his palm flat on the closed lid of the gas grill.

"It's cold," he said.

"Because we grilled the steaks hours ago," Dana pointed out. "Where on earth did you two go?"

"We needed a screwdriver." Cutter picked up one of the oversized cookies, smelled it and broke it in half. "Peanut butter?"

"Yes."

He ate both halves in two bites. "I may have to marry you."

"Pretty sure not," Sophie said dryly. Despite all her efforts, her gaze still slid to Meyer. He wore his usual jeans and a dark T-shirt, but in her mind, she was still seeing him with his unbuttoned shirt.

And it didn't matter that she'd had a perfectly good reason to do that unbuttoning. She still felt flushed now. She was going to have to figure out a way to stop that because she couldn't very well get hot and bothered by her best friend's…whatever definition Meyer fit where Meredith was concerned.

She set the plate on the table where Dana and Alexa could reach. "The rest of the steaks are in the fridge," she said. "If you want to grill them, you'd better get a move on." With perfect timing, a wave broke against the boulders below her deck, sending up a tall spray of mist that curled over the plexi. "That's only going to get worse."

In response, he lifted the grill lid. "I'll take my chances."

She shrugged as if she didn't care what he did.

"What're all the shells?" Another cookie already in his hand, Cutter's attention had moved on.

"She makes jewelry with them," Alexa said. "Show him your earrings, Sophie."

Feeling self-conscious, Sophie pushed her hair behind her ear. Cutter reached out and touched a dangle, and Meyer hit the ignition on the grill, sending up a whoosh of flame.

Sophie looked away.

"Awkward much?" Alexa asked sotto voce.

"Alexa," Dana muttered as she stood. "I'll get the steaks."

Sophie was perfectly aware that Cutter's sly amusement was aimed at his brother. She just wasn't sure what he thought he'd be accomplishing by flirting with her.

"What's Meredith doing tonight?" she asked deliberately.

Meyer returned her look with an impassive one of his own. "You'd know better than me."

She wondered if Meredith had said something to him about Sophie missing her calls. Then she decided she was being stupid. He and Meredith had better things to talk about than her. "I'm sure she's getting ready for Grange's party tomorrow," she answered her own question.

"Here." Dana returned with a package wrapped in butcher paper and handed it to him. "Already seasoned with salt and pepper, and that's all they need. So don't go asking for steak sauce—" she looked sideways at Alexa "—or ketchup."

"There's salad left, too." Sophie escaped into the house.

The girls had been just fine when it was the two of them.

And Meyer and Cutter had been just fine when Sophie had been with the two of them before.

But now, with all four of them? Tension had filled the air just as tangibly as the mist from the waves.

She took her time gathering the salad and place settings, but she could only procrastinate so long before it would be obvious.

She carried everything outside again. The waves were breaking even harder against the plexi. The decking glistened with water only a few feet from Meyer standing at her gas grill, where two steaks sizzled over the flame.

"Alexa?" Dana nudged her sister. "We still have boxes to deal with. Beds to make up."

Alexa looked like she was prepared to argue, but she unwound her legs and handed Sophie her throw. "We should do this again," she said.

Sophie maintained her smile, but it took an effort. "Sounds fun." She looked beyond Alexa to Dana. "I'll bring the wine."

Dana smiled and looked around again at the deck. "Might be worth a very cold and very wet night," she said. Then she surprised Sophie entirely when she gave her a quick hug before she followed Alexa down to the sidewalk that led to her carport.

"More for me," Cutter commented and reached for his third cookie. He stepped inside the house. "Mind if I snoop around? See what kind of improvements we should be making at our place?"

She minded being left alone with Meyer a lot but would never say so. And besides, Dana and Alexa had wanted to do the same thing shortly after they'd arrived. "Help—"

He was already gone, moving down the hallway.

"—yourself," she finished faintly.

She let her gaze skid over Meyer again before quickly focusing on folding the throws and returning them to the basket next to her fireplace. Then she retrieved the sweater near her front door and pulled it on. And even though she had pretty strong feelings when it came to overindulging, she opened another bottle of wine and poured herself a glass.

"Liquid courage, Fifi?"

She didn't bother looking at Cutter. She just pulled out another wineglass and filled it partway. "Save the effort, Cutter. You're not really interested, and even if your brother could hear us, it wouldn't matter."

His lips quirked. "Who says I'm not interested?"

She gave him a sidelong look. "I am."

"Figure you have good powers of observation, then?"

She slid the wineglass toward him. "Good enough."

He surprised her by not taking it. Instead, he winked. "We'll see, won't we?" Then he went outside where Meyer had just flipped the steaks.

She shook her head.

Just then she wished that both of the Cartell-slash-Cardinale men were anywhere other than her back deck.

She poured Cutter's wine down the drain, washed and dried the glass and returned it to the cabinet. She moved her seashell collection back to the spare bedroom where it belonged and, with nothing else left to do, picked up her wine and went into her own bedroom, closing the door.

Yes, it made her a terrible hostess.

But then again, she hadn't exactly invited her guests, either.

The bodyboard that she'd bought Grange for his birthday was sitting on her bed.

Even though there was no hope of disguising what it was, she set her wineglass down on the nightstand and unfurled the bright blue-and-green wrapping paper and began taping it in place.

When it was finished, she added the gigantic green bow that she'd also bought and left her bedroom again, intending to carry it out to her SUV.

Meyer sat at the table on the deck, his attention on his nearly empty plate.

There was no sign of Cutter.

Her hands felt suddenly nerveless, and she left the bodyboard propped against the wall next to the front door and turned to head back to her bedroom just like the coward that she was.

That was when she noticed the small floral plate sitting on the breakfast bar.

Her heart skidded around unevenly as she walked over to it and slowly traced the scalloped edges with her fingertip.

Her grandmother's plate.

When she looked up, Meyer was watching her.

Her mouth dried. She lifted the plate slightly. "I figured you'd lost it or something."

"Or something."

She set the plate down again with excessive care. "Any more panic attacks?"

His gaze narrowed. "No."

"The magic of love," she muttered.

He still heard. "I'm not in love with Meredith."

She chewed the inside of her cheek. "I don't care if you are." She went outside, walking past him to the grill. "But if you hurt her, there won't be enough left of you for anyone to find when I'm finished." John had already done enough damage. Meredith didn't deserve more.

Meyer had already turned off the burners and closed the lid. She checked the gas valve, finding it, too, already closed. She shook out the protective cover and fought the growing breeze until she'd fastened in place once more.

When she turned back, he was standing behind her. "She is not in love with me."

Her teeth set on edge. "What are you doing here, Meyer? Is the idea of spending your first night under your father's roof so terrible that you'd rather be *here*?"

"Sophie—" He broke off, looking irritated.

She lifted her chin. "What?"

"Just shut up," he said roughly and kissed her.

Shock drilled right through her like electricity going to ground and she yanked back, but he caught the hand she would have slapped him with.

"You don't want to do that," he said softly.

Her fingers curled. All she had to do was twist her hand away and she could free herself.

So why didn't she?

"You don't know what I want."

His thumb pressed along her wrist, feeling unbearably intimate as their pulses throbbed. "Don't I?"

"Meredith—"

"Has nothing to do with us." Her hair was blowing between them, and he moved it out of her face. "Meredith's my *family*," he said gruffly. "I owe her everything." He lowered his head until she could feel the warmth of his breath against her temple. Her ear. "But that doesn't mean I want her like this. That I ever have."

His hair brushed her cheek when he kissed the side of her neck, and she shuddered. Weak. She was just weak and somehow, instead of fighting the thumb on her wrist, her fingers were twining with his and she was arching over the arm he'd slid behind her back. Then he was kissing her throat. Her jaw. And thoughts of anyone else but him were slipping from her mind like grains of sand.

She stared blindly up at the dark sky, pinpricks of starlight flickering, feeling the rush of another wave spend itself against the deck.

She couldn't think, couldn't do anything but feel. The cold, salty mist that drifted over them even after the wave receded, only to gather up all over again and surge with even more force. The heat coming off him that melted everything inside her, leaving her hollow and wanting.

She twisted her free hand into his hair and found his mouth with hers.

How many times had she dreamt about this?

How many nights had she wrenched awake, aching and pulsing and desperately empty?

None of it—none of it had been remotely close to reality.

She twined her arms around his shoulders, gasping as he lifted her off her feet, dragging her slowly up his body until she was pinned between him and the thick plexiglass that vibrated from the force of an inexorable ocean. His hands were between them. Under her shirt. On her breasts. Then between her legs. Swirling. Delving.

And then *he* was there. Hard. Perfect. Filling and more inexorable than any ocean could ever be.

She shattered around him, so easily, so profoundly, that she didn't care that she cried out. Didn't care about anything except him and the endlessness of that moment until she felt the waves crash through him, too, and she cried out all over again for the undying pleasure of it.

Then finally, finally, he let her slide slowly back down again. Limp. Undone.

He cradled her face in his hands and slowly, gently kissed her lips. Her cheeks. "You okay?" His voice was low. Raw.

She wasn't. She never would be again. Because she couldn't deny the truth anymore.

Despite everything, she was in love with Meyer Cartell.

Her breath hitched inside her chest, and she nodded silently, gathering his hands together and kissing his knuckles. She knew there was no future for them. Not when there was too much in the past.

Tomorrow, she'd deal with the guilt of Corinne. Of Meredith.

But just this once, she needed to have something to hold onto. Even if it was only for one night.

She took his hand and led him inside.

She pushed the slider closed with one hand and turned on the fireplace. She shivered despite the flames that leapt to life. Then she slowly pulled off her wet clothes, leaving them in a pile on the floor as she dragged his equally wet shirt over his head and he toed off his shoes.

"You're cold." His warm, deft hands slid over her goose-pimpling flesh.

"So are you." She pushed her hands down his jeans, dragging everything off in one smooth sweep. Then she gathered it all up in her arms.

"Wait. Where are you going?"

"To put your stuff in the dryer," she said.

He gave a strangled laugh. "*Now?*"

"I'll be back." She boldly looked him up and down. Not a nurse at all. Just a woman. "I'm sure you can…entertain yourself for a couple minutes."

Then she smiled tremulously and walked down the hall, feeling his gaze on her bare backside as certainly as a caress.

Chapter Seventeen

"I *can* fire you, you know."

"You can do that after I bring you back." Sophie patted the wheeled transport chair she'd brought with her. "Come on, Otto. Let's go. It's time you got out of this room. I've already talked to a guy I know with beach security down at Friars," she said. "I'll be able to get you so close to the players you'll be able to see the beads of sweat on their brows without your binoculars even if you decide not to leave the car."

His eyes narrowed. "You're in a good mood."

Sophie raised her brows. "Aren't I always?"

"Not this good." Otto tapped his chin with a long, bony finger. "Something's different," he mused.

She was *not* going to blush. She patted the chair again. "Let's go. I've already got your walker loaded up in my SUV."

"Walker," he muttered, dismissively. "Might as well wear a sign that says you're old."

"They're an assistive device to help with mobility and balance."

He sniffed, waving away her help when he slid off the bed to stand on his good leg. "My balance is fine." He hopped slightly and pivoted, landing on the chair with a huff. "Stupid cast," he muttered, grunting slightly as he lifted his cast onto the footrest.

She hid her triumph, unlocked the wheels and pushed his chair across the room to the mirrored elevator doors.

His hair was particularly Einstein-ish that morning, and the white silk shirt he wore with khaki-green sweatpants from his seemingly inexhaustible collection of them looked as if it had been splashed with scarlet paint. She'd seen bloody emergency room traumas that were less garish.

And she couldn't seem to get the smile off her face.

Otto's gaze met hers in the mirrored reflection. "Ah. World turned sideways," he said knowingly.

The door opened, and she quickly pushed his chair inside. She set the wheels and closed the elevator door. The car jerked smoothly and a moment later deposited them on the main level.

She hadn't presented the trip out as a real choice to him but had simply acted as if his cooperation were a foregone conclusion. But she was quite aware that—until he was actually strapped into her SUV—he could choose to call a halt at any moment, which was why she didn't waste any time rolling the chair through the big house and out onto the red-bricked drive.

She'd left the passenger door open on her SUV when she'd loaded up the walker, and she locked the chair wheels again when she reached it. "We'll take it slow—" She broke off, watching him reach up to the top of the door with one arm and pull himself to standing. Then he turned and landed on the front seat. "All right, then," she said, more than a little surprised at how easily he'd accomplished the task.

The man was progressing faster than they'd expected.

She'd pushed the passenger seat as far back as it would go, which allowed plenty of length to accommodate his cast, and as soon as he was settled, she hurried around to the driver's side and they set off.

It took about thirty minutes to drive down to Friars Beach, and as she'd arranged with the beach patrol, she nosed her way through the crowds and pulled up into a spot that had been held. She stuck her head out the window and waved. "Thanks, Chris," she yelled.

He raised his thumb and turned back to directing the traffic.

She looked at Otto. "Well?" She waved her hand across the windshield that looked directly onto one of the sand courts. "Want to get closer or sit right here?"

His attention was on two female spectators who were rubbing sunblock all over their tanned limbs. "This'll do."

She checked her watch, making a bet with herself that Otto would be out of the vehicle and, walker or not, getting a closer view before the morning was through.

She rolled down all the windows and got out long enough to retrieve two cold sports drinks from the ice chest in her back seat. She gave one to Otto and got back into her seat, settling in for the show.

And a show it was.

For two solid hours, Otto was so enraptured, he didn't try to put his hands on Sophie's knee even once.

But she'd been wrong about him wanting to get closer. "If you're worried about the sand getting in your cast, I'm prepared."

But he shook his head. "You're a natural-born caretaker,

Sophie Lane. But this is more than enough." He rested his head against the backrest. "I've seen enough."

"Not natural-born enough to realize how tiring this would be for you."

"Just drive, my dear. No need to remind me how old I am."

She carefully worked her way back out of the crowded area. "Is there anywhere else you'd like to go while we're out? I still have an hour before I need to be somewhere." It would cut it close, but she didn't *have* to go home to change first for Grange's birthday party. And really, the more she filled her time before the party, the less she had to think about how she was going to tell Meredith what had happened between her and Meyer…

"Where's the airfield?"

She felt a jolt. She knew she'd be seeing Meyer later at the party, but would he be at the airfield? He hadn't left her place until nearly dawn, and she hadn't seen his truck at the beach house when she'd left that morning for Otto's. "Not far. We have time for a drive-by at least. The biplane is almost always parked out on the grass, if you want to see her."

He smiled faintly. "Sure."

She could have drummed her glee onto the steering wheel, but she contained herself and headed inland.

It took less time than she'd expected to reach the airfield; all of the traffic turned out to be concentrated down at Friars for the tournament. She turned onto Perimeter Road and pulled off to one side when Otto requested.

He hunched forward, looking out the window at the buildings in the distance. Two JCS jets were visible, as was the biplane parked out on the grassy fairway strip. But other than that, the place looked quiet.

"When I was young, this place was nothing but dirt," Otto murmured.

"Did you grow up here?" He'd only said he'd bought his mansion on a whim.

He shook his head. "I never grew up."

Sophie chuckled. "Maybe I should start calling you Peter Pan, then."

"Not the worst name I've heard." He winked and sat back in his seat. "Now, take me home so you can get on with—" he waved a hand "—whoever's really put that rose in your cheeks."

She felt her cheeks get even warmer. She didn't exactly want to be late for the party despite the cowardly part of her that did, but she also didn't want to lose any momentum where Otto's progress was concerned. She was almost convinced that if she could just get him to see Ollie up close, her allure would draw him in just as surely as it did everyone else. "Are you sure you don't want to get closer?"

"Haven't you learned? I'm an observer, Sophie my girl."

She let it go. Progress was progress, and now that she'd gotten him out and about once, it would be even easier the next time. Regardless of the activity.

"An observer," she repeated as she pulled her SUV around and headed the way they'd come. "Why is that?"

He lifted his skinny shoulders. "Eh. Why's the earth round? Why's the sky blue? Sometimes it's okay not to question. Sometimes it's okay to accept that some things just are." He folded his arms across his scarlet-spattered shirt and closed his eyes.

The wind from the opened window was having a field day with his hair even more than hers, which was at least contained in a ponytail. By the time she returned him to his third-floor bedroom, he looked like an escapee from a wind tunnel.

"Olivia will be here tomorrow," she reminded him before she left.

"Thank you, Sophie."

She smiled at him, but he was once more ensconced in his window, long fingers slowly adjusting the knob on the side of his scope, and didn't even notice.

It wasn't until she got back in her SUV and had brushed out the mess of her hair that she saw the text message from Meredith on her phone. Expecting it to be something about the party again, at first the words didn't even make sense to her.

And then they did.

OMG! He proposed this morning.

Everything inside her fell. Of course he had. She had a perfect track record, didn't she? She pinched her eyes together for a long moment, then shakily composed her reply.

Congrats. I knew you and Meyer were meant to be.

The response came immediately.

Are you crazy? I'm talking about Walker. What do I do?

"Happy birthday, dear *Gra-ange*, happy birthday to you!"

More than two dozen kids crowded around the picnic table in Meredith's backyard and hooted when Grange bent over the blazing candles on his baseball diamond–shaped cake, extinguishing all but one with his single blow.

Grange just laughed at the jeers from his friends, licked his thumb and forefinger and squeezed the remaining flame out of existence.

"John used to do that," Meredith muttered to Meyer before working her way through the sturdy bodies to reach the table, where she began slicing the cake.

Meyer looked down at Sophie's blonde head.

Grange's party had been well underway when she'd finally arrived, looking hardly any older than the teenaged guests in her bike shorts and a sports bra, her wind-tossed ponytail situated high on her head.

But when he'd headed toward her, she'd given him a warning stare that had stopped him in his tracks, and in the time since, there had been no evidence of an early thaw.

He could still taste her skin on his lips, but it was as if the previous night hadn't happened at all.

As if they were right back to where they'd always been.

Maybe even more so.

"That's about the fifth time she's mentioned John since I got here," he commented in a low voice.

She didn't look up at him, but he knew she'd heard him. "What do you want me to do about it?" Then she moved away again to plunge her hand into the barrel full of ice and drinks.

"Ice cream," Meredith said over the noise of Grange's friends. "I forgot the ice cream." She looked as frazzled as she sounded. "Meyer, would you mind? It's still in the freezer."

What he wanted was to know what kind of bug had gotten into Sophie's bonnet. But this was Grange's birthday party and Meyer was already struggling with the specter of John Skinner that seemed to loom over them.

The adults, at any rate.

Grange, at least, seemed to be doing fine.

"On it." He jogged up the back porch steps to go inside the house.

Under the best of circumstances, Meredith's place was

chaotic, and hosting a birthday party with close to thirty kids had only made it more so.

He found two gallons of ice cream in the freezer behind a red leather purse. It was Meredith's.

Her idea of security with a houseful of kids?

He shook his head and left the purse where it was and carried the ice cream out to the party, where Sophie snatched the containers out of his hands as if they were in danger of contamination.

Then she edged her way through Grange's friends until she reached Meredith.

Whatever her problem was, he couldn't do anything about it. Not now. Not here.

Which meant he just stood there, increasingly frustrated while the two women worked silently next to each other. One petite and fair, the other statuesque and dark. Both making their mark on his life for very different reasons.

If John hadn't died, would Meyer have come back to Cape Cardinale at all? Would he have finally lived up to his promise, and they'd all be here together now, celebrating Grange's birthday?

Or would Meyer still be somewhere on the other side of the world, eating and breathing military life and never knowing there was someone like Sophie out there?

Both women looked up at him, as if they'd heard his thoughts.

But Meredith's gaze went past him and widened slightly. Her cheeks paled. The piece of cake that she'd just sliced slid out of her fingers, and despite Sophie's quick attempt to catch it, fell onto the grass.

Meyer looked over his shoulder. The relief of seeing Walker Armstrong standing there and not the ghost of John Skinner was almost humiliating.

Meredith handed the cake knife to Sophie and rushed

past Meyer. She grabbed Walker's arm and yanked him back into the kitchen, slamming the door shut after them.

Meyer looked back at Sophie. She'd focused her frown on the closed kitchen door. Then she seemed to shake herself and smiled determinedly at Grange and his buddies.

She rapidly added a fresh slice of cake to the plate that was still waiting and handed it to her next customer.

Meyer joined her, taking up the job of ice-cream scooper that she'd abandoned while taking on Meredith's duties.

"I've got it—" She broke off when their hands brushed reaching for the next paper plate. Her fingers retreated in a curl.

For years, Meyer had been pretending life was normal. He ought to have felt pretty practiced at it by now, but he didn't.

Not after last night.

"How long are you going to act like nothing's changed?" he asked under his breath and plopped two scoops of ice cream onto the plate before holding it out for her.

"This is *not* the time." Her lips barely moved. She slapped down a slice of cake next to the ice cream and smiled brilliantly at the next kid in line. "Enjoy!" Her voice was overly bright.

Meyer grabbed another plate. Plop. Plop. "And what's your excuse going to be then?" She'd had an ax to grind where he was concerned too long for there not to be. "There's never gonna be a time. Is there?"

Her brown eyes flashed then shifted away. She dumped another slice of cake onto the plate. "Just. Scoop," she enunciated through her teeth.

He did.

Serving up one plate and then another and another until the ice cream containers were empty and misshapen from his attacks and the only thing left of the cake were globs of green and brown clinging to the edges of the waxy cardboard.

Too many things in his life were things he couldn't control. He'd be damned if this was going to be one more. "Sophie—"

"Just don't Meyer. Last night should never have happened." Her sudden words came out in a rush.

"That's not the message you delivered last night."

She snatched up the thick cardboard and manhandled it into a fold. "I guess the cold light of day helped me to see sense." She stomped down onto the cardboard with one foot, flattening it with the ferocity of a sledgehammer. Then she shoved it into the trash bag that was already overfull of discarded plates from the hamburgers that Meredith had grilled.

He wondered if she was imagining his face on the cardboard, but then her expression went oddly blank and he realized that the kitchen door had opened, and Meredith practically stumbled out of the house.

Her color was high, her expression agitated, and Meyer's protective instincts reared. "If he's upset her—" He took a step toward her, but Sophie grabbed his arm, spinning to face him while at the same time blocking his way toward Meredith.

"Just hold on," she said urgently. "Don't…don't do anything crazy. Not where Grange can see—"

Meyer could feel the distinct imprint of each one of her fingers on his arm. Could feel, too, the warmth of her torso and the press of her thigh against his. He was feeling more than a little crazy, and it had nothing do with Meredith. "Grange can see the same thing I do. His mother looks like she's put her finger in an electric socket!"

She made a strangled sound and released him.

In a flash, she'd moved over to Meredith and tucked her arm through her friend's and drew her away from Meyer.

He frowned, then felt like an idiot when Meredith suddenly turned her back on everyone, and he realized she was adjusting the misaligned buttons on her shirt.

Grange and his friends—preoccupied with the new basketball hoop that had been Meredith's gift for him—didn't notice a thing.

At least, not until Sophie's loud "*Just tell Walker you'll marry him!*"

Everyone stopped what they were doing and looked toward her.

Meredith was staring at Sophie as if she'd announced there were aliens among them. "Easy for you to say! You won't even let yourself trust *Meyer* and he's the most trustworthy guy I know! But you actually thought he proposed to me this morning!"

Sophie's head whipped up, and she looked at Meyer. The guilt in her eyes was plain.

Realization tasted acrid.

Even after last night, Sophie believed Meyer had proposed to Meredith.

He exhaled and turned away only to run into the trash can and send it crashing. He swore and knelt down, shoveling the mess back into the big rubber can, heedless of whether it made it inside the bag or not.

Sophie knelt beside him, grabbing the flattened cake board to help scoop. "Meyer—"

"Don't bother." He grabbed the cardboard out of her hand and pitched it after the piles of paper plates and half-eaten hamburgers and plastic cups still sticky with soda. "I see what happened."

"But you don't." She followed on his heels when he started carting the can toward the garage, where Meredith kept her curbside bins stored. "You can't possibly. It was just a knee-jerk reaction. For a minute. It didn't last."

He shoved open the side door of the garage. The fact that he noticed the old door had a loose hinge was strangely appropriate. He was feeling old and a lot unhinged.

He flipped open the lid on Meredith's bin and let the contents inside the trash can rain down into it. "If it didn't last, then why was last night a mistake?" He slammed the lid back down and tossed the trash can aside. It rolled and hit the side of the canvas-shrouded Camaro that occupied the rest of the old garage. "Why the hell is it so hard for you to admit that there's something more between us?"

Her hands twisted in front of her, and even in the dingy light, he could see the glistening in her eyes. "Relationships never work out for me, all right? All I could think was *four for four* and—"

"Four for four?" He kicked the rubber can again because it was that or punch something, and he wasn't sure the garage walls would stay standing if he did. And he damn sure wasn't going to let a few tears soothe it all away. "You know more about me than even Meredith. And you're right. Relationships will never work when you won't even try." She was a runner's wall that he'd slammed into, and he didn't have the stamina to keep going. "Go home, Sophie. Just go home."

Chapter Eighteen

Meyer was sitting behind the wheel of John's old Camaro when Meredith came looking.

"Sophie left." Her voice was quiet.

He nodded.

"She told me what happened."

He nodded. He'd expected that, too.

"Do you think there's a possibility that you might have been too hard on her?"

He rolled his gaze her direction. "I never claimed to be a catch, Meredith. But she's always going to jump to the worst conclusion where I'm concerned. She won't let herself trust—" He looked back at the dashboard of the car. There was enough that he was responsible for without inviting blame for the things that he wasn't. "I can't," he concluded wearily. "Shouldn't you be supervising Grange's party or something?"

"After cake, half of them always leave." Meredith slowly moved around the Camaro, tugging off the dust-ridden canvas cover the rest of the way and letting it fall to the ground. "The other half, including our new thirteen-year-old, have gone to the park down the block."

Thirteen. For about the hundredth time, Meyer thought about John.

He was the one who should have been here.

Not Meyer.

And now, apparently, there was Walker.

Sophie's words were still echoing inside his head. "I take it that Walker wants to marry you," he said.

Meredith was slowly moving through the dust motes that glimmered in the light, her hand caressing the car's racy lines. "How many hours d'you suppose you and John spent trying to restore this old thing?" she asked instead of answering.

"God only knows." It had been built in 1969. It had been old even before John had bought it. "It wasn't even running when we first met in college."

"Because he needed you to fix the engine," Meredith murmured. "Which you did." Her lips quirked sadly, and she pulled open the passenger door. It stuck slightly and squeaked, but she managed and slid down into the bucket seat. "Just like you fixed so many other things for him."

He'd been too late to fix what mattered most.

"I didn't expect to feel this old at forty-three," he admitted.

"Shouldn't have run off Sophie, then. She'd keep you young even when you're eighty-three."

The fact that she was right didn't make him feel any better. He pressed his hand against the wheel, and the horn tooted. He swore. "Didn't expect it to work," he admitted.

Meredith traced the scrolled letters on the dashboard. "John used to honk when he'd pick me up."

"I remember. Always told him to get his lazy ass out of the car and go to the door."

She chuckled sadly. "He did once. When we first started going out? Driving his grandma's car back then. That's how he knew how bad things were with my mom. I think he fell in love with me the same way he was always picking up stray animals. Couldn't stand it when someone didn't have a home."

"Because he knew how it felt. The only one he had was his grandmother."

"I know. He got to feel like he was rescuing me, and I got to feel like I was some hot stuff. High school girl running all over town with the hottest car and the hottest college guys. Nobody talked about poor Meredith with the mother who liked to forget she existed." She closed her fist over the knob on the shifter. "John was the first person who made me feel like I mattered. And despite everything that came after, I never stopped loving him because of that. You remember my last year of high school?"

More vividly than he wanted to. "It was twenty years ago."

"Kind of you. Twenty-one now."

Corinne had made the same correction. "What are you going to do about Walker?"

"Nothing." She leaned her head back against the seat. "Yet."

"He proposed this morning." A fresh stab slid through him.

"Yes." She let go of the shifter and adjusted her seat. It fell back until it was nearly flat, and she laughed a little. "Some things don't change." She pulled it back up, struggling with it a little until it stayed in place.

"You didn't say yes."

"No."

"Did you say no?"

"No."

"Mmm."

"Did you know John got Corinne pregnant?"

He jerked, knocking his knee on the hard steering wheel. "Pregnant!"

Meredith's eyebrows lifted. "I'll take that as a no."

He shifted uncomfortably. The car's seats had never been all that great. "I knew she was after him, but no, I did not know."

"Sophie believes you were the father."

"How the fu—" He broke off. "Corinne tell her that?" It explained a hell of a lot.

Meredith lifted her shoulders. "You'd have to ask Sophie. Or Corinne, I guess. Assuming she's learned the art of honesty since then. Sophie says she had an abortion. And that you broke her heart."

"I never touched Corinne." But there'd been plenty of times when they'd all piled into this very car while Corinne's mother had watched, thin-lipped and disapproving, from the front door and little Sophie had watched from around the curtains in a window above the garage "The only heart she had was to take what belonged to someone else," he said flatly.

"John could have said no."

"Why aren't you pissed off?"

Meredith gave that same sad, weary laugh. "I spent plenty of time being angry. But it takes a lot of energy to maintain it. And how do I know that all of it wasn't my fault, anyway?" She exhaled, slowly rocking her head back and forth against the seat behind her.

"You didn't cause John to cheat on you," Meyer said flatly. "Not with Corinne. Not with the others." Third strike, she'd said. That was two more than he'd known about.

"In my head—" she tapped her forehead once "—I get that. But in my heart? Well. Tougher terrain."

"Is that why you haven't told Walker yes?"

"That's what Sophie asked, too." She turned sideways in her seat, hitching one knee beneath her. "You need to go and talk to her, Meyer."

"She doesn't trust me. She'll never trust me."

"Because she was a kid when she thought she learned all about you."

"She's not a kid now. She should judge me for the man she *knows*."

"Now, you sound like wounded male talking." She lifted her hands peaceably when he glared. "No offense."

Offense taken.

"I've known her for ten years, Meyer. Do you know how many times she's been serious about a guy?" She held up her fingers. "Three. You know how many times they've broken it off and married someone else? And I don't mean eventually. I mean, like, within months. Sometimes even weeks." She waved her fingers in front of his face. "Three. And then along comes you. The guy she already feels disloyal for falling for and—"

"She hasn't fallen for me," he dismissed roughly.

"Then you're not as smart as I've always thought you were."

"It wouldn't matter anyway," he forced the words out. Not because they weren't true, but because they were. "I'm like the old man. Itchy feet. I wouldn't stick."

Meredith laughed. Not wearily. Not sadly. "Wow. You *are* really not as smart." She patted his arm. "I hate to break it to you, Meyer, but you're about as un-itchy as they come."

She was wrong, but he didn't have the heart to correct her. "The two of you going to be okay?"

"Me and Walker?"

He didn't smile, but it was tough not to. "You and Sophie."

It wasn't often he saw Meredith blush. "We'll be fine, too." With another squeak and a shove, she got the car door open. "Do you think I should save the Camaro for Grange's sixteenth?"

"Leda's going to be sixteen before Grange."

"God no. She's already the worst kind of beautiful—the kind who doesn't know it. Add a vintage hotrod?" She shook her head. "Not going to happen while there's breath in my body."

"Then save it for Grange."

"Ach." Meredith grimaced impatiently. "Just find a buyer." She leaned against the car door to close it.

"What's wrong with him having it? Something to remember his father."

"They can remember something else. Something that didn't involve another woman." She headed for the doorway.

"Meredith."

She glanced back.

"What's the deal with the purse in the freezer?"

Her cheeks got red again. She jabbed her finger toward him. "*You* try keeping your wits about you when you get a marriage proposal before coffee!"

Sophie shoved the filter in the coffee maker and stabbed the Power button with a fierce finger before she turned to face her sister. "All Dad wanted to do was tell his daughters that he and Francesca are getting married. And you couldn't even give him that."

It was Monday evening. She might have corralled some of her anger on the traffic-jam of a drive from Cape Cardinale to her sister's apartment, but it had escaped all over again when she'd found Corinne sprawled on her couch in a drunken stupor.

Sophie had nearly gotten right back into her car.

"Don't glare at me like that," Corinne said, her head propped on her hands.

"Have you been to *any* meetings since you called me last week?"

"What for? I'm just gonna fail again."

Sophie crossed her arms and leaned back against the cluttered kitchen counter, steeling herself. The coffee maker was burbling behind her, almost in accompaniment to the emotions churning inside her. "With an attitude like that, you probably will." Her voice was flat. She looked from her sister to the rest of the apartment that looked like a recycling center for spent beer cans.

Every other time this happened, she'd gone around, cleaning up. Putting things to rights. As if by having some order around her, Corinne might find a toehold to push herself up.

"Is that why you came here?" Corinne's voice was dull. "To spread your vast wisdom?"

"I came here to tell you that dad was really hurt, Corinne! You promised to be there for lunch, and instead you were—" She waved her hand tellingly.

Their lunch at the Cliff should have been a time for celebration. Instead, between Sophie's misery from the afternoon before and Corinne's absence, it had been anything but.

"What're you going to do next month when it's their wedding?" she demanded. "You going to pull the same thing? Because I'd rather they elope than see that disappointment on his face again!"

"Next month!" Corinne picked up a beer can, swirled it and found it empty. She tossed it aside. "So soon?"

"What's the point in waiting? They love each other." The words felt like splinters in her throat. Not because she didn't want to see her dad and Francesca happy, but because it only underscored her own misery. "What really went on between you and Meyer Cartell?"

Corinne squinted at her. "When?"

Sophie threw up her hands. "*When do you think?*" She ground her molars and tried again. "The summer you dated," she managed in a calmer tone.

Corinne grimaced. "It doesn't matter. It was a long time ago." She reached for another one of the cans in front of her, and Sophie snatched it out of her hand, tossing it aside.

It clattered into a half dozen others, sending them tumbling like bowling pins. "Was it really?"

Corinne jumped like she'd been bit. "What's your problem!"

"Too many to mention," she muttered.

The coffee pot gurgled and spat, and Sophie turned away from Corinne. She found a lone mug in the jumbled cupboard and washed and dried it before filling it with the fresh brew. She'd made the coffee for Corinne, but she found herself in need of it, too.

She sniffed the milk in the refrigerator and grimaced. Definitely not adding that to her coffee.

She poured it down the sink drain instead and sat at the small dining table, silently drinking her black coffee while the clock on the wall softly ticked and the self-recriminations inside her head mounted.

Eventually, Corinne got up and left the room. Sophie poured herself more coffee. The caffeine sat uneasily on the scallops from the Cliff, and she knew she should stop, but she couldn't seem to make herself.

Corinne returned.

She'd showered. Her wet hair was combed severely back

from her face. She pushed aside a jumble of thick books on the chair opposite Sophie and sat. She was pale and looked older than she really was, and her hand trembled when she took Sophie's mug and lifted it to her own lips.

She grimaced after one sip. "Needs cream."

"You don't have any. And your milk was sour."

Corinne took another sip and set down the mug, turning the handle back toward Sophie. "What do you want to know about Meyer?"

"You dated."

Corinne's lips twisted. "Not really."

"You and Meyer. Meredith and John. I remember, Corinne."

"The four of us hung out for a while."

"And then you got pregnant. And you had an abortion. Because being pregnant didn't fit in with his plan. That's what you told me. Do you remember?"

Corinne's jaw whitened. "You think I'd forget? Not even two decades can wipe away some things."

"Is that why you drink? Because Meyer rejected you?"

"Meyer." Corinne gave her a pitying look. "Why are you fixated on Meyer? It was *John*, Sophie. It was always John." She exhaled. "I was good enough to sleep with when Meredith wouldn't have him, but she was always the one he wanted."

Sophie suddenly felt truly ill and it had nothing to do with too much caffeine or seafood. "You got pregnant... by John Skinner."

"Isn't that what I just said?"

Sophie swallowed hard. She clasped her hands together so tightly her nailbeds turned white. "Who else knew?"

"John."

Sophie gave her a look.

Corinne exhaled impatiently. "Everyone knew."

"*I* didn't!"

"You were a kid!"

"Mom and Dad? Did they know?" She could see by Corinne's expression that they had. Sophie placed her clenched hands on the table. "What about Meredith? Meyer?"

"Meyer." Corinne looked skyward, obviously remembering. "He caught us in the back of John's Camaro. God, the argument that they had." She grimaced. "Not about me, of course. But about *Meredith*. How she deserved more. She had everything I wanted, but even back then I couldn't bring myself to hate her. I tried, though. I tried hard. But she was always so…*nice*." She spit out the word as if it were a curse. "And maybe she didn't know that first time, but—"

Sophie shot back in her chair. "*First time?* How many times were there?"

"Over the years? More than I can count. But not enough to get pregnant again," Corinne said. She was staring at the palms of her hands. "But I tried." She sniffed and a tear slid down her cheek. "And then she found out we were having an affair again, and he knew she'd leave him for good. That's why he killed himself." Her eyes reddened even more. "Because of me."

Sophie covered her eyes. She'd never once thought to connect Corinne's unhappiness with John Skinner's death.

And just then, she wondered what the man had done to inspire such misguided devotion that he'd left behind two women who both blamed themselves for actions that might or might not have been deliberate.

"Meredith blames herself, too," she told Corinne, even though she'd promised Meredith she'd never speak of it to anyone. "Seems to me, letting the past go is long overdue for both of you." She looked around the depressing mess that was her sister's apartment. "The wedding's in a month.

First Saturday in July at Dad's house. Try to be there. Sober. It's probably the only wedding gift that really matters to him." She walked to the door.

Corinne's voice followed her. "What's the deal with you and Meyer?"

"There is no deal."

How could there ever be one now?

She opened the door and left.

Chapter Nineteen

"Mind telling me what this nonsense is about?"

Sophie looked up from the examining table that she was sanitizing. Doc Hayes stood in the doorway of the room, holding the envelope that she'd left for him on his desk. "It's my resignation." She turned back to what she was doing. Word had rapidly gotten around town that he'd returned a week early, and his appointment schedule had been packed all week.

The only thing good about that was that they'd all been so busy, it hadn't left room for awkward conversations.

Or awkward silences.

"Want to tell me why?"

She snapped the roll of paper into place. "I'm going back to Portland."

He entered the room and closed the door. He was a tall, spare man with a fringe of graying hair and kind eyes. He held up the letter between two fingers. "So you said in your letter. But that still doesn't answer my question. Why?"

She exhaled. "I miss the emergency department."

"Sophie," his tone was chiding. "You have exemplary skills that any ED would welcome. But do you really think I don't know you better than that? You thrive in private practice. Most of my patients tolerate me just so they can see you."

Her shoulders sank. "I just can't stay anymore." It was too much. Knowing about Corinne and John. About John and Meredith.

And Meyer—

"Have you told Meredith?"

"Not yet." Since the doctor was blocking the door, she busied herself filling the apothecary jars with gauze pads and tongue depressors. "I was going to do that later after I'd told you."

"Guess that'll teach me to go away when I come back and three of my best employees have decided to desert me."

"Three?"

He set the envelope on the counter next to her. "Talk to Meredith," he advised. "Maybe you'll both come to your senses."

He left the room, and Sophie folded the letter and slid it into one of her many pockets. She finished wiping down the counter and then went to find Meredith, but she'd already left for the day. Only Doc himself remained.

He'd gone back to his office, and she could hear him talking on the phone.

She carried her backpack out to her SUV and climbed behind the wheel.

She knew she was a coward when she texted instead of just dropping by Meredith's place on her way home like she so often had done.

Are you really leaving Doc's?

She waited, her pulse pounding slightly in her head, but when no response came, it seemed like answer enough.

She tossed the phone onto her passenger seat and went home. But not even there did she get any peace because Cutter was sprawled on one of her deck chairs when she got there.

She was so weary inside that she ignored him while she changed out of her scrubs and into a knee-length T-shirt dress. Then she unlocked the slider and went out onto the deck, folding her arms and waiting silently for him to finish whatever he was doing on his laptop.

"Half a month," he said eventually. "That's how long it's taken for them to lose their minds."

"Them being—"

"Alexa and Dana." He closed his laptop. "You need a better password on your Wi-Fi," he told her. "Your signal is strong as hell out here, but anyone could be using it."

She raised her eyebrows. "I think *anyone* is. And if I knew how to change it, I would."

He opened the laptop right back up. "I'll do it for you right now."

"Nice of you, but I have a feeling you'll make it something long and complicated that I'll never remember."

"Maybe." He didn't sound the least remorseful. "You wouldn't happen to know where Meyer is, would you?"

She pushed her hands into her pockets. "No." She rolled it around in her mouth before finally giving in. "Why?"

"Haven't seen him since yesterday." He closed his laptop once again. "*Bilgewater92*. Capital *B*. Numerals *9* and *2*. Think you can remember that?"

She spread her hands. "I don't know. I guess." It wasn't as complicated as she'd expected.

"Did you know your dad checks in on us?"

"What? No." She shook her head. "I didn't know."

"Says it's part of the duties he has where Pietro's will is concerned."

"He doesn't talk to me about that sort of thing."

"He's come by three different times. If his schedule holds true, that means he's due to come by again this evening."

"I'm sure Meyer will turn up. He wants his fortune just as much as the rest of you."

"Not for himself."

Naturally. Because Saint Meyer had turned out to be pretty darned close to one. It was Sophie who'd tarred and feathered him all because she'd been clinging to the faulty lens that she'd formed when she'd been a kid. "Check the airfield. Or Meredith's. He'll be at one or the other."

"Already did that. They haven't seen him."

"His apart—" She broke off when Cutter shook his head.

"Not there, either."

She let out a huff. "I don't know what you think *I'd* know." Since Grange's party when he'd told her to go away, she hadn't spoken to him even once.

She'd seen him plenty.

But only because she'd discovered that if she used her binoculars from the third step down on her deck stairs, there was a spot through the trees where she could see their entire house.

In the last week, he and Cutter had pulled down the cedar deck from the front of the house and put up a temporary ramp from the doorway down to the ground. They'd also erected a tent next to the house, though she wasn't sure who was actually occupying it.

She doubted it was Dana or Alexa. But then, considering her faulty judgment, she was probably wrong about that, too.

She'd also decided that she'd picked up one too many

habits from Otto when she'd frittered away nearly half a day perched on that step, watching them work on the deck.

She palmed the binocular case where she'd left it sitting on the patio table. "If it helps any, I happen to know that my dad's annual dinner with his clients is tonight. I doubt he'll be checking up on anything besides that. And now, if you'll excuse me, I have things to do."

He stretched out on her lounge and grinned. "Don't let me stop you."

She shook her head and went back inside.

She didn't really have things to do.

But anything was preferable to standing around discussing his brother's whereabouts.

She didn't need one more reason to think about Meyer when she was already consumed by them.

She changed into her yoga gear and left the house. She hadn't planned to go to a class that evening, but she also hadn't planned on having Cutter Cardinale camped out on her deck. The yoga studio was near the senior high school, and she took her usual shortcut via the cemetery.

It was only when she reached the roundabout that it came to her.

She slowed and took the roundabout back the direction that she'd come and, relying on long-ago memories, turned onto a narrow lane that ran over a small crest.

There, on the other side, was Meyer's truck.

And there, sitting fifty yards away with his back against John Skinner's headstone, was Meyer himself.

Her heart squeezing, she parked behind his truck and quietly got out. The door of her SUV still sounded loud when she nudged it closed.

The sun was still high, but its beams were lengthening. Another few hours and it would be sunset.

She moistened her lips and started across the green,

green grass of the cemetery, walking between the head-stones. Despite his dark aviators, she still felt his gaze on her every step of the way until she stopped a few yards away from him.

"I guess you needed some quiet."

He didn't answer, and she walked over to crouch next to him. Her fingers shook a little, but she reached for his glasses and flipped them up.

His intense blue gaze met hers. "Go home."

The words hurt now as much as they had at Grange's party. She let the glasses back down where they belonged. "Cutter's worried about you. Seems to think you're risking your inheritance." She sat down and hugged her knees. "I told him he didn't have to worry about my dad. Not tonight at least. He has a work thing."

"Client dinner. I know. Meredith's going with Walker."

Sophie plucked the laces of her tennis shoe. "That's, um, that's— I'm glad to hear that."

"She didn't tell you."

She shook her head. "We haven't had a lot of chance to talk since…" She trailed off and moistened her lips. "I'm glad she's gone with him, though. Maybe there's some bright spot waiting for them."

She could just make out part of the inscription on the headstone Meyer was leaning against. But she remembered helping Meredith get through ordering it.

John Skinner. Loving Husband and Father. Slipped the Surly Bonds of Earth.

The last line was part of a famous aviation poem, but she couldn't remember the name of the author. Just that he'd died much, much too young after having written it.

"How long have you been here?"

"Not as long as John." His voice was deadly dry.

She went back to focusing on her shoelaces. "Corinne

told me about the two of them. I… I never knew. I thought it was you." She chewed the inside of her cheek. "I know it doesn't excuse anything." She blinked away the burning behind her eyes. "But I am sorry for…misjudging you so badly."

"I'm sorry that I didn't know she'd gotten pregnant."

"What would have been different if you had?" She plucked a blade of grass and held it into the faint breeze. "Would John have married Corinne instead of Meredith? Would he have been any more faithful?" She let go of the blade and watched it drift along before it slowly fell back onto the ground. "Would Leda and Grange even exist?"

He lifted his knee and propped his elbow on it, pinching his eyes closed. "So many mistakes."

She let out a long breath. Her biggest one was falling for Meyer. It had been impossible before, thinking that he'd caused her sister's heartache. It was even more impossible now, knowing that he hadn't. Knowing that her sister was inextricably woven into Meredith's grief.

"I'm going back to Portland," she said abruptly.

He dropped his hand and frowned at her. "Running doesn't help, Sophie. That's the one thing I can say with honest-to-God authority."

"I couldn't bear it if Meredith ever learned the truth."

"She told me you knew about John's cheating."

"Yes, but not that it was with my own sister! Meredith didn't even know who it was—"

"Maybe not always. Or not for certain, but she figured it out. Same way I did when I learned Corinne had gotten pregnant even before Meredith and John got married."

"So many mistakes," she repeated his words. Her whisper felt raw. Almost as raw as her flayed emotions.

"Don't add to them by leaving."

"I still can't stay."

"Why?"

Her throat closed. She could only look at him, mutely.

He swore under his breath and shifted, only to yank his cell phone out of his jeans pocket. "Thing *never* shuts up." He started to toss it aside but stopped, arrested by the message on his phone.

The color drained from his face.

She instinctively reached toward him. "*What?*"

"Leda's missing."

The world jarred to a halt. Then suddenly, everything inside her swooped, dizzyingly. Nauseatingly. "That's not possible."

He wasn't listening. He was punching numbers. She could hear the line ringing when he put the phone on speaker.

"Meyer!" Meredith sounded frantic. "Thank God. Nobody's been answering their freaking phones." Her voice broke.

"Are you with Walker?"

"I'm here." Walker's deep voice spoke over Meredith's sobs. He wasted no time. "Leda was supposed to be with Danielle Dowling since last night, but her parents were at the client dinner. They said Leda hadn't been with them at all. They're trying to locate their oldest boy, Scott, in case he's involved."

"I should have given her a phone." Meredith's voice was choked. "She can't even c-call—"

Sophie pressed her fist to her mouth, stifling any noise.

"We've already talked to the police," Walker said.

"We're still at the station," Meredith's voice hitched. "They're checking with all of Leda's other friends as well."

Meyer closed his hand tightly over Sophie's ankle. "Where's Grange?"

"At home."

"We'll go there now." Meyer pushed to his feet and held out his hand to Sophie. She took it, and he pulled her to standing.

"We? Are you with Sophie?"

She swallowed the knot in her throat. "Yeah. I'm here, Meredith."

"Thank God! *Why* haven't you been answering your phone? I've been calling for the last hour!"

Tears squirted out the corners of her eyes. "I'm sorry. I didn't know."

Walker came on again, this time sounding quieter. At his end, he'd taken it off speaker. "She just needs to know everyone else she loves is where they belong," he excused.

Sophie's nose burned. She swiped her cheeks. It was probably the most words she'd ever heard him say, and some of the most important. "Thanks, Walker."

"We'll be with Grange," Meyer said. "Call us the second—"

"We will."

Meyer's hand shook as he pushed his phone into his pocket. "Ride with me?"

She nodded and ran to her SUV, grabbing her yoga bag and keys and taking precious seconds to hunt for her phone that had fallen onto the floor and slid beneath the seat.

It blinked with a half dozen messages and missed calls.

She pushed it deep into her yoga bag where it wouldn't have a chance of escape, locked the vehicle and jumped in Meyer's waiting truck when he pushed open the passenger door from inside.

She dropped her bag onto the floor, shoved the buckle home on the seat belt and dragged the door closed even as he put the truck into motion. "Leda's a smart girl," she said, trying to comfort herself as much as Meyer.

He squeezed her hand tightly and drove a little faster.

Grange was pacing the living room when they got there, and the abject relief when he saw Meyer was enough to break Sophie's heart all over again.

Meyer hugged the boy. "We're going to find her," he promised.

"I knew she wasn't with Dani," Grange muttered, pulling back, obviously trying for a manful tone that would have worked if not for the way his voice cracked. "I should've told Mom last night."

Sophie caught his chin in her fingers until he met her gaze. "Don't," she said firmly. "There're enough people going around blaming themselves for things already."

Meyer abruptly turned away, and she realized he was looking at his phone again.

She tugged Grange down onto the couch beside her, keeping Meyer in her periphery. "Have you eaten anything?"

Grange shook his head. "Not hungry."

Nothing could have underscored his worry more.

She wrapped her arm around his shoulder. Thirteen or not, he was still the same little boy she'd pushed endlessly on the swings he'd loved.

Meyer turned back to them. "They've located Scott. Leda's not with him." His jaw looked tight. "But she was."

"Where?"

"Cannon Beach. The police are already looking for her."

"Cannon is small," Sophie said. "A fraction the size of Cape Cardinale."

"With a lot more tourism," Meyer muttered. "Thanks to the sandcastle contest tomorrow." The annual event drew thousands. "Rat bastard kid dumped her on her own today and left her there."

His gaze touched on Grange for a moment, and Sophie swallowed her *why?*

Leda was smart, she reminded herself again. If she'd had

money, she'd have used it to call home, get a bus ticket. If she didn't have money, she'd have found the police. On an ordinary day, it should have been simple enough.

Toss in thousands of tourists packing into the small community for the sandcastle contest?

The possibilities of a young, teenaged girl in a town on her own were endless and horrifying.

Fifteen minutes crawled by. Thirty. An hour, then two, and their phones—Meyer's, Sophie's *and* Meredith's cordless house line—remained silent.

Grange had finally pulled out one of his video games, but it just sat there in his lax grip, unused.

Sophie finally pushed off the couch and went into the kitchen for a glass of water that her roiling stomach wouldn't allow her to actually drink. Instead, she just hung there, her arms propped on the edge of the sink, the water from the faucet overflowing the glass, and when Meyer spoke her name, the glass fell with a clatter.

She looked at him. He held up his finger, his phone pressed to his ear. His eyes closed. "I'll meet you at the airfield," he said, then dropped the phone onto the table.

Sophie could barely breathe.

"They've got her. She's okay."

Her knees felt weak. "Thank God," she whispered and flew into his arms.

His arms closed around her like a vise, lifting her onto the tips of her toes. "Meredith wants me to fly her up there and get her. Seaside Muni's the closest airport."

Realization was too slow. Sluggish. She blamed it on the abject relief still flooding through her. But when it hit, she pulled back as far as his arms allowed and looked up at him.

He was pale. Beads of sweat already forming on his forehead.

"Another pilot?"

He shook his head. "Everyone's out on charters. The sandcastle contest helps us down here, too."

She managed to wedge an arm between them just so she could draw in a normal breath. "Do you even have a plane available? What about Hannah? She's still a pilot, right?"

"Yeah, we've got a plane. But Hannah went down to Eureka to visit her sister for the weekend. It's a six-hour drive. Even if she could find a plane there and go straight up, it'd still take longer than us just driving from here in the first place."

To drive would take the better part of three hours. Add in tourism traffic on the coast highway—

She rubbed her hands up and down his arms. "Just tell Meredith. She'll understand."

He shook his head. "She'd want to know why."

He was still holding her off her feet. She wondered if he even noticed. She could see over his shoulder into the living room. Grange looked like he'd fallen asleep. "Why you're having panic attacks about flying? It's anxiety, Meyer. She'd understand."

He set her on her feet and let go. He looked over at Grange, then pulled her by the hand outside through the kitchen door. "She blames herself for John's accident. But it wasn't her. Never was. It was the business."

"What are you talking about?"

He clawed his fingers through his hair. "JCS was going bankrupt. They were going to lose everything. Not just the business. But their house. Their car. Their personal savings. All of it. He'd put everything they owned as collateral on an aircraft he had no business even trying to buy considering the state of JCS. And if I'd have known, just been here, been his partner like we'd planned when we were both too freaking stupid to know our tails from holes in the ground, instead of focusing on the trajectory of my own damn career, none of that would have ever happened."

"That's what you've thought? All this time?" Too many people, she thought. All feeling responsible for the acts of one fallible man.

"It's what I've known. All this time."

"Meyer." She cupped his face. "Meredith knows the business wasn't exactly a raving success."

"She didn't know *how* bad," he said grimly. "I made sure of it. She already had enough to worry about, having two kids to raise."

"Sometimes an accident is *just* an accident."

"No."

"Yes." She followed his gaze with her own until she felt that whoosh of connection that so many times before she'd tried to avoid. "Why's the earth round?"

"What?"

"Why's the sky blue?" She stroked his bristly jaw with her thumb. "John died. And he left a terrible, awful void. That doesn't mean there has to be anyone at all to blame. Sometimes things just *are*." Just like she was going to love him whether there was any hope left or not. "Is Meredith on her way to the airfield or not?"

"Yes."

"Then I guess you'd better get going. Because one way or another, she's going to get to her daughter, and if that needs to be by four wheels on a road, you need to at least tell her so." Then, because she couldn't stop herself, she stretched up and pressed her lips to his. His fingers flexed on her waist, and she pulled away, quickly. Her heart was pounding so hard it hurt.

She peeled his grip from her waist and turned toward the house.

"Where are you going?"

"Someone needs to stay here with Grange."

She pulled open the kitchen door and went inside, closing it after her.

He puked twice doing the walk-around.

Meredith and Walker were inside the plane already, impatient as hell to get to Leda.

Meyer didn't blame them. But he still couldn't rush through what had to be done more than he already was.

He hadn't flown in nearly two years.

It was a nighttime flight, and he'd be landing on a runway that under normal circumstances would be questionable even for the light jet.

His alternative would be to land at Astoria. But that meant a longer drive to Leda.

He'd flown fighter jets, for God's sake. He'd landed on carriers. In LZs that no sane person would ever choose.

He could do one measly half-hour flight.

He *would.*

Checklist completed, he went on board. Another checklist. And then finally, he powered up.

The plane had been built for two pilots but cleared for a single. He'd never wanted a second-in-command more than he did then.

He hit the intercom. "Wheels up in five. Strap in."

Then he put his hand on the stick.

Small steps. Sophie had said it herself.

He took a deep breath and closed his eyes.

For once, the face in his mind wasn't John's.

It was Sophie's. Brown eyes luminous. Pink lips curving as she looked up at him from where she sat in Ollie's front cockpit.

He opened his eyes, gave a soul-deep exhale.

"Right," he said to no one at all. "Let's get Leda."

* * *

"There." Sophie pointed to the faint light blinking in the sky as it approached the airfield. She and Grange were in the control tower. "That's them, isn't it?"

The controller yawned and nodded. "Right on time." He adjusted his headset. "Niner—"

Sophie hurried Grange down the stairs and out of the quiet terminal building. She'd tried to stay at Meredith's house. She really had.

But neither she nor Grange had been able to relax, and since her own SUV was still parked at the cemetery, she'd finally located the spare set of Meredith's car keys and they'd driven out to the airfield.

Less than two hours had passed since Meyer had left.

The blinking light grew stronger, and in the quiet night, the plane engine was soon audible.

She rubbed Grange's arm. "Doing okay?"

He nodded. "I ever see Scott Dowling again, I'm going to feed him to the alligators."

She wasn't sure which alligators he meant, but she appreciated the sentiment all the same.

She rested her head against his, and they stood there, waiting for the plane to finally land.

It touched down as smoothly as a bird, then taxied closer to the terminal before the engines finally cut. Sophie held Grange in place until she saw the door open and the short set of stairs fold out. "Now—go."

He ran across the pavement just as Meredith and Leda appeared.

Leda jumped down the rest of the steps and caught up Grange in a hug. Meredith joined them, and when Sophie saw Meredith stick out her hand toward the man coming down the steps, she smiled through her tears.

Meyer appeared last and stood at the top of the stairs,

his eyes taking in the knot of Meredith and her kids and Walker.

Then he looked toward Sophie, and she brushed her hands down her sleeves, feeling suddenly very self-conscious as he came down the stairs and walked toward her.

"Guess you did it," she said when he was but a few feet away. Tall. Rumpled. No sign of the rust in his hair at that hour but still so ridiculously handsome that she felt breathless.

He didn't answer. Just kept walking right up until the toes of his boots met the toes of her tennis shoes. Then he pulled her close. "I love you. Just in case you were wondering."

She lifted her chin. "I wasn't."

"Liar."

Her eyes flooded. "Okay. Fine. I love you, too. Satisfied?"

"Not nearly." He stroked her cheek. "But I will be. Let's go home."

Her heart leapt even higher. "Whose?"

"What do you think?"

"I think you still have nearly a year before you get to call the beach house yours."

"And you have some explaining to do about this business of moving back to Portland." His lips whispered along hers. "But *later*."

It turned out to be much, much later.

And by then, Sophie knew there was no reason to run after all.

No matter where she went.

Her heart was always going to be right where Meyer was.

Epilogue

"All right, step down on the seat. Just like the last time."

Sophie gingerly climbed over the side of Ollie, dropping down onto the seat. "You're not going to pull anything funny once we're up in the air, are you?"

Meyer smiled at her. "I'm a serious pilot. What kind of *funny* do you mean?"

It had been a week since he'd retrieved Leda in the middle of the night.

A week in which Sophie had told Doc that she wouldn't be going anywhere after all. But he was still losing Olivia. And Meredith.

Meredith, who'd tearfully shown Sophie the engagement ring that she'd accepted—and shared the news that she and Walker and the kids were moving to Colorado, where Walker would be joining his father's law practice.

It's time, she'd said. And even though they'd both cried—a lot—Sophie knew their decision was a good one. They had an entire future ahead of them.

And it's only a few hours by plane, Meyer had reminded Sophie later. *And I have a connection or two on that front.*

"I mean *funny,*" Sophie said now. She twirled her finger in the air. "No spins or rolls or whatever."

He leaned over her, fastening the harness that seemed designed to hold a person in place for just that sort of thing. "Would I do that to you?" His fingers lingered over her breasts as he adjusted the straps.

She caught his fingertips before they could do any further marauding. "You've been doing that to me from the moment we met," she accused.

His eyes glinted. He brushed his mouth across hers and gave the harness a final tug. Then he handed her a leather cap that looked straight out of the 1940s with a, fortunately, more modern headset attached to it. "So we can hear each other," he said.

She pulled it on, feeling a little foolish. The thing fit like a skullcap. "My mother would not approve," she said.

He grinned and adjusted the headset. "Your mother's not here. And even *she* would want one—gets windy up there in an open cockpit." He handed her a small bundle of rolled-up rags. "Push 'em in that metal box there." He pointed at a latching box near the floor.

"What are these for?"

He shrugged. "Cleanup." He hopped down from the wing, conveniently avoiding her reaction.

"Cleanup after *what*?"

He just laughed and walked around Ollie's wings. Checking this. Adjusting that. Then he was back up on the wing again. "All set?"

She nodded wordlessly, sliding her fingers around the harness, surreptitiously tugging. She'd never liked roller coasters, and it felt like she was strapped into the wildest one possible.

"If you're having fun…" He stuck his thumb up. "Do that. If not…" He turned his thumb down. "Do that."

Her hands immediately went to the bulky headphones on her head. "I thought you said we'd be able to hear each other."

He winked and slid his aviators down onto his nose.

Not even craning around allowed her to see him in the cockpit behind her.

She exhaled.

Then the engine cranked, and the propeller spun slowly a few times before seeming to catch its breath and speeding up.

Her stomach was bouncing around in all manners of ways, and she was suddenly glad, after all, for the bundle of rags. Just in case.

"Here we go." His voice was suddenly in her ear. Deep. Intimate. "Ready?"

Her throat was too tight. She nodded. Then poked her hand in the air. Thumbs-up.

She thought she heard him laugh, but a voice from the tower overrode it, and she listened to the incomprehensible gibberish that passed as instructions between the tower and Meyer. The noise of the engine grew louder, and they were suddenly moving.

She couldn't see one darn thing straight ahead of her, and she kept craning her head one way and then the other, looking out from the sides as the plane jostled over a few bumps in the path until it seemed to turn almost on a dime.

Then the engine revved and picked up speed as it raced down the runway, seeming to go much too long before it suddenly swooped off the ground, leaving her stomach somewhere far behind.

She grasped the metal rails on either side of her old-fashioned seat. Who had ever thought it was wise to fly around in a plane that had been built at least eighty-five years ago?

"Sophie." His voice was in her ear again. "Open your eyes."

Her eyes popped open. "How did you know they were closed?"

"Mirror up on the wing above you."

She looked and then noticed it. "I can't see you."

"I'm not as pretty."

The plane banked to the right, and she swallowed hard, transferring her grip to her harness straps.

"Meredith's house is off your right," he said in her ear. "See the basketball hoop in front of the garage?"

"I don't feel as high up as I expected."

"Hot-air balloon was probably higher," he said. "You said you'd do it again in a heartbeat."

"I spent the entire time clinging to one of the corners of the basket," she admitted. "We landed at Friars. I thought we'd end up in the water, but we didn't."

"And we won't now, either."

They banked again, to the left this time. And she saw the cemetery. The schools. They passed her father's five-story office building, and then they were over Friars Beach, where the surfers looked like toys bobbing among the rolling waves while the plane climbed higher, heading south, following the coastline.

It was so incredibly beautiful that she forgot her nervousness and stopped clutching her harness so that she could lean closer to the edge of the cockpit to see even more.

Eventually, though, he turned farther out to sea, and they were heading northward once again. She smiled, pressing her head back against the seat and feeling the sun on her face. "Ollie, you're amazing."

Even whispered, Meyer heard her. "She'll make you love

her every single time." His voice seemed to deepen. "Some females do that to you."

Shivers danced down her spine. "How long before we're back?"

"Why?"

"I'm feeling a sudden need to *do that*."

He laughed, and the plane suddenly dipped wildly, making a long spiral down before swooping almost straight up. She felt gravity give way as the horizon upended itself and she was staring up at the waves instead of down, and then the circle completed itself as Ollie leveled out again.

Exhilaration flooded her veins. "You promised!"

"Having fun?"

Her hand shot in the air. Thumbs-up.

"That's my girl!" The engine throttled, and she laughed as they flew, up and down and over and around. Dancing in the sky as if they were birds on the wind.

Then she realized where they were and pointed. "Look! That's Otto Nash's place." The sprawling house looked even more impressive from the air with its multiple wings and red-tiled roof. "I have *got* to get him up here. He'd love it!"

"Don't miss your house." The right wing dipped again, allowing her to see her house farther down below the cliff. It looked small and tidy even with the long, meandering staircase working in and out of the stand of spruce.

She laughed at the sight of the man lounging on her deck. "Cutter's using my Wi-Fi again."

"Need to start charging him."

"I don't know. He's been letting us sleep in his tent."

Meyer's laughter was low and sweet in her ear. The plane swooped lower, almost skimming the waves as he shot farther out to sea and then looped back around leisurely, going so slowly that she could almost make out the planks of zigzagging wood on her walk where it reached the glittering golden sand that swept out in a smooth, perfect crescent.

And then she saw it.

Written in huge letters in the damp sand.

Her eyes welled.

There was no question the message was for her. Not when her name was right there for all the world to see.

MARRY ME, SOPHIE?

The outline of a huge daisy was drawn beneath the question.

How could a girl ever resist a flower like that from a man she adored?

She wiped her cheeks. "Yes," she whispered. Then she laughed. "Yes," she said louder, to be certain the wind hadn't carried it away.

"Are you sure?"

"Never more," she promised, throwing both her arms in the air. Thumbs up.

Then he laughed, too, and throttled the engine once more.

And they flew.

* * * * *

Don't miss Alexa's story,
the next installment in Cape Cardinale,
the new Harlequin Special Edition miniseries by
New York Times bestselling author Allison Leigh

On sale October 2024,
Wherever Harlequin books
and ebooks are sold.

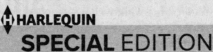
#3039 TAKING THE LONG WAY HOME
Bravo Family Ties • by Christine Rimmer

After one perfect night with younger rancher Jason Bravo, widowed librarian Piper Wallace is pregnant with his child. Co-parenting is a given. But Jason will do anything—even accompany her on a road trip to meet her newly discovered biological father—to prove he's playing for keeps!

#3040 SNOWED IN WITH A STRANGER
Match Made in Haven • by Brenda Harlen

Party planner Finley Gilmore loves an adventure, but being snowbound with Professor Lachlan Kellett takes *tempted by a handsome stranger* to a whole new level! Their chemistry could melt a glacier. But when Lachlan's past resurfaces, will Finlay be the one iced out?

#3041 A FATHER'S REDEMPTION
The Tuttle Sisters of Coho Cove • by Sabrina York

Working with developer Ben Sherrod should have turned Celeste Tuttle's dream project into a nightmare. Except the single father is witty and brilliant and so much more attractive than she remembered from high school. Could her childhood nemesis be Prince Charming in disguise?

#3042 MATZAH BALL BLUES
Holidays, Heart and Chutzpah • by Jennifer Wilck

Entertainment attorney Jared Leiman will do anything to be the guardian his orphaned niece needs. Even reunite with Caroline Weiss, his high school ex, to organize his hometown's Passover ball with the Jewish Community Center. Sparks fly,..but he'll need a little matzah magic to win her over.

Get 3 FREE REWARDS!

We'll send you 2 FREE Books plus a FREE Mystery Gift.

FREE
Value Over
$20

Both the **Harlequin® Special Edition** and **Harlequin® Heartwarming™** series feature compelling novels filled with stories of love and strength where the bonds of friendship, family and community unite.

YES! Please send me 2 FREE novels from the Harlequin Special Edition or Harlequin Heartwarming series and my FREE Gift (gift is worth about $10 retail). After receiving them, if I don't wish to receive any more books, I can return the shipping statement marked "cancel." If I don't cancel, I will receive 6 brand-new Harlequin Special Edition books every month and be billed just $5.49 each in the U.S. or $6.24 each in Canada, a savings of at least 12% off the cover price, or 4 brand-new Harlequin Heartwarming Larger-Print books every month and be billed just $6.24 each in the U.S. or $6.74 each in Canada, a savings of at least 19% off the cover price. It's quite a bargain! Shipping and handling is just 50¢ per book in the U.S. and $1.25 per book in Canada.* I understand that accepting the 2 free books and gift places me under no obligation to buy anything. I can always return a shipment and cancel at any time by calling the number below. The free books and gift are mine to keep no matter what I decide.

Choose one: ☐ **Harlequin**   ☐ **Harlequin**   ☐ **Or Try Both!**
             Special Edition   **Heartwarming**   (235/335 & 161/361
             (235/335 BPA GRMK) **Larger-Print**   BPA GRPZ)
                                (161/361 BPA GRMK)

Name (please print)

Address   Apt. #

City   State/Province   Zip/Postal Code

Email: Please check this box ☐ if you would like to receive newsletters and promotional emails from Harlequin Enterprises ULC and its affiliates. You can unsubscribe anytime.

Mail to the Harlequin Reader Service:
IN U.S.A.: P.O. Box 1341, Buffalo, NY 14240-8531
IN CANADA: P.O. Box 603, Fort Erie, Ontario L2A 5X3

Want to try 2 free books from another series? Call 1-800-873-8635 or visit www.ReaderService.com.

HSEHW23